"A sexy, thrilling novel. You will feel transported,
as if you are speaking French and drinking a little
too much wine with your best friend and
a dangerously handsome man."
—TAYLOR JENKINS REID,
author of *Maybe in Another Life*

"Dunlop's captivating debut ardently delivers
the joy and exquisite pain of being young and
in love: with a friend, with a lover, with a
country, with a life, with the future."
—LAURIE FRANKEL,
author of *The Atlas of Love*

"Fine wine, dark chocolate, a French love triangle,
and the perfect best friend (at first) are only a
handful of the decadences awaiting you—not to
mention the shocking twist that keeps this succulent
debut lingering long after the final page."
—MIRANDA BEVERLY-WHITTEMORE,
New York Times bestselling author of *Bittersweet*

"Dunlop's smart and suspenseful debut
richly evokes the heady emotions of
friendship, lust, and betrayal."
—*BOOKLIST*

Losing
the Light

Losing
the Light

a novel

ANDREA DUNLOP

WASHINGTON SQUARE PRESS

New York   London   Toronto   Sydney   New Delhi

WASHINGTON SQUARE PRESS
An Imprint of Simon & Schuster, Inc.
1230 Avenue of the Americas
New York, NY 10020

First Washington Square Press trade paperback edition February 2016

WASHINGTON SQUARE PRESS and colophon are registered trademarks of Simon & Schuster, Inc.

For information about special discounts for bulk purchases, please contact Simon & Schuster Special Sales at 1-866-506-1949 or business@simonandschuster.com.

The Simon & Schuster Speakers Bureau can bring authors to your live event. For more information, or to book an event, contact the Simon & Schuster Speakers Bureau at 1-866-248-3049 or visit our website at www.simonspeakers.com.

Interior design by Kyoko Watanabe

Manufactured in the United States of America

10 9 8 7 6 5 4 3 2 1

Library of Congress Cataloging-in-Publication Data

Dunlop, Andrea.
 Losing the Light : a novel / by Andrea Dunlop.—First Washington Square Press Trade Paperback edition.
   pages cm
 "Washington Square Press Fiction Original Trade."
 1. American students—France—Fiction. 2. Foreign study—France—Fiction. 3. Young women—Sexual behavior—Fiction. 4. Triangles (Interpersonal relations)—Fiction.
 PS3604.U5554S65 2015
 813'.6—dc23
                    2014042904

ISBN 978-1-5011-0942-3
ISBN 978-1-5011-0941-6 (ebook)

For Pat Geary,
who first made me believe

ICAN'T BELIEVE you're leaving Manhattan. How am I supposed to handle our friendship becoming a long-distance relationship?"

I collapse back onto my couch with a long sigh and stare out the window. The air has that thinness today as if it might snow. "You're being dramatic. And if you think you're the first person to make a joke about upstate being 'long distance,' you're sadly mistaken. The house is only thirty minutes on Metro-North—it takes longer to get to the Upper West Side."

I decide I want it to snow. Chalk it up to the overabundance of cozy feelings of home and hearth that I'm currently experiencing. I'm dreaming of the working fireplace in our new two-bedroom Victorian house in Riverdale and of living there with a man whose father taught him how to build a fire. It's not a large house, but it dwarfs this apartment, and the idea of living in a space where I might occasionally be alone with my thoughts is incredibly novel; it's been years since I've been able to hear myself think.

Kate lets out an exasperated click. "First of all, since when do I go to the Upper West Side? Secondly, I don't do Penn Station. You can't make me!"

"Ha! Grand Central. You can't even complain about that. There's a Cipriani near there!"

"How can you do this to me? First the engagement and then the suburbs? And don't think I don't know what's coming next."

"*Don't* you dare. Are you trying to make me break out in hives?"

"I'm just saying"—Kate gives a triumphant little laugh—"I know what happens to people when they leave Manhattan."

"Babies don't just *happen* to people. At least not people who paid attention in health class."

"I'm from Alabama. Abstinence-only education, remember?"

"We've strayed so far from the point I don't even know what it was."

"The point is you *are* coming to my party tomorrow. No excuses. You owe me that."

"I just have so much packing to do," I say weakly, knowing I'm not unwilling to be cajoled into going. James and I have a lovely life together, but I can't say I don't miss my single days now and then, the best of which I spent with Kate, who is easily my most glamorous friend. Kate and I have known each other for seven years, since she was an assistant at *Vogue* the year I was a junior copy editor there. She always looks professionally styled in that way that's engineered to look incidental, with scarves and expensive T-shirts and perfectly done smoky eye makeup. She's forever going to restaurants where she is on a first-name basis with the owners and runs into at least ten people she knows; new places with no sign by the door and no reviews online. Ever since I've known her, she's been the kind of girl who is always on the list.

"I'll help you pack!" she says.

"No, you won't," I say, smiling. "But I'll come to the party anyway. Just for you."

"Hurray!"

"Did you send me the invite?"

"Only like three weeks ago! Whatever, you're so busy and important. New Museum at seven o'clock tomorrow. Gotta run to meet Alejandro. Love you!"

Mission accomplished, Kate gets off the line.

I put down my phone and look around, knowing I should do some more packing before bed but feeling too exhausted. Already half of my life is in boxes. I'll miss our little apartment downtown. I've been trying to convince myself that being outside the city won't matter, giving myself the same argument I just gave Kate: the thirty-minutes-on-the-train case. But it won't be the same. And I've decided that this is okay with me. I've already given in and let my head and heart be commandeered by dreams of a different life, one with real furniture and counter space, a little yard, and maybe a dog.

I look at the clock and wonder where James is; it's past ten already. His boss is fond of dragging him to dinner with clients since no one else in the boutique advertising firm where James works has quite such an affable demeanor and honest face. He puts people at ease. He won't want to come to this party with me tomorrow, but I'll ask him anyway if for no other reason than to watch him do his spot-on impression of Kate's too-young, dimwit boyfriend, Alejandro, a model/DJ from Brazil ("But, uh, we make the party, yes?"). James does like Kate, but not enough to want to come and hang around her fashiony crowd. It's not his scene and I love him for it. It's not mine either, but I'm more willing to take an anthropological stance on the beautiful people.

I pour myself a glass of red wine. It has a slight hint of vinegar, but I ignore it and drink it anyway. I haven't packed my party dresses yet, so I wander over to my closet to thumb through them. How did I ever end up with so many? I cringe when I realize that I've worn several of them only once, one of them not at all. I wonder for a moment about the imaginary life I bought these for. Not the life of a freelance copy editor who works from home and spends many of her nights happily eating takeout with her new fiancé. I must have thought I'd end up with Kate's life.

I go back to the couch where my laptop is open and search my e-mail for the invitation from Bliss & Bliss, the PR firm where Kate's a senior account manager, run by two terrifying blond sisters in their fifties who've been pulled back nearly into their thirties by top-of-the-line plastic surgery. I've met them a dozen times but they never remember me. Ah, here it is. I'd completely skimmed over it. The subject line is cut off by my in-box: *Bliss & Bliss invites you to spend an evening at the New Museum with . . .* I maximize the e-mail to see who it is that Bliss & Bliss is inviting me to spend an evening with . . . *photographer Alex de Persaud to celebrate the release of his book* GFY: Paris and New York by the Night.

I push back from my desk as though adding the extra bit of distance might change the words on the screen, then laugh out loud; a shrill, manic laugh. Taking a deep breath, I scroll down the screen a bit. I'm greeted with an image of the cover of Alex's new coffee-table book of party photographs. This I've seen before. A couple of weeks ago I had a small fit of post-engagement nostalgia and found myself mentally cataloging all of the various romances that had led me to the man I would marry. So with the usual trepidation in my heart I googled Alex's name and news of this book came up.

In the beginning, when I first moved to the city, I searched for him regularly, with the vague notion that New York was the sort of place he might have ended up. I looked for information about him if for no other reason than to confirm he still existed somewhere other than in my memory and imagination, in which he loomed so large. That was before everyone was online, before everyone's entire social and professional life was cataloged there. Now, given how easy it was to look up and contact completely unexceptional people you'd once known, you would think that someone prominent—even a little famous within certain circles—such as Alex would have every last detail about him recorded somewhere.

He wasn't so famous in the mainstream that someone like me—unconnected to his industry—would necessarily know of his work if I hadn't gone looking. But living in downtown Manhattan, you tended to hear of such things as the popular photo blog *By the Night*, to which he'd become a contributor five years ago. The blog covered the posh international party scene: film festivals and music festivals with the right kind of celebrities in attendance, polo matches, and myriad other fêtes for fancy people. Alex covered Paris and the south of France; he photographed soccer players and models, French actresses, and visiting Russian oligarchs. After a couple of years the site was defunct, but Alex's career seemingly continued on its upward trajectory. He, or someone who worked for him, maintained a website with a sleek catalog of his editorial work, but the only contact information was for press.

Other than a couple of interviews in *Paris Match* and *BlackBook*, there was nothing about his personal life anywhere. Every time a new social-networking site became popular—MySpace, Facebook, ASmallWorld—I looked for information about him, to no avail. The closest I ever came was a Facebook fan page devoted to his work with a couple hundred members.

A therapist I went to see years ago told me that I had to focus on accepting that I would most likely never know what happened after I left France. But how do you come to accept something like that? She didn't seem to know, so I stopped seeing her. But that was all years ago.

If any tenuous connection existed now between Alex and me, it would be through Kate. A cold chill suddenly runs through me. Does Kate *know* him? Has this connection been there all this time?

I text Kate: *Party looks fun! Do you know the photographer?*

She texts me back uncharacteristically fast: *No. Some French guy. Tracey Bliss is in LOVE with him! So happy you're coming! Xoxo*

I want to pepper Kate with more questions about him, but for some reason I hold back. I've never told Kate about France, about Sophie. I haven't told anyone I've met since I've been living here. I've never known quite what to say about it, so I don't even begin; how could I tell one part of the story without telling the rest? It was all anyone could talk about during my last year of school, and selfishly it was a relief to get away, to be somewhere where no one knew. It hurt too much to keep rehashing it.

Without being completely aware that I'm doing it, I find myself pacing our six-hundred-square-foot apartment. At least I have a day to mentally prepare. What if I hadn't looked at the invitation? Does this mean he's been living here in New York? Could I have stood next to him on a subway platform? Brushed by him on the sidewalk? Had my back to him in a crowded bar? The thoughts make me dizzy.

I hear James's key turning in the door and my heart races as though I'm about to be caught doing something and it's too late to hide the evidence. He opens the door and sets his messenger bag down.

"Hi," he says, and then immediately, "What's wrong?"

"Nothing," I say a little too quickly.

"You sure? You're looking a little shell-shocked."

Putting my wineglass down, I go over and bury my face against his chest, still cold from being outside. I love that he's so much taller than I am; it gives me an instant sense of security. I wrap my arms around him under his overcoat.

"I just have a lot on my mind," I say, my voice muffled.

He strokes my hair. "Is that all? Jesus, I don't know what I thought you were going to tell me with that look."

I shake my head. "It's a lot, with the move and everything. I guess I'm just feeling unsettled."

He pulls back and gives me a searching look. His blue eyes are as arresting close up as they were the first time I saw him. I remember it vividly. We were at a friend's barbecue out in Brooklyn and he stepped right into a shaft of late-afternoon light. His eyes appeared illuminated and I stared right into them; not until a moment later when he stepped out of the light could he actually see me looking at him, and he smiled.

Later it would seem that I knew right then we'd fall in love; that I could see from his eyes and his slightly crooked smile everything that was within him; that he would be funny and kind and even-keeled in the face of my worst moods and most unreasonable requests.

"Good things," I say. "I feel good about everything, but transition is always stressful."

"Okay." He pulls off his overcoat and hangs it on the hook by the door. "And you would tell me if it was something else?"

"Of course," I say, feeling guilty as soon as the words are out of my mouth. I resolve that I'll tell him about all of it at some point. I know I should have told him already, but I am not yet accustomed to the sort of full disclosure that an impending marriage warrants. What's the harm in taking it slow? I'll tell him later. Soon.

"I know I'm an old man to say this before eleven, but I'm beat!" He leans down to kiss me on the cheek. "I'm gonna head to bed."

I nod. I wonder if I've drunk too much wine to take a sleeping pill. No, I decide, it was only two glasses, counting the one I had with dinner. I know that otherwise a restless night is the only thing waiting for me in the bed; and that at some point I'll get unreasonably mad at James for sleeping so soundly next to me.

I slip away to the bathroom to brush my teeth and take the pill.

"You don't have plans tomorrow night, do you?" James asks from the other room.

Immediately I'm awash in anxiety all over again. "I told Kate I would go to her party," I say cautiously.

"When is that?"

"I think it's seven to nine."

"Can you meet me for dinner after? Stan wanted us to come out with him and Maria." James appears behind me in the bathroom and reaches over me for his toothbrush. Stan is James's dull, cheerful boss; Maria, his second wife. "I think she needs a friend."

I give him a look.

"Come on, she's sweet."

"She's a desperate housewife. And I'm a little scared to be living near them soon. I feel like she's going to want to come over to play bridge."

"I don't think Maria plays bridge," James says, laughing.

"Whatever it is they do in the suburbs, then. I'm sorry, I'm being a bitch. Of course I'll come to dinner." Standing on my tiptoes, I kiss his cheek. He smiles at me through the toothpaste foam, then leans over and spits.

"Does it help that dinner is at Babbo?"

"It helps a lot." I don't ask him about the party on the off chance that this night of all nights would be the one he decides to come with me.

⁓⁓

The next evening I try on most of what's left in my closet before deciding on the faithful black dress that I've worn a hundred times before. Tonight is not the night to wear something I feel even slightly uncomfortable in.

I take a cab down to the New Museum and am faced with a clutch of impossibly young-looking, dressed-up partygoers having one last cigarette before they go inside. It's so cold tonight, I cringe at the sight of their bare fingers shakily pull-ing cigarettes to their lips and away again. I haven't smoked a single cigarette since France, but I suppose I can't really judge—they all look about the age I was then. There's always a preponderance of terrifyingly chic teenagers at things like this.

The kids at the check-in desk don't look any older: one a young, black guy with eyeliner and his hair done in an elaborate asymmetrical swirl, the other a girl positively in-terchangeable with every other young fashion PR intern I've ever seen.

After I give them my name, they smile obsequiously and point me to the coat check; they're cautiously polite in case I'm someone important.

I go up to the roof-deck bar where the party is being held. Making my way into the room, I have a visceral sense of not belonging. Kate, my only friend here, will be running around all night working. But that's not what I'm really doing here, I remind myself. The space is beautiful with 180 degrees of windows looking out over downtown. Searching the room for him, I wander over to the edge of the party where I feel a little less conspicuous and pretend to be looking at the spec-tacular view. During the day the Lower East Side is not much to look at—nothing like the grand, gilt-edged buildings of the Upper East Side—but in the darkness when all that can be seen is the sparkling topography of lit windows, it's breath-taking in its way.

"Darling!" Kate makes her way through the quickly thick-ening crowd. She has a glass of champagne in her hand and grabs another from a nearby waiter.

I'm genuinely pleased to see her and the champagne. We exchange cheek kisses.

"I'm so glad you're here," she says.

"You look stunning." She does. Kate is a gorgeous red-head with a tiny waist and an unfairly generous bustline. Her hair gets a bit blonder every time I see her, which I can only chalk up to the time she's been spending in the L.A. office.

"You do too!" she says, perhaps on reflex.

"How's the event shaping up?"

"Good, good. Alex is really charming. I'm not super familiar with his work, though I used to read *By the Night* all the time. Remember it? I don't think it's around anymore."

I nod. It's completely surreal to hear her talk about Alex. My Alex. For a moment I feel as though I must be mistaken, that it can't possibly be the same man.

Kate's BlackBerry buzzes. She reads the message. "Fuck, my idiot interns forgot to make two copies of the list and now they're getting slammed at the door. I'll be right back." She's already turning to walk away. "You okay?"

I nod, holding up my champagne glass as though it's all I need to get through this night. Hardly, I think, but keep it coming.

Letting my eyes float across the room, a couple of vaguely familiar faces pop out at me, though I don't know from where. Just this city, I think.

Then I see him. He's standing in the middle of a group of people only a few feet away, in between Tracey and Megan Bliss. The way that both of them are flipping their assiduously highlighted hair, I would say that Kate has it wrong. Both sisters are in love. I can't help but stifle a nervous laugh with my free hand; it's just too absurd that this is how I would come across Alex again. When I look back over, he's staring right at me. Shifting my weight nervously from one hip to the other, I look down at my hands and take a deep breath, knowing I'm not prepared to face him yet. When I risk another glance in Alex's direction, he's still looking at me, smiling now. I watch him make his excuses to the Bliss sisters, or at least that's what I glean from their matching crestfallen expressions. I stare into my glass, my heart pounding so hard it seems as if I can feel it in my nose and fingertips.

"Excuse me," he says, and I look up. I've decided in the brief moments since I've seen him that I'll pretend at first not to recognize him. Admitting that I remember him right away will put me in a weak position, particularly since I'm alone at his party. It could much too easily look as if I had contrived this meeting. I feel somehow that I unknowingly *have* contrived this meeting, perhaps only because I knew about it before he did. It suddenly occurs to me that he might also have known, that he might have been sent a guest list with my name on it, seen that I would be here.

"I have to ask. What did you find so funny just now?" My stomach flips. He looks the same. How can that be? Ten years have passed, but he has the same beautiful eyes, same thick, dark hair, only the attractive sprinkling of gray at the temples is new.

"I was just wondering how long it's going to take those two women to claw each other's eyes out over you."

Laughing, he runs his fingers through his hair with a shrug; overt flattery was never lost on him. "They're throwing me this party. A fight would certainly get them some press coverage. Maybe not the kind they want."

"What's that saying? No publicity is bad publicity?"

"Are you in PR?"

I shake my head. "Freelance copy editor."

"You're far too beautiful for that kind of job; *quel dommage*, as we say in Paris."

I smile and stare at the remaining champagne bubbles in my glass; they're moving more slowly now.

"What's your name?"

"Brooke," I say, watching his eyes. Nothing, not even a flicker of recognition. I feel sick and empty, as though I've drunk too much without eating first.

Ten years. Unlike Alex's, my appearance has changed. The hair that once fell past my shoulders is now cropped just beneath my chin in a serious bob, with blunt-cut bangs that hang low over my eyebrows. One of the editors at *Vogue* suggested the style—saying it would make me look like a young Anjelica Huston—and I've kept it ever since. I'm thinner as well, which I can probably also attribute to my time working at fashion magazines. But is that really enough—different hair, slightly sharper cheekbones, better clothes—to render me unrecognizable to a man I'd once been with?

"Alex de Persaud," he says, shaking my hand, something he would never have done back in France, something he must have picked up in the States. Plenty of pretentious kissing of cheeks goes on among this crowd, but maybe he has deemed, correctly, that I am not one of these people.

"So this party is for you, then?" I ask helplessly, given no choice but to follow his lead.

He sighs and nods. "Yes. It's for my new book. My agent won't let me get away with turning things like this down, I'm afraid. How, may I ask, did you end up here?"

"My friend Kate works for the company. I don't know where she is now." I look around, suddenly desperate for Kate to appear and validate my story. "What is your new book about?"

He rolls his eyes as though embarrassed by the whole thing. "It's a book of photographs I've taken. Mostly at parties; it isn't exactly what I would consider my real work, but it's what keeps me in champagne and radishes. It's called *GFY: Paris and New York by the Night*—catchy, no?"

I note that he maintains that his paying work is not his *real* work. "Very. And what does *GFY* stand for?"

"Can I tell you a secret?" He leans in so close to whisper in my ear that I can feel his breath on my neck.

I nod.

" 'Go fuck yourself.' "

"Excuse me?"

"That's what *GFY* is for." He grins. "Not what I told my publishers, of course. I told them it stood for a 'generation of fabulous youth.' Can you believe I sold them on that bullshit?"

"That's bold. What do you have against your publisher?" So that much hasn't changed, I think. He always claimed to be bothered by people like this—the people in his book, the people at this party—and yet here he is.

He turns his shoulder toward me so that we are mostly hidden from the rest of the party by a nearby pole. I know that these moments alone with him cannot possibly last; my mind reels wondering what to say next.

"You see, *chérie*, everyone wants these photographs to be something more than they are. Everyone talks about how they capture some ineffable moment, some excitement, but in reality they are pictures of pretty, young people, pretty, young, *rich* people mostly, doing what they do—which is party. They dance, do drugs, and prepare to fuck each other. When I see these pictures, I see the emptiness behind them, the unhappiness, but that's not what people want to see. In any case, my publisher kept asking me, 'What is the concept?'—so there you have it."

"And they can go fuck themselves."

"I knew you would understand. I can see you're not one of them. You don't think this kind of thing is art, do you?"

I shrugged. "I wouldn't presume to say." He was a bit cynical when we were young—so adamant about who was real and who was not—I suppose it makes sense that he would be even more so now.

He laughs again, and the uninhibited moment triggers in me some long-lost and yet familiar yearning. Mercifully, a waiter approaches with glasses of champagne, and Alex grabs two and hands me one, taking the empty one from my hand and setting it on a nearby table.

"Can I tell you another secret?"

That you knew me in another life? That you haven't entirely forgotten those events that were so important to me?

"I want to leave this party with you right now."

"But it's your party. You have to stay." How can it feel the same to stand next to him after all these years?

"This is true. One of those formaldehyde blondes is bound to come and take me away at any moment, aren't they?"

"I think you mean *peroxide*."

"*Ah, non.* I was referring to what keeps the rest of them intact, not just the hair."

I laugh and give him a rueful look. His English is much improved to make a joke like that.

"In any case, before this happens, you must give me your phone number. I have to go to Paris next week to promote the book, so you must agree to meet me for a drink before then."

My mind races. He's right that someone will swoop him away momentarily; the party's filling up around me. I can't blurt out everything I need to say in the next two minutes—what all that might be, I don't yet know, but I do know I need more time.

"Be brave, *chérie*"—he pulls a phone out of his pocket and awaits my number—"take a chance with the mad Frenchman."

I tell him my number.

"Good. I will call you." Those immortal words.

"I really should go find Kate." I need to be the one to walk away first this time. "*Bisous.*" I lean in to kiss him on his cheek. Blushing as I do so.

"*Ah, tu parles français?*"

"Yes, a little. I studied there when I was in college."

I wait for something to register. Nothing does. I can see it in his eyes, he doesn't remember. I know now that this isn't a game; he has gone on with his life and doesn't remember my ever having been in it.

"It's so charming when Americans speak French," he says.

"*À bientôt.*" I turn on my heel. Looking back over my

shoulder, I see that he's watching me walk away. I admit that I am somewhat gratified by this.

There's no way I can stay at the party now. I'll find Kate and make my apologies. I also feel an urgent need to see James. I tell myself that what I've just done is in no way a betrayal. I don't want Alex, I just want some answers to the questions that have been haunting me all these years. And after tonight's strange interlude, to some new questions. Does he really not remember me? Remember us? Does he comprehend the impact he had, purposefully or not, on my young life?

More champagne certainly isn't the answer, but as I pass yet another waiter with a full tray of glasses, I pluck one off to accompany me on my search for Kate.

I try to look purposeful instead of desperate as I navigate the crowd. Then I see them, the prints of Alex's photographs that have been hung on the back wall. I momentarily forget all about leaving as I'm captivated by the images. They're tastefully small and depict something aspirational and un-touchable: beauty disguised to look ordinary, waifs peeking out from under large hats and wound up in impractical scarves, modern dandies with elaborately manicured beards and full sleeves of tattoos. The people in the photos are posed to look approachable and relaxed, but it's impossible to imag-ine any of them at the DMV.

Then, there she is, like a shot between the eyes. I feel as if I've stumbled on something illicit and my cheeks burn.

Girl, ocean, reads the caption beneath.

I might not have known it was her if I hadn't been stand-ing right beside Alex when he took the photo all those years ago. Her lower half is submerged in the water, her bare back to the camera, wet hair snaking across her shoulders, only a whisper of her face visible in profile.

Sophie.

Does he even know that she's dead?

I GREW UP on a dusty street in a small house in Chino, a part of Southern California that outsiders don't visit unless they have a good reason. It lies in the vast expanse between Los Angeles and Palm Springs, misleadingly referred to as the Inland Empire. It's a place so choked with smog that it seems to be fading right before your eyes, filled with palm trees that look as if they'd rather be anywhere else.

Thanks to my mother, our house was immaculately clean, with a picture of Jesus above the toilet in our one full bathroom. From the time I was little, she was employed as an admin in the registrar's office of the university where I would one day be a student. Since she had started out on the cleaning staff, she was proud of working her way up into a professional job. She tended to win people over if they knew her for any length of time, endowed as she was with a sort of slightly beaten-down enthusiasm that made people want to do things for her, that made people feel especially good about helping her.

We had always gotten along, she and I, but by the time I was preparing to go to the university—on a scholarship that was the result of my good grades and her goodwill—I was saddled with the uncomfortable knowledge that she had spent the last decade of her life scrimping and saving to give me this opportunity. My dad lived in San Diego with a second wife and two small children, and I spoke to him a couple of times a year. By the time I was eighteen we didn't seem to have much to do with each other anymore, given that he was relieved of the burden of his child-support payments and I the burden of his palpable absence, which I had long since gotten used to.

Instead, it was my mother who selflessly and tirelessly worked so that I could go to college with a bunch of rich kids who'd grown up with swimming pools in the backyard and stables nearby where they boarded their horses. And here I was with a shot at the same education they had; naturally I would try to sabotage a thing like that.

I felt in control when I embarked on an affair with my Contemporary Literature professor, Regan Douglas, during my sophomore year of college. Perhaps other women figure out much earlier how to tell when a man thinks they're attractive, but I hadn't needed this sixth sense until I was closer to twenty. It wasn't that no one had ever flirted with me before, but I'd had a jealous boyfriend all through high school, so I didn't interact with other boys much. Kevin was the kind of guy who never leaves Chino, even though his every sentence about the future was preceded by "When I get out of this shithole . . ." Besides his jealous streak, he wasn't very nice to me in general. He only told me I was beautiful twice over the three years we dated, and both times he was blackout drunk. Luckily, he did me the favor of breaking up with me when I went to college. I was getting way too full of myself, he said.

Since I'd had such limited experience with men, I would probably never have taken any particular interest in Regan if I hadn't noticed the ways his eyes clung to me for a split second longer than they needed to, the way they would flicker to me for an infinitesimal moment even when other students were speaking. Aware of his glances, I couldn't stop watching for them and would feel a small thrill of vindication every time I caught him looking. He always seemed a little startled when he looked at me, as though my features were a puzzle that he was attempting to solve.

Once I realized what was happening, I was unstoppable. It wasn't that Regan was so very attractive. The fledgling half men who were my classmates didn't interest me much, and the sentiment seemed to be mutual—with my prominent nose and my dark hair, my curvy but solid frame, I was not the California boy's type. Older men had always paid me a bit more notice, and there were other professors around who were much better looking than Regan. Still, I liked his longish, sandy hair and his intense blue eyes magnified by his glasses. I liked his delicate-looking bones, the angles of his elbows. I'd probably look better with a burlier man, but I've always preferred this elegant, whippetlike build. Here was a man who could never have been anything but a professor of English literature. He would have looked pathetic in a suit sitting in a swivel chair in some corporate office with his narrow shoulders and slightly hunched neck, but here he was lovable and even noble.

As you get older, you have fewer and fewer of the kind of crush that I had on Regan, the kind you organize your day around, where a flitting glance or shoulders nearly brushing against each other can make your afternoon, where every action, no matter how small, is an indicator of the waxing or the waning of feelings, of possibilities.

I found many reasons to go to visit Regan during office hours; never had my appetite for knowledge been so fierce. I would latch onto anything he said in class that could be construed as warranting further discussion. My interest in the subject matter was genuine. Always a voracious reader, I had started experimenting with writing short stories after spending my teenage years filling up my notebooks with fraught poetry about Kevin.

Regan's office was like an outward extension of his mind: cluttered, shabby, and disorganized, but charming all the same. We would spend a cursory twenty minutes or so discussing whatever issue I had ostensibly come to him with and then inevitably veer off, usually onto something in our personal lives tangential to the text we'd been discussing. The inventiveness of these leaps of logic was surely good for my cognitive development, so it can't be said he did nothing for me as a teacher. Before long, I was talking about my mother and he was talking about his young marriage, how it was faltering.

At first I was always the one to make excuses to leave, feeling that if I sat for too long, I would appear pathetic, but as our meetings became more regular, I grew bolder. Our goodbyes became longer and more drawn out. First he would rise from his chair, say he should be leaving since the end of his designated office hours was long past, but instead linger by the door for another ten minutes.

Then one day after a ninety-minute discussion of *Of Human Bondage*—one of our favorite topics, as much for its easily mined sexual undertones as for its literary value—he began to go through the motions of ushering me out the door. He got up from behind his desk to walk me the couple of feet from my chair to the door as was our usual routine. The physical contact had progressed during these send-offs, but not in any way that would seem untoward to the casual observer, if this casual observer saw nothing untoward about my spending so much time there in the first place. Reaching for a shoulder to squeeze, he would sometimes pat me lightly on the back or take me by the elbow and gently steer me toward the door, but that day he took my hand. The hand is fraught territory, partly because it seems so innocuous with its relative distance from any of the textbook dangerous places: breasts, thighs, ass. Still, someone taking your hand is crushingly intimate. He held on to my hand a moment too long, enough to be fairly described as *lingering*, and I tightened my grip, fearing he'd pull away.

"I'm sorry," I whispered, unsure why. But our hands stayed clasped, and after what seemed like an eternity, he took a step closer to me and shut the door. Another interminable silence followed.

"Brooke," he said, his eyes downcast, and for a moment I feared he'd reject me. Dropping his hand, I stared at my feet. I had an entire fantasy built around Regan, and I could feel it unraveling at a breathtaking speed. But as if in a dream, he put his hand to my face and kissed me. I was so shocked my knees nearly buckled.

After the first kiss, the rest unfolded quickly. I had to suffer the burden of Regan's conscience, which ebbed and flowed. One minute he was brazenly screwing me on his desk (more his fantasy than mine, as it was my back and not his that had to endure it), the next he was sobbing in his car at the end of the dark road blocks away from my mother's house about his wife and his job and how he was ruining me, an innocent, a girl not even old enough to join him for a cocktail.

I wished he wouldn't talk about his wife; I didn't want her to be my concern, and as long as she remained abstract enough, I could tell myself that we had nothing to do with each other. As far as my age, I thought he was making too much of it. At twenty I considered myself fully in and of the adult world, and I resented being treated as though I weren't. What was also true but that I didn't tell him—or that I tried once to tell him but retracted when I saw that it only made him cry harder—was that I wanted to be ruined. My innocence, as I saw it, wasn't of any use to me. I felt that I had the right to screw up. After all, for a girl whose dad had left her to start another family elsewhere, I'd never done much acting out.

The affair doesn't bear telling much more about. It's notable, like so many romances, only for its beginning and its end, and in this case the unexpected direction in which it sent my life.

It ended in his home on a hot day near the end of my sophomore year. Despite my growing boredom, which I couldn't have articulated at the time, I was still waging a minor campaign to get Regan to leave his wife. Regan seemed to expect me to comfort him whenever he was feeling guilty about her, to remind him that he was still a good man despite his indiscretion. But my conviction on that point was weakening, and I suggested that if he was really so unhappy in his marriage, perhaps he should leave it; then we could be together without all of the drama. The thought of their marriage made me a little sick, partly because I was intruding upon it and felt guilty, partly because I was horrified by the idea that this was what most marriages were actually like, that this could be my eventual fate too. Yet Regan seemed aghast at the suggestion of his leaving. Wounded by his reaction, I curled myself on one end of his couch, refusing to look him in the eye as I spoke.

"Well, do you love her?" I pulled my legs in closer to my chest, sweat pooling behind my knees, Regan's antiquated air conditioner doing nothing to combat the mid-May heat wave. He had one elbow propped up on the opposite arm of the couch, and with his free hand he was scratching the uneven beginnings of a beard that dotted his jawline. I hated him when he gave me the look he was giving me now, as if I were a student who was boring him with a question to which the answer was obvious. Truthfully I never listened to him when he spoke in class anymore. For one thing my grade was hardly a concern, and for another I couldn't focus; half the time I would be fantasizing about him, and the other half, increasingly so lately, I spent thinking up reasons to pick fights. During these lectures I made a deep and nuanced study of his reactions and facial expressions. Horrifyingly, he made the same face when a student he had been leading to a certain conclusion finally reached it as when he finally achieved orgasm and let out a similarly triumphant "Yes," and his deep look of focus when considering a well-made point was just like the face he made when getting a blow job. Recently this had made me prone to horrible bouts of giggles not only in his classroom but occasionally also in the bedroom.

"It's a fair question," I said now, poking him in the rib

cage with my big toe. I meant it to be a playful gesture, but it felt aggressive on contact. He seemed so tired these days that even the slightest movement made him seem like a weary, beaten-down dog. He hadn't been sleeping, he'd told me, and it was putting him on edge. I wasn't sympathetic to this since I naively couldn't quite imagine having done something that kept me up at night.

"You know what the answer will be," he said, irritation edging into his voice. A flush swept over his face; his transparent, pale skin always made it difficult for him to hide his emotions.

"If that were true, I wouldn't be asking the question. I thought you said you didn't even sleep together anymore." I was tempted to move closer to him on the couch, but I was suddenly gripped by a nauseating fear that he would push me away if I did so.

"We don't," Regan said, now facing me. He didn't wear his wire-rim glasses in the house though I liked him better with them on. Without them his eyes looked beady and the skin around his eyes appeared looser and more damaged, making him seem older than thirty-six. "I'm not *in* love with her. There's a huge difference. You'll understand someday. . . ."

"Oh, don't you dare." I stared straight ahead. "Don't you go there."

The subject of my age, or rather my age relative to his, was our mutual weapon in these fights, the double-edged sword that we would take turns threatening each other with. He used it to remind me that he had wisdom on his side; I to remind him that other people would think that he was taking advantage of me if they ever found out about us.

There was a long pause. I examined the army of tchotch-kes that was stationed on every flat surface of the living room: little ceramic animals, Russian nesting dolls, miniature silver picture frames. None of this could have been Regan's; how could I not have noticed before that it was all her? I suddenly fantasized about walking over to the cabinet and sweeping off a whole batch of them with my forearm. I could practically hear the dozen little pops of the tiny ceramics as they smashed to the floor.

"Brooke, I'm sorry. What do you want me to do, lie to you?"

"Ha! As though you don't lie every day."

"Lies of omission are different. You asked me a direct question, and I gave you a direct answer. There is a difference between love and sex."

Normally in these kinds of arguments, I solved the problem by crawling into his arms and kissing him. Right now nothing sounded less appealing, not to mention that I would, in essence, be proving his point. The truth was that my sympathy for his passionless marriage that he seemed incapable of leaving had turned into a sort of disgusted pity, and pity has a way of extinguishing desire. The heart is simply not equipped to feel these two things simultaneously.

After a few more minutes, I got up wordlessly and left. He didn't try to stop me.

A pleasant breeze was blowing outside, and as I made my way up the walkway to my car, I passed through a pocket of orange-blossom fragrance and momentarily felt better. Mulling over our discussion, I drove back to campus past parched hillsides dotted with billboards and sad little houses surrounded by chain-link fencing. My stomach was growling. I could never eat in front of Regan; I wouldn't even feel hungry when he was around. However, after spending a few hours with him I would leave and instantly become ravenous. This nervous energy that extinguished my appetite was yet another thing that I mistook for love.

Something had changed between Regan and me. I reminded myself that what we were doing was risky and dangerous, and if people found out, he would be fired and I would be scandalized. Yet in reality it was all starting to feel pretty commonplace.

The next morning Regan was not in his Contemporary Lit class. Instead, poor, nervous Mr. Flannigan was filling in for him. I was distracted throughout class. Regan hadn't been sick the night before and hadn't mentioned being out. I racked my brain for a possible explanation.

After class, Flannigan motioned me away from the stream of students leaving the stuffy lecture room and said, avoiding eye contact, "Brooke, Dean Keller asked me to send you up to see him after class."

"Oh," I said stupidly. "Um, I have a meeting with Professor Miller in a few minutes."

"She's been informed, Brooke, you should go." As he said this, he gave me a strange look: sympathetic and accusing at the same time. It didn't make me feel any better. The idea of getting caught out with Regan had always been thrilling, but now that it seemed to be happening, I felt nothing but an empty thud of dread in my stomach.

"Okay," I said, "thanks for letting me know."

Flannigan shot me a tight smile.

I was anxious walking up the hill to the admin building, so much so that I was short of breath by the time I arrived. At the door of Dean Keller's office, his assistant, Patricia, greeted me and asked me to wait. The bristly seat covering on the chair scratched at the back of my legs and I regretted having worn shorts.

Eventually Keller appeared at the door of his office. "Come on in, Brooke."

Keller's affable nature was a thin veneer, as he was a vicious old disciplinarian with a penchant for Jerry Falwell's brand of Christian values. As a child, I would come with my mom to work and visit him in his office, where he would ask me what new words I'd learned since the last time I'd seen him and give me a few pieces of the candy he kept in his desk. Now that she worked in the registrar's office, my mother didn't see him much, though he loved talking about us: the university's hard-luck charity case.

"Brooke, how is your mother?" Dean Keller began. He never had any conversation that wasn't padded on either side with small talk, as if that changed what came in between.

"She's fine. Dean Keller, why am I here?" I blurted, feeling unable to withstand chitchat.

Dean Keller let out a long sigh before telling me the news that would change my young life. Regan had resigned. He would be relocating with his wife, Michelle, to his home state of Ohio. He had broken down the night before and told Michelle everything, and she had gone straight to Dean Keller early the next morning. Until that point, I had carefully avoided knowing her name, and just like that, she became a real person. I imagined her showing up in person, puffy-eyed and ragged, to stake out Keller's office. Or maybe she filled up his voice mail with angry tirades. I imagined Michelle would want to be reassured that the girl would be dealt with, would have reminded him of the moral code that the students were obliged to sign during freshman orientation. Maybe she was unsatisfied that only Regan should pay for the affair and decided that she, who'd gotten nothing out of it except perhaps for the endless contrition of her husband, must be vindicated. Or maybe she'd done none of this and only the dean himself was so concerned with my behavior.

I sat stunned in Dean Keller's office as he spoke, nodding from time to time when some sort of response or affirmation seemed necessary. But I wasn't listening. My own thoughts overwhelmed me. I would never see Regan again. And now the wife was not an abstract but a person named Michelle who'd just found out her husband was a philanderer. Was there a way around my mother ever knowing about this? I wondered. I felt as long as she didn't know, all was not lost.

The administration was full of promises that the situation would be kept quiet as long as I cooperated. Keller told me I was still an important and valued asset to the university and that they didn't wish for me to leave permanently. Fortunately for me, the moral code contained no language specific to fucking one's literature professor. So they were left to their own creative devices for an acceptable solution.

Miraculously, my fellow students didn't seem aware of what had happened. If there were rumors, they never reached my ears. I added this oversight to the mounting evidence that I was a person who could slide through life without anyone's noticing, even, evidently, if I did something outrageous. At that time, I felt this trait would eventually prove useful, as though I might be called to espionage or a career as an anthropologist.

I must give Keller his due; he promised I wasn't going to be punished and so I wasn't. Instead, a "sojourn," the word he jauntily used, to France might be a good option since I was a strong student of the language. This was something of an overstatement, however. I was an adequate student of French, but I spent a fair amount of each class trying to avoid eye contact with the professor. I knew that Keller's encouraging me to spend a year abroad was more influenced by his desire to have me far enough away that he could distance himself from the scandal than by his belief that I would benefit from the experience.

It didn't matter. Getting away would be welcome, and a year in France appealed to me as a measured adventure with little risk. The language choices at my high school had been slim and limited to Spanish—which half of the students at my school spoke fluently already—and introductory French, and I chose French because it fit much better with my idea of a future self. I liked the language, the preponderance of lazy vowel sounds, and the extraneous consonants. Even the fact that the language was less rich and diverse than English had its own special appeal and gave me the idea that the French were less pedantic, more laissez-faire, than Anglophones. *Je t'aime,* darling, "I like you, I love you." What's the difference? Imagine not needing different words for *love* and *like*; half of the girls I knew practically lived and died by this nuance.

And what about Sophie? We weren't exactly friends in

those days. We knew each other from French class, but we weren't close, and friendship is something girls of that age take quite seriously. If I was the kind of girl who could slip into class ten minutes late unnoticed, Sophie was the kind of girl whose arrival might as well have been heralded by a marching band.

She was the kind of gorgeous, athletic blonde that California specializes in. She was from a small, wealthy town on the coast, where everyone has enormous, gleaming kitchens full of granite and steel and knows how to play tennis. You wanted her to be an idiot just to prove that the world was fair, but she was at the top of her class of econ majors, a permanent fixture on the dean's list. I wanted to hate her, but I couldn't find anything to justify it.

Our worlds didn't cross much in those days. She was occupied with the volleyball team and the boys I would always see following her around campus, hanging on her every word. We sat by each other in French class and occasionally got coffee afterward, a casual flirtation. Part of me wanted to know her better, but I was a little intimidated by her, and I was a little awkward then. I had friends, but not a lot of them. The bonds that seemed to come so naturally to girls like Sophie and her friends often eluded me, and I was simply more comfortable alone.

At college, I did have something of a best friend in Allegra. The daughter of wealthy hippies from Berkeley, she was a fellow English major who was pretty in a pale, ethereal way that no one seemed to quite appreciate the way she felt they ought to. We talked mostly about books and moving to New York or Berlin after school.

But our friendship had been strained recently by my relationship with Regan, since the burden of keeping the secret left me with little energy for other relationships.

Now I found myself facing a void, alleviated only by the school year's drawing to a close.

I smiled to myself when our French professor brought up the study-abroad program in a medium-size French city called Nantes. She gave some stats about the city: the sixth-largest in France, located on the Loire River. None of it meant much to me. All I cared about was that it was France, which was enticing no matter which city. My enthusiasm was only slightly tempered by the knowledge that my own bad behavior had landed me the opportunity. My eyes swept over the other students in our small class of ten. Sophie looked rapt; I caught her eye and she smiled.

As the class spilled out into the baroque corridor of the old Arts and Letters building, Sophie grabbed my arm and pulled me toward her conspiratorially. The intimacy of this startled me, since we'd never touched before.

"We're going," she said, giving me a sly smile. Her eyes were lit up with excitement.

"Where?" I asked, struck a little dumb by her torrent of energy.

She leaned away from me to playfully smack my arm and let out a peal of laughter, a melodious sound that most men and almost as many women found completely irresistible. "To France! We're going."

I admit the *we* thrilled me. And though I knew I was going, I felt as if I had to seem to be still considering it. "It does sound cool. I worry that my French isn't strong enough, though."

She dismissed this with a wave of her hand. "Your French is fine. And it will get better so fast."

"I've never been out of the country before," I said, suddenly embarrassed that I'd admitted to her what was actually a sizable understatement: I'd never even been on a plane before.

"Brooke!" she said, stopping at the top of the stairwell. "Come *on.*" She held my shoulders with both hands, her grasp had an almost violent cheerfulness.

I relented. "Okay," I said, as though the decision were both spontaneous and wholly my own. "I'll try to make it work, I promise."

"Ha!" She hugged me with one arm.

Turning the corner, we found Stacey—Sophie's teammate and most recent sidekick—waiting for her, staring at her phone disconsolately. Stacey looked like a cheap facsimile of Sophie with her harshly dyed blond hair, and unlike Sophie, Stacey did actually seem a little bit stupid.

"Stace," Sophie said, causing the girl's head to snap up, her brow furrowed and looking as if she was on the verge of tears. "Oh my God, no. I told you not to text him!"

Stacey sighed and her shoulders drooped as if someone had deflated her. She looked straight at Sophie, without seeming to register me. "It's not like I'm being crazy! I just asked him how his Tuesday was going."

"And he didn't write back."

"Maybe he's just busy."

"What is Brad busy with? He barely goes to class."

"Water polo . . . ?"

Sophie shook her head. Suddenly both of them seemed to

remember that I was still there. "Stace, you know Brooke?" It was something of a rhetorical question: almost everyone at our school of fifteen hundred knew each other on some level.

"Hi," Stacey said with a smile as if she'd smelled something a little sour.

"Brooke, we'll talk later."

With that, the two blondes glided off down the hallway, Sophie taking Stacey's arm, presumably comforting her. Their world seemed no less foreign to me than France.

❧

Even if I hadn't already been going to France, Sophie might easily have convinced me. She was a difficult person to say no to. She had the robust sheen of a girl who gets what she wants in life, usually without trying too hard. And she was adventurous in a way that made you think that going along with her wasn't something you'd regret. In the middle of her sophomore year, she had taken time off from school to go on a mission trip to Peru with her cousin. That she'd somehow convinced the famously uptight administration to let her go was a testament to her powers of persuasion; that she'd caught up with schoolwork so quickly after her absence was a testament to her smarts. I was slightly in awe of her, as was almost everyone I knew.

The joint adventure in front of us gave Sophie and me a reason to get closer.

"Oh, please come," she said to me of her volleyball game the following Tuesday night. "I'm afraid no one will show up in the stands!"

I dragged a pouting Allegra with me. Despite Allegra's

obvious disdain for the game, she was clearly happy to have me back from my affair with Regan, and she agreed to accompany me there and to a handful of other places Sophie invited me: a frat party where I was introduced to every member of the men's water polo team, including the infamous Brad, who looked rather worth the fuss that poor Stacey had made over him. He was, like his teammates, flush with good health despite the vast quantities of beer and pizza they all seemed to consume, tall and impossibly broad shouldered, golden tan from the sun with chlorinated hair sticking up in a way that gave him a vulnerable, boyish quality. My mom would have called him a hunk.

A long, torpid summer followed that semester. Sophie went away to coach volleyball at the resort where she always spent her summers, and I stayed home working at the same drive-through Starbucks where I'd been three summers running. I was long past caring if the men who came by in their pickups looked down my shirt when I handed them their change, especially if it meant a bigger tip.

Sophie called me often, as though she had already decided we were best friends. It seemed as if she were watching every movie ever set in France, reading Fitzgerald and Hemingway and Anaïs Nin—in other words, giving herself over completely to the fantasy of what our trip would be like. I, on the other hand, was somehow too afraid to do this. I was worried about being disappointed, I was afraid to hope too hard.

Sophie even came for dinner one night, after my mother had invited her spontaneously when she'd called and I'd been in the shower. I didn't say anything for fear of hurting my mother's feelings, but I was ashamed for Sophie to come out to Chino. But if she'd found it vile, she hadn't shown it, as she charmed my mother, complimenting everything from her cooking to her skin to her taste in dishware.

My mother was deliriously excited for me, though it was a bittersweet happiness, as I could plainly see her longing to be in my place. Well, not in my place precisely, but to have once been in my place. At least once a week she would mutter apropos of nothing, "I always wanted to go to France . . . " and then trail off dreamily, with the eyes of someone watching a ship they wished to be on recede into the distance. She had taken French lessons long ago with a friend of hers at the local community center, and she seized upon this opportunity to make up decks of flash cards to quiz my vocabulary. My mother and I switched off cooking dinner each night, and as soon as the trip was planned, she dug out her old but completely untouched volume of Julia Child's *Mastering the Art of French Cooking* with the idea that we would make dinner from it every night, but after a few days of the strenuous recipes we retreated back to our old basics of meatballs and marinara and store-bought roast chicken. During these long evenings together I often wondered what might have happened if my mother had found out about Regan, and it hit me how much I'd had at stake, that it would have killed me to see her as disappointed as I knew she would be.

"Are you going to be okay without me for a whole year?" I asked her cautiously one night while I was standing at the sink rinsing our dinner dishes.

"Of course I will. I did manage to survive before you were born, you know." She poked me lightly in the ribs as she went by.

"I just don't want you to get too lonely."

"That's sweet, honey, but I'll manage. I hope *you* don't get too lonely over there. You know the French can be a bit prickly."

"I'll be fine." Finishing the dishes, I wiped my hand on a towel. "Besides, there will be other Americans there. Sophie is going."

"I like Sophie. She will be good for you."

"Yeah, she's great." I rinsed the last remnants of food into the drain and paused to let our ancient disposal do its worst. "Wait, what does that mean exactly? That she'll be good for me?" I poured myself tap water and followed my mother out to the porch, where she liked to sit and drink a glass of chardonnay on warm evenings.

"She just seems very friendly is all. Very . . . healthy."

"And I'm not?"

"You withdraw sometimes." My mom looked at her fingernails in apparent consternation. "I just worry. It's not a criticism," she continued when I was silent in response, "it's probably my fault."

"No, Mom"—I curled my legs underneath me and stared out into the street that was still half-lit with waning sunlight—"it's not your fault."

❧

I left on a Saturday and arrived in Paris after the twelve-hour flight disoriented and disheveled, my every nerve ending frayed from excitement and stress. I wished that Sophie had been able to make the trip with me, but she was meeting some girls from the volleyball team who were also studying abroad for a week in Greece before the school year started. I knew from class that her French was better than mine, and she tended to walk decisively, she wouldn't dither from one terminal to the next looking like a dazed newborn animal the way I did.

From De Gaulle I took a train to Gare Montparnasse, where I was to board a train bound directly for Nantes. Dazzled and terrified, I arrived at the train station, my eyes still dry from the stale, recycled plane air and blinking at the massive departure board, which looked delicate and antique compared to the one at LAX. One of the wheels on my large, cumbersome rolling suitcase broke, and I was forced to drag, instead of roll, it through the crowded tunnels. I was reminded of my inferior language skills upon being nearly robbed when I took several moments too long to understand that a man next to me was telling me that the two teenagers behind me had their hands in my backpack. Sophie would have fended them off, I thought, and she would have done so using the *subjonctif*, and everyone whom she'd have asked for directions would have understood and obliged. A small twinge of jealousy was followed by a wave of relief that she would be with me soon and that we were going to be in France together.

I was not completely shy, but people could exhaust me quickly, and sometimes I got so caught up in observing that I forgot to actually interact. I was comfortable with this. I felt it gave me a secret sort of upper hand to absorb the details of people's lives without having to offer any of my own.

Shaking with exhaustion, I emerged aboveground from the station in Nantes. I could feel tears swelling under my lids and thought if even one more person looked at me with that mix of sympathy and disgust that I had seen on the faces of strangers all day, I would definitely cry. I was relieved by the complete indifference of the cabdriver who awaited me outside the station, the sole cab waiting at the stand. During the short drive, I tried to compose myself. Soon I would have to meet new people, many new people, some who spoke no English. I felt as though I would lapse into a coma if I lay down that moment, and I tentatively leaned my head back on the seat and closed my eyes for a blissful second, only to be jolted back into the present as we hit a pothole hard while careening down a narrow alley.

"C'est par là," the taxi driver said, pulling up beside a narrow drive that ran between two buildings. The streets had a surreal, anonymous feel to them, like a movie set, and street signs were plastered obscurely to the sides of buildings. No entrance was visible nor any sign indicating the school was here.

"Ici?" I asked incredulously. My voice sounded weak, as though I were talking to the driver through a drainpipe.

"Oui, oui. Six rue de Cadiniers." He gestured to a small plaque affixed to the side of the brick building as he got out of the cab to help with my bag. I scrambled out onto the sidewalk and handed him the fare I was clutching tightly in my sweaty palm.

"Merci." He flipped through the bills, never quite making actual eye contact. He grunted as he settled back into the driver's seat, then he was gone and I found myself alone on the empty street. I looked at the sign more closely, getting increasingly nervous. What would I do if I discovered I had been abandoned on the wrong street? I had no cell phone. I would have to walk along the street until I found somewhere

with people and a phone, dragging my gigantic suitcase along with me.

I stood on the sidewalk next to my massive case that had been brand-new when I left but already looked beat-up after the long journey. My mother and I had found the navy-blue canvas suitcase with cream piping on sale at Marshalls, and we'd both thought it looked pretty chic. I dragged it behind me toward the foyer of the ground floor. Peering into the breezeway that led to the entrance, I finally spotted a small handwritten sign that read L'INSTITUT FRANCO-AMÉRICAIN TROISIÈME ÉTAGE and felt a great flood of relief, as if I'd just stepped out of the way of an oncoming bus.

"Oh, thank God," I said aloud, and my voice seemed to echo throughout the street. Pulling back the screen of the ancient elevator, a new problem presented itself. The elevator was tiny, not at all equipped for a vulgar American with her supersize suitcase. Either I was going up to the third floor or my luggage was, but not both, not simultaneously. I heard the slamming of a car door behind me in the street and turned around to the welcome sight of a face, obscured by blond hair, leaning down to a driver, that I recognized in an instant.

"Sophie!"

Her head snapped up and her hair fell away. She smiled and pulled her sunglasses off, despite the bright glare in the alley.

"Brooke!" Leaning back down to the open window of the cab, she quickly addressed the driver and handed over money.

She had a monogrammed carryall with telltale brown and tan Louis Vuitton squares slung around her shoulder and a matching suitcase that had already been deposited on the street—both bags looked broken in and well loved. She left her luggage on the sidewalk to run over and throw her arms around me.

We hugged each other, jumping up and down.

"Let me get that." I relieved her of the carryall.

"Thanks! My cabdriver was so nice. He says he has a daughter our age in California. She even plays volleyball. Can you believe that?"

That the cabdriver had a daughter who was Sophie's doppelgänger or that Sophie had befriended one of the first people she'd encountered on French soil? I wondered. "Amazing," I said in answer to both.

It was a warm day and I was sweating from the exertion of hauling luggage. Glad for the coolness of the shaded stone foyer, I got a better look at Sophie as my eyes relaxed from the sun. "Quite a tan you've got there," I said, noting with envy how brown her skin was, how blond her hair. People exposed themselves to all manner of chemicals to get this look, only to come out looking like rejects from a bodybuilding competition. Yet on Sophie it was both perfectly natural and naturally perfect.

"I worked very hard on it this summer," she said, white teeth gleaming. "It won't help me fit in here, though."

"You can just pretend you spent your summer on the Côte d'Azur. No one has to know it's an American tan."

"And Grecian." She checked out the elevator situation.

"You go up first and then I'll send the bags. I don't see how else we can get them up to the third floor."

"Genius," she said, stepping into the elevator, "thank God we both arrived at the same time!"

She pulled the screen closed and let out a surprised little laugh as the elevator began to lurch and groan around her.

After we finished our luggage procession, we found ourselves facing a grand doorway from behind which the faint murmur of voices could be heard. I noticed a tiny doorbell in the frame and buzzed it. After a shuffling from within, the door slowly opened with such a creak that one would have thought it had been sealed for a century. An older woman about five feet tall appeared in the threshold, her wide eyes bearing a wary and somewhat accusatory look as they darted back and forth over Sophie and me.

"Bonjour," she said hurriedly, then mumbled something in the direction of the floor as she turned back toward the foyer, from which I gleaned that we were meant to follow her. So the two of us dragged our luggage awkwardly behind us into a foyer with a worn wooden floor and an elaborate but threadbare rug. An enormous mirror with a gilt gold frame took up the wall that faced the door. I was greeted and momentarily startled by my bedraggled reflection, my hair pulled back in a sloppy knot with errant curls sticking out all over my head, the little eye makeup that I had applied before the journey pooled in the corners of my eyes and my face flushed. I wanted desperately to shower before meeting anyone new. The tiny woman said something and gestured to a smaller room off to the side where luggage and coats were piled high, before disappearing down a hallway.

"It's smaller than I would have thought," Sophie remarked as we picked our way through the luggage and jostled our bags into place. Most of us would be studying primarily at the institute itself, with some of the more advanced students taking classes at the university with our French peers. I tried to discern something about our fellow Americans from the suitcases, but the rolling bags obviously borrowed from parents and the backpacks with slogans and patches sewn onto them revealed little. Sophie looked at me. "How many of us are there again?"

"I don't know." I glanced out a nearby window onto the street, where a man walked briskly with a baguette underneath his arm, a small dog trotting along at his feet. "Thirty maybe?"

We stood there for another minute to collect ourselves before walking back into the main room.

"*Bonjour, les filles,*" a bright voice came from the other direction. A middle-aged woman burst forth from the hallway, her arms opened. This must be Madame Rochet, *la directrice.* She had on a tight white top that offered up a modest but astonishingly perky décolletage, and a fitted black pencil skirt finished off with a smart, wide belt and four-inch heels. Her extremely youthful figure nearly excused the age-inappropriateness of the outfit. She wore her graying blond hair in a perfectly coiffed bob that evoked a sexier Anna Wintour and had luminous eyes and a bright, crooked smile. Ah, I thought, a fresh bit of delight creeping through me, how very *French.* There is something intimidating about a beautiful older woman that a younger version could never match. She looked at Sophie and me with a broad grin, as though we were exactly whom she had been hoping to see.

"*Bonjour,*" Sophie and I offered quietly in unison.

At that moment the doorbell buzzed. Madame Rochet

strode with admirable dexterity in her high, high heels to the door and opened it, issuing another warm welcome to a boy and a girl as they walked through the door with their luggage. The boy was tall with fair hair cut close to his scalp; he had broad shoulders and a wide, friendly face. He smiled at us as he glided by in long strides. His carriage, slightly prim expression, and somewhat showy gestures when he spoke to his companion were recognizable as those of someone who is newly inhabiting their sexuality, who has turned up the volume of a recently discovered self. The girl was shorter and a bit stocky; she had shoulder-length blond hair and an ordinary face that was not unattractive save for its beleaguered expression.

The four of us reconvened in the main salon and Madame Rochet came in with a list. *"Alors, nous avons Brooke Thompson, Adam McNeil, Lindsay Adams et Sophie Martin, n'est-ce pas?"* Madame Rochet spoke slowly with careful, deliberate enunciation. I marveled at the sound of my name from the mouth of a native French speaker, the *b* and the *r* nearly buried beneath the melodious double *o* and the definitive, emphatic *k*. I never wanted to hear it said any other way.

She explained to us in painfully slow French that our respective host families would be coming by in a few hours to pick us up. In the meantime, a number of cafés were right next to the institute if we would like to pass a little time there. After Madame Rochet left, Sophie introduced me to the new twosome and suggested that we go find coffee.

We settled for the small, dingy café across from the institute. I could tell Sophie wanted to venture farther and find something better but acquiesced when Lindsay started to sigh impatiently. Since it was so pleasant out, we sat at one of the sidewalk tables.

"You two know each other already?" Lindsay asked after the waiter took our orders.

"Yes," I said.

"We're good friends from school," Sophie added. Mortifyingly, I felt myself blush to hear Sophie describe us as good friends.

"Oh, yes?" Adam asked in a light, utterly disarming drawl. "We're boyfriend-girlfriend."

A pronounced moment of silence descended on the table before Lindsay and Adam simultaneously burst out laughing. "I'm messing with you, *les filles. Je suis* gay."

"Good thing," Lindsay said as the waiter brought out coffees. "I wouldn't date you anyway."

Adam lit up a cigarette and took a deep drag. "Be nice, Lindsay, or I'll tell all the boys in the program you have back hair."

"All ten of them? I don't have back hair, by the way."

"As opposed to how many girls?" I asked.

"Twenty? Twenty-five, I think?" Adam said. "Not good odds, ladies, and even less so for lonely little old me."

"You're not old," I said, "and I'm sure you won't end up lonely."

"Past my prime already, twenty-two! Why, it was just yesterday I was a young fag and Lindsay here a young hag."

"I wish you wouldn't use that word," Lindsay said, scrunching up her face.

"What are the chances, though," Sophie said, sidestepping the awkward moment, after the rest of her cappuccino disappeared in her mouth, leaving only foam in her cup, "that no other guy here in a *French* program will be gay? I think you have luck on your side, *mon chéri.*"

"Thank you, lovely Sophie, but it doesn't matter. *Je cherche un homme français; il faut faire comme les Français*—if you know what I mean." His accent was not as perfect as Sophie's, and the words came forth a bit laboriously, but he was competent and spoke with an enviable self-assurance. My fears were renewed that I would be the worst speaker here.

"You'd like to do as the French do? As in you'd like to do the French?" Sophie asked.

I laughed and Lindsay rolled her eyes.

"Why, yes," he said, affecting his best Southern-belle imitation. "But really we all have to have French boyfriends. Our grandchildren will be so disappointed if we can't tell them stories about the French boyfriends we had *long* before we met their grandfathers."

"You've come with big plans," I said.

"I'm here to work on my French," Lindsay said with a sniff, "and, you know, actually *learn* something about the world."

"Lindsay"—Adam rolled his eyes—"will you please stop acting like a surly virgin!"

"I'm not a—"

"I said *acting.* No one needs a little *amour français* more than you. Just saying."

Adam and Lindsay registered our slightly uncomfortable smiles and laughed.

"Don't mind us," Lindsay said, the edge gone from her

voice. *"Ce n'est que l'amour."* She and Adam beamed at each other.

"You guys both speak French really well," I said. "How long have you been taking classes?"

"Since I was five," Lindsay said. "I went to school in Geneva, so it was required."

"Fancy," Sophie said.

Lindsay shrugged.

"I *technically* learned in high school, but the French classes at my school were abysmal," Adam said. "I learned more from watching the old Yves Allégret films I borrowed from the library."

"I'm a little surprised that they had things like that where you grew up," Lindsay said. "No offense, just seems a little outré for small-town Georgia."

"None taken." Adam twisted his cigarette into the ashtray. "I grew up in Shit Town, Georgia. Most people there could barely be said to actually speak English, let alone anything else."

A charity case like me, I thought, smiling. I knew I liked him.

By the time we got back to the institute, my host family was already there. They had showed up earlier than expected, but I was still a little embarrassed that I'd made them wait. Muttering an apology, I clambered out of the common room with my luggage.

I was spirited off by my new host parents, Pierre and Nicole Dubois, in a small blue Peugeot. They were modestly dressed, with kind smiles that I found immeasurably reassuring. I imagined that the family might become important to me. But that was before I'd met the man whose presence would eclipse every other moment of my life in France, before I had an inkling of what Sophie would mean to me.

The house was like all the others on its street: four stories of red brick, with a steep roof topped with a crooked weathervane, tucked snugly in between two other houses. Tall, wiry Pierre navigated my enormous suitcase up the narrow staircase. He smiled intermittently and reassured me that he was *"très fort!"* even though the strain showed on his weathered face. Dinner with their three children—teenaged twins and an adorable, mouselike ten-year-old named Maximilian—was as awkward conversationally as one could expect given the circumstances, despite their efforts to speak slowly on my behalf. The meal was simple—roasted chicken with vegetables—but was followed with fruits, cheeses, and yogurt, a procession that seemed both formal and habitual.

My host mother urged me to bed early and brought a tisane to my room, a cozy attic space with a slanted ceiling that housed a desk and a simple brass bed with a blue coverlet.

"Bientôt tu rêveras en français," she said just before closing the door. *Soon you will be dreaming in French.*

W HEN I arrived at the institute the next morning, I found Sophie in the small kitchen adjacent to the coatroom. The rest of the students had arrived and a low hum of chatter filled the rooms, punctuated by the occasional squeal or exclamation.

"Good morning," Sophie said when she saw me.

"*Bonjour*. There's coffee?"

Sophie was wearing black jeans and a black-and-white–striped T-shirt, her hair wet from the shower. She handed me a round cardboard container. "No, actually, there's Nescafé. Coffee facsimile. I need it anyway, my host family only keeps tea in the house. I assumed for some reason that all Europeans drank espresso; that's the first of many things I'll be wrong about I'm sure." She yawned, mouth broad as a jungle cat's.

"Tired?" I added hot water from the electronic kettle to the dubious-looking dark powder.

"Yeah. Went for a run this morning."

"Oh, God, you didn't. I hate you and your discipline."

She laughed. "You're welcome to join me next time. Although I will warn you that my host family thought it was totally bizarre. But if I get out of my routines, I'll never get back into them."

"It is odd being in someone's house all of a sudden, with

their family. I can't quite relax yet. How's your family, other than the no-coffee thing and the reaction to your exercise habits?"

"Sweet." She winced as she finished the dregs of coffee in the bottom of her cup. "The parents anyway. There's an eighteen-year-old girl who's kind of a brat, but then, she's eighteen."

We both nodded knowingly, as though eighteen were so young. It felt like a big two years back then.

"What about your family?"

"Oh, I like them, they seem nice." My eyes searched the counter for something to add to the bitter instant coffee and located a sugar bowl. Leaning against the door to the kitchen, I sipped my coffee, which was nearly bearable with two spoonfuls of sugar, looking around at the other students. Nearly indistinguishable, they all looked vaguely sporty, collegiate, and earnest. In other words, American. I saw only three boys, all wearing the tattered, white baseball hats so common on college campuses. I doubted they would make any effort to fit in, and they were unwelcome reminders of what I was surrounded with back home. The room was filled with the particular din of many women speaking at once. The words that could be picked out were mostly English. I suspected we all felt timid with French and would for some time to come. Suddenly I saw Adam's face weaving through the crowd several inches above the surrounding brunette and blond heads.

"Adam," Sophie called out.

"*J'arrive!*" He made a dramatic show of struggling through the crowded hallway and into the kitchen. "*Bonjour, les filles.*"

"*Coucou!*" we heard Madame Rochet call from the main

salon, beckoning us all to the buses going to La Rochelle. We were headed to the beach resort for a welcome trip, a chance to bond with each other and to see the seaside before we settled into life in Nantes.

Sophie and I shared a room at the Ibis chain hotel from which we could see a sliver of the ocean from the dingy balcony if we craned our necks just right. I remember that the room smelled like smoke, not in an off-putting way, just another little reminder that you weren't in America, where virtually nothing smelled like smoke anymore.

"I like this place," Sophie said, stepping out onto the balcony. "Not the hotel, I mean, but La Rochelle. I'm afraid by the time we leave I'll wish that we were here instead of in Nantes."

"Don't you like Nantes?"

"No, I do. But this place is so charming. I think since I grew up on a coast, I'll always prefer to be by the ocean. You know?"

"Yeah," I said, though I knew nothing about preferring places that reminded me of where I grew up; I always preferred the opposite.

We had time before dinner, so we took a leisurely walk around La Rochelle. The posh and polished seaside town had tidy cobblestone streets and gleaming sailboats knocking against each other in the harbor. Vast moorings contained boats of all sizes. It sparked my imagination to see them all sitting there without their owners. What sort of life would bring someone to this harbor in one of these beautiful boats? I was shot through with longing to have such a life and wondered if it could ever be possible.

"Which one is yours?" Sophie asked, smiling and perhaps, I thought, reading my mind. People had so often told me I was stoic, yet Sophie seemed to know what I was thinking just by looking at me. Magical, all-seeing Sophie.

"That one." I pointed to a striking white sailboat with gleaming brass finishings and a line of small portholes in a tidy row.

"You're such a romantic to choose a sailboat. Well, now we have to go and see what its name is." She took off trotting down the pier. I laughed and followed her. Our sandaled feet smacked the boards of the dock, and an older couple who were sitting on the deck of their small yacht glared at us. I didn't care.

"La Puissance."

"I don't know what that means."

"Neither do I."

We looked at each other and laughed.

"I think it's pretty bad to not know the name of your own yacht; it's like having a tattoo in a language you can't read. But moving on, which one is yours?"

"Definitely that one," she said, having already chosen. She pointed to one of the larger, newer-looking yachts.

"You would need a captain and crew for that one, I think." I put my hand over my eyes to shield them from the sun and marveled at the huge vessel.

"I can obviously afford it," she said, tossing her hair. "I mean, look at the size of my yacht!"

We walked over to investigate, peeking around the corner surreptitiously as though the owner might come above decks at any second to shoo us away.

"One Fish, Two Fish," Sophie read. "I'm such a cheese ball to pick an American boat. Santa Barbara, CA. Wow, they're a long way from home"—she glanced back at me—"just like us."

"It's strange to think there are other Americans here right now."

"Why's that?"

"I don't know. I just don't want there to be." Maybe I'd been naive to think we'd be the only ones.

"Oh, we're *everywhere.* The Australians are just as bad, though, and the Germans! They take up half of Greece in the summer! But we don't have to be that kind of American. We can be *Franco-américaines.* We can be hybrids." She reached out to nudge the edge of the boat with her foot as though testing to see if it was real. "Come on." She suddenly hoisted herself up over the railing and onto the stern.

"Sophie! What are you doing?"

She shrugged and smiled. "It's not like I'm going to rob them. I just want to look around." She held out a hand to me and I didn't see how I could do anything other than follow her.

"Holy crap," she said, opening the sliding glass door to the inside, "they just leave it open!"

"Which probably means they're coming back any second!" I craned my neck to look nervously back down the dock.

"Will you relax?" She leaned down to the minifridge, exclaiming "Aha!" as she pulled out a couple of beers.

I put my face in my hands, smiling at her through my fingers.

"Let's take these up front." She popped the tops off with a wine key that was sitting on the counter.

We sat on the wide bow drinking the beers in the waning sunlight.

"This is where we would sunbathe. Topless, of course," she said.

"Of course."

"You know," she said, leaning back on her free hand and stretching her legs out, "I'm really glad we're here together. I always wanted to get to know you better."

"Really?"

"Yeah! You've got this whole mysterious vibe going on. It's intriguing."

"Mysterious? Honestly?" I closed my eyes to the sparkling bay. "I never do feel like I fit in at school."

"Yeah, but in a good way. You're surprised I think so?"

"I'm surprised you thought about me at all." Embarrassed, I added, "I mean you're the Volleyball Goddess and all."

She rolled her eyes. "I'm not all about volleyball, you know. I have other hobbies. I wanted to study art history, but my parents wanted me to do econ. More practical. I still paint, though, and take art classes when I can."

"I didn't know that." I tried to picture shimmering blond Sophie among the tattooed, sallow-cheeked art majors I knew. "Can I see some of your work sometime?"

She shrugged. "Maybe in five years when it's decent."

A seagull landed on the railing and looked at us, cocking his head accusingly.

"Maybe it's his boat," I said.

She laughed and for a moment we were both quiet.

"I don't think fitting in is the point," she said thoughtfully.

"The point of what?"

"Of anything."

❧

Back in our room, Sophie threw herself facedown on her bed with a heavy sigh. "I'm *so* tired," she said, her voice muffled by the pillow.

"You don't want to go out?" I didn't want to choose between staying with Sophie and going out.

"Uhggggnnnnnn."

"Come on! It's our first night with everyone."

"Hmmmph." The tone was lighter, though, less certain.

"Don't you want to see who's going to be the first person to get wasted and make a fool of themselves on foreign soil?"

She flipped over on her side, a little more animated. "Why? You gonna go big tonight?"

"No"—I smacked her playfully and bounced onto my knees on the end of her bed—"not me. My money is on one of the quiet girls from the Christian college."

"Repressed Christians Gone Wild."

She yanked me down next to her and snuggled up to me. "Let's take a nap for like ten minutes and then I will rally. Okay?"

"Okay." The cheap bedspread was rough against my cheek, and Sophie's hair had an airy, soapy smell that was more pleasant than the scent of the stale smoky smell of the room, so I didn't move my face from where it was, practically nestled in her long hair.

I drifted off and slept deeply until Sophie, still dripping from the shower, shook me.

"Wakey, wakey. Looks like I'm not the only one who needed a disco nap." She made her way over to where her suitcase was propped open in the corner, rummaging around for clothes. As soon as she'd found a pair of underwear, she dispensed with the towel. I couldn't help but stare at her while her back was to me, not that I imagined Sophie minded anyone staring at her, nearly naked or otherwise. Her body was an ideal and impossible mix of teenage and altogether womanly features: long, lean limbs and a compact, curvy torso with a soft, flat stomach.

"I think my boobs got smaller," she said suddenly, snapping on a bra and turning to face me as though reacting to some vibe of scrutiny that I was inadvertently sending off. "I think I lost a couple of pounds and it all came off my boobs."

"You're crazy." I laughed nervously. "You have such a good body. I'm jealous." Though I'd meant it as flattery, the latter part was all too honest and I blushed, deciding now would be a good time to leave the room and shower. I swung my heavy limbs off the edge of the bed, and as I stood, I expanded into a full, involuntary stretch accompanied by a huge yawn.

"Why would you be jealous? I wish I had *your* boobs."

Girls like Sophie never saw the truth: they could make other women feel lesser simply by existing.

"Do you want the ass as well? I'm afraid it's a package deal."

Sophie craned her neck as though considering this. She

suddenly dashed over to me and smacked my ass hard enough to leave a mark.

"Sold!" she said, laughing as she went into the bathroom.

≈§≈

They assembled us in the lobby for a dinner that was served in predetermined courses like at a wedding. When a beet salad was served, Madame Rochet, with a look of horror, halted our conversation to explain that we mustn't use the word *beet* because in French it is popular slang for a certain part of the male anatomy. We giggled like third graders and a running joke was thus born, as beets are utterly ubiquitous in France.

Afterward, we went to a local bar, where we posted up in a booth in the corner, gleeful at being allowed to drink in public, and stayed there late into the night. When our waitress appeared, Lindsay and Adam amused us all by ordering increasingly exotic drinks, a sidecar, a Harvey Wallbanger, a caipirinha, and then making an impressive show of explaining to the waitress in French what was in each of them. They insisted each time that Sophie and I had requested them, that we were important guests from Russia who didn't speak a word of French and they were only trying to accommodate us. Sophie and I played along by looking stern and every so often muttering *da* or shaking our heads. California had never felt farther away.

T HE NEXT morning we were woken up at what felt like an ungodly hour. I could feel the town around us still sleeping. We were taken to a large conference room where we sat down at small desks and were handed thick test booklets. Had there been mention of a test? Yes, I suppose Madame had said something about it, but we'd been told it was nothing to worry about: *Ne vous inquiétez pas*. We all struggled to keep our hangovers at bay while finishing the exhaustive grammar exam.

❧

It was already late afternoon when we arrived back in Nantes. I opened the door with the key that Nicole had given me. I knew I was welcome and yet it felt strange, as if I were breaking into someone's house. Setting my duffel bag down gingerly at the foot of the stairs, and hearing no one else home, I was slipping into a kind of tired reverie when suddenly the family's young son, Maximilian, and another young boy sprang from the garden and ran through the tall grass up onto the porch.

"*Salut Brooke.*" Maximilian kissed me and smiled his mouse smile at me, big, round eyes sparkling. His friend, a boy several inches taller than he with short, dark curls, laughed. Maximilian shoved at him.

I felt an almost irresistible urge to ruffle Maximilian's hair but resisted and instead asked where the rest of the family was. At a party, he said, motioning for me to come with them. *"Viens avec nous!"*

I followed him and his friend as they barreled through the house, snatching two Ping-Pong paddles off the kitchen table and sprinting out into the street without locking the door behind them. They led me to a narrow side alley where banners and scarves were strung between the windows of the two tall town houses like laundry lines. People congregated in the street around folding tables laden with cheese and fruit, bottles of wine that were down to the dregs, and an enormous punch bowl. Music was coming from a stereo in someone's garage, and a few older couples were dancing in the street. Maximilian promptly abandoned me, dashing off with his friend to the Ping-Pong table. I wished I could stand there for a while, invisibly watching the party.

I searched the alley for Nicole and finally spotted her. She was wearing a white linen dress and was smiling and laughing with two other people. It still felt like summer in the air, and I felt suddenly as though I were being allowed into something secret and special. Nicole and I caught eyes across the alley and she motioned me to her.

"This is my brother Franck and his wife, Madeline." Nicole gestured to each of her companions. I stepped in to kiss them on the cheeks, certain it was the right thing to do. Franck and his wife accepted the kisses but looked at me askance. Had Franck tried to offer me his hand first? My cheeks burned; surely a slightly overdone greeting was not truly offensive? Wouldn't it have been worse to shove my big, dumb American paw at them if I wasn't supposed to?

They politely asked me about myself, using the slow, enunciated French that everyone seemed to have been told in advance to use with Americans. I found to my dismay that even making casual conversation was surprisingly difficult, and several times my attempted word or phrase was met with a subtle but unmistakable look of confusion. Nicole made a gracious attempt to cover my ineptitude by telling her brother and his wife how I had been away with the other Americans for two days and how tired I must be.

Later back at the house, Nicole assured me that it would get better. She'd had students with her before and she'd seen their progress. I hoped she was right.

We'd been placed in grammar classes, and I'd been put in a lower group than Sophie, Lindsay, and Adam.

"Oh, well," Lindsay said, seeming to appear at my elbow just as I was tracing the remedial list and locating my name, "you're lucky, really. I think our class is going to be *super* hard."

I refrained from making a snide remark about how not all of us went to Swiss boarding schools.

"Anyway," Sophie said, sensing my embarrassment, "you don't learn French from a grammar class. We're going to learn French from all of the fabulous friends we'll make here."

"*Club de conversation* starts soon!" Adam reminded us. The institute was bringing in local university students to meet with us and practice French and English in a casual setting, using the main room of the institute one evening a week.

After a couple of reschedulings due to illness, unspecified "personal matters" of Madame Rochet, and a bus-driver strike, the club at last began. Mercifully there was wine, which Adam, Sophie, and I availed ourselves of right away.

We were each assigned a partner—English-speaking if one was French-speaking and vice versa. The class was led by Madame Rochet.

"Now, my children," she said, holding her hands out to each side as though preparing to receive us collectively in an embrace, "you may speak to your companion about whatever you like. Doesn't matter what. Your families, your studies, sports, interests. Whatever pleases you. Off you go."

My companion was a pretty, dark-haired French girl named Véronique. She spoke in a slow, melodious voice and smiled brightly at me whenever I managed to produce a complete question or observation. The source of her enthusiasm for English turned out to be a year that she had spent in California, which had left her bewitched by America. She was longing to go back; she was an actress and planned to spend a short time in Paris studying theater at the Sorbonne before moving to Los Angeles. I told her I thought California had nothing on Paris, which she pleasantly, laughingly disagreed with, and after all, I'd only seen the train station in Paris. But California was her Paris. It pained me to think of what a place like Los Angeles might do to Véronique, and I shuddered to think of her spray-tanned and siliconed. But maybe she would have some innate Gallic resistance to these forces.

Every so often I stole a glance at Sophie, facing off with an enraptured-looking young Frenchman with closely cropped hair and bulging, round, brown eyes that gave him the appearance of an eager woodland creature.

After the hour was up, I reconvened with Sophie and Adam by the wine, and we discussed what to do with the rest of our evening. Adam had a blind date with a university student whom he met online, and we were admonishing him to send us an SMS afterward to let us know he was safe. We'd quickly become fond of sending each other these on the little prepaid cell phones from Orange that we took everywhere with us. I noticed out of the corner of my eye that several of the boys crowded around Véronique as soon as our time was up. They must know each other from the university, I thought. Adam excused himself to use the restroom.

The moment we were alone, Véronique materialized by our side.

"Excuse me, girls?"

"Hi," I said, then introduced her to Sophie. They both nodded and smiled at each other.

"Listen, girls, I am having some friends over tonight to my apartment. Thomas and Mathis will be there," Véronique said, gesturing with her shoulder in the direction of Sophie's conversation partner and another tall, round-cheeked, blond male student, "and some other people from school. It will be very small, but I would love for you to meet our friends. Will you come? *Pour pratiquer le français, non?*"

"Of course."

"Yes," Sophie and I answered simultaneously, trying to contain our enthusiasm at having been invited to someone's apartment. After all, we'd been warned that this would likely not happen, that young people in France often had the same social circles from childhood on and that they might not be especially keen to add anyone new. I had assumed this was doubly true for Americans.

"Let us just tell our friend where we're going," I said.

"Perfect," Véronique said, "come find us after."

Sophie and I looked at each other with frank amazement; we imagined ourselves epic in the pantheon of students who had gone abroad throughout time. Look at us, I thought, making it seem so easy. Amazingly it didn't seem to be only Sophie who had gotten us in the door; after all, it was my conversation partner who had done the inviting.

Véronique returned to the boys, who appeared to be waiting eagerly for her report, and whose faces lit up when she delivered it. Mathis's smile was small and nonchalant, but Thomas was beaming. He believes he has a chance with Sophie, I thought, and perhaps did. Not that he was in Sophie's league, but then, who was? He was not bad looking, I supposed. And it didn't hurt that he was French, which gave him the allure of seeming remote and intriguing. A Frenchman would feel like a conquest, even though it was well-known that they were more than willing to sleep with American girls. One of a great host of contradictions: that Americans girls were thought to be easy because of our endemic national friendliness, when truthfully we were generally more prudish about sex than the French.

What it came down to, I thought, as Sophie and I watched Adam walking back toward us, was that no matter what else was at play here, the French had the upper hand in the situation: we were on their turf.

"Adam, we're hanging out with French people tonight, aren't you proud?"

"*Mais oui!* Did you girls pick someone up in a bar this week that I didn't know about?"

"Actually it was the two of us who got picked up," I said, "by our new friend Véronique."

Adam looked over and, when he saw that Véronique was looking in our direction, gave her a little wave. "I think perhaps that had something to with *les mecs* there."

Sophie laughed and I just nodded.

Véronique's apartment was above a café and Laundromat just on the other side of the *centre-ville*. The small one-bedroom had red wallpaper and gilt mirrors on the walls alongside re-creations of vintage film posters. It should have been garish but somehow wasn't. The only furniture was a little couch and chairs that looked just shabby enough to be well loved and between them a solid, black lacquer hutch that served as the coffee table. A television set on a stand was placed inconspicuously in the corner. I hadn't watched television since I'd been in France; it seemed intimidating, and unlike when I spoke to real people, it made no concessions to my helplessness. I missed it so little that I lamented the hours I had spent with it all my life, the hours I would surely spend with it in the future. To be without it gave my life in France a cultural purity.

For a short time it was only the five of us, and Véronique dominated the conversation with her questions and reminiscences about California. Do you surf? she wanted to know. Do you skateboard? She had learned to do these things while abroad and seemed disappointed that neither of us counted them as hobbies. She talked about the wide streets and the palm trees, the tan, smiling faces. She was so unexpectedly warm that I became momentarily suspicious of her; had she secretly been assigned by the institute to befriend us? Certainly someone from our country had laid some important groundwork with her that we were now benefiting from. My guess was that she must have met a guy there.

Before long others began to arrive and Véronique's apartment filled up with people. Thomas used the burgeoning crowd to position himself next to Sophie, and I could hear him peppering her with questions: What did she think of France? What was she studying at home? Her French sounded so fluid and perfect that I felt suddenly alone in the room as the only American who couldn't pass. *You have only a tiny accent,* Thomas said to her, *c'est charmant.* He leaned in when he talked to her, eyes wide with frank interest and attraction that no American guy I'd met would have the courage for since, back home, something far less than this would be considered way too much.

Véronique was a wonderful hostess, introducing me to everyone she spoke with and presenting my Americanness as something special, and indeed her friends—too chic to all be students, I decided—reacted in kind.

"Ah, vous êtes Américaines? Génial!"

After a couple of glasses of wine I relaxed. I was falling into the sweet spot of these conversations, the divine intersection of alcohol and foreign language where just enough drink meant that my tongue was loosened and those words and phrases I knew came easily, but not so much that my thinking and speech were generally impaired, in which case my French would go right out the window. The trick now was to maintain this level and neither sober up nor get much drunker. Watching those around me drink more or less like adults, it struck me anew how differently the French students seemed to feel about alcohol than Americans. It was not at all like back home, where the general idea was to get as much in the bloodstream as quickly as possible, in pursuit of which we chugged vile things at parties like jungle juice, a mixture of cheap synthetic fruit juices and grain alcohol.

Wandering off in search of a bathroom, I suddenly felt shy passing through the crowd without my new dear friend and guide. People stared openly at me, not in a way that felt hostile, just interested. I was under the impression that the group around me was tight-knit and that Sophie's and my faces were something of a shock, though hopefully a pleasant one.

I checked myself out in the small gilt mirror that hung above the scalloped edge of the sink. The bathroom was pretty and spotless, if a bit overtly feminine for my taste with its frilly hand towels and small porcelain angels on the narrow windowsill. The bathtub was the odd type I had seen several times now, with a long shower hose. The lighting was soft, and for this I was grateful, as it had been many hours since I'd applied my makeup and I most likely didn't look as good as the wine would have me believe. I wiped away the eyeliner that had pooled in the corners of my eyes.

I exited and carefully closed the door behind me. As I turned around to head back to Véronique, I nearly collided with someone.

"*Pardon,*" I exclaimed, proud of myself for speaking French even when taken by surprise.

"No, no," the man said, "it was my fault. I startled you." Tall and dark haired, he had a smile that seemed to burst from his face and white, but not too white, teeth. He seemed relaxed, and a glaze of color lit his skin as though he had just returned from a vacation. "And then, no harm done," he said, holding aloft two glasses of wine, both still full. After what appeared to be a split second's consideration, he handed one of them to me.

"Oh, but . . ." I looked at him quizzically. Had he been walking around the party looking for someone he wanted to talk to, armed with an extra glass in case he should find the person without a drink?

He shrugged. "It was for my friend Serge, but I think he can fend for himself." This was even better, I thought; he hadn't been just wandering around, he was on his way else-where and had changed his direction. His eyes flickered over me. "You must be one of Véronique's Americans."

"Is my accent that bad?"

He chuckled. "No, no. Your accent is fine, *chérie*. We simply don't see that many new faces around here and you look American."

This didn't seem likely to be a compliment and I made a sour face at him. He laughed again. It thrilled me that I amused him.

"This is not an insult. It's the perfect teeth"—he drew back his lips to reveal his own, which looked no less than perfect themselves—"and the shiny hair." He reached out and lifted a strand that hung over my shoulder. With someone else I might have bristled at this overly intimate gesture, but I could feel myself subtly leaning into his touch. I nervously took a sip of wine.

The seconds passed rapidly while a silence opened up around us. I feared if I said nothing, he would walk away, and yet I felt frozen. Abruptly he laughed, and I blushed as though he'd been reading my thoughts.

"Don't tell me I have somehow offended you already, *ma jolie Américaine*. What a terrible ambassador I am."

"No!" I said, too quickly this time, too emphatically. "It's okay." My French, so fluid moments ago, was threatening suddenly to abandon me completely. "How do you know Véronique?"

"*Elle est ma cousine,* we've been close since we were *très petits.* In fact I have not really gotten to talk to Véronique yet tonight. She was engaged in some very deep discussion with someone when I came in, but maybe we should go and see if she has emerged from it, no?"

I felt a wash of disappointment that we would lose the intimacy of this corner so soon, but as I felt myself floundering with the language, Véronique—with her patient enunciation and, if necessary, her English—could only be a help. After all, I would still be near him. Him. I realized I still didn't know his name. I wanted to ask him before we joined the others, but he had turned his back to me and reached out behind him, his hand blindly finding mine and grasping it to lead me through the crowd. I didn't even need to know his name. I wished we had a long corridor or an expansive room to cross hand in hand and not simply the ten feet or so of the living room of this small apartment.

When she saw us, Véronique squealed with delight and jumped up from the couch where she'd been chatting with a girl who was perched on the armrest and deposited four kisses on his cheeks. Four! A number I had heard rumor of but had not before witnessed.

"Alex!" she said. Alex. He released my hand to put his arms around her and I wished he would hold it again. But why would he do that? I reminded myself that we didn't even know each other.

"Brooke," Véronique said, "I see you have already met my darling Alex."

"Yes," Alex answered for me, "we have already become good friends. She was quite horrified that I knew she was American without her telling me so."

"Oh, but you must not be, *chérie*!" Véronique admonished.

"Véronique loves Americans, as I'm sure you have already discovered."

She scowled at him and turned around suddenly as though she'd forgotten something important on the couch.

"And you?" I said quietly. Such a simple question, yet it felt so bold given the circumstances.

"I am not generally predisposed either way," he said, his tone unreadable, or at least unreadable to me, focused as I was on deciphering his French and distracted as I was by his eyes, his voice, all of him. "So it is you as well who must be a good ambassador."

"*Voilà,*" Véronique said as Sophie appeared by her side, "the other." Véronique had not made quite such a point of introducing us as a pair to any of the other guests who had woven through our conversations saying their hellos. Alex was clearly important to her.

"*Bonjour, je m'appelle Sophie.*" She had taken to saying her name as the French did, with a swift emphasis on the last syllable. I watched Alex's face for a reaction, for the momentarily stunned look that I had come to expect would pass over a man's features upon first meeting her. But he betrayed nothing, had just the same cool smile.

"What a lovely accent you have," Alex said, "how charming."

"Alex lives in Paris most of the time, but he's come home to Nantes to take care of his grandmother," Véronique explained. "And where have you been before this, Alex? With this tan?"

"To the house in Cap Ferrat. The weather was unusually warm for this time of year. My family has a charming little house down south," he explained to Sophie and me. "We must all go there sometime."

Was this casual invitation something that could actually materialize? It seemed so far-fetched. How had we been so lucky to meet Véronique and Alex on the same day? I was sick with the desire to make them like me. Taking advantage of my not facing Alex directly, I studied his face. I had never met anyone our age so self-assured; he seemed settled into himself. I wanted to ask how old he was but could not see a way to do so casually.

"Is your grandmother ill?" Sophie asked.

"Sadly, she has some quite advanced dementia. My mother is not coping very well, I'm afraid"—he smiled slightly when he said this—"so I've come back to help for a little while. I can do my work here, so it's not really a problem."

"What sort of work do you do?" I asked.

"I'm a photographer." Alex held his hands up in front of him to pantomime a camera.

"Come sit," Véronique instructed us. Sophie and I settled back into the plush couch as Véronique wended her way through the crowd to fetch glasses and another bottle of wine. Shrugging off his elegant olive-green coat, Alex sat next to me, the complete length of his thigh pressed tightly against mine in the compact space.

"How is your mother?" Véronique asked when she returned.

"Fretting and smoking all day long, drinking too much in the evening, not eating enough. Generally playing the victim." His harsh words made me tense up, and I wondered if he had felt me do so. He took another sip of wine before turning to Sophie and me. "It's complicated with my family."

"It's complicated with all families," Sophie said.

"Yes," Alex said with a sanguine laugh, "that is very true, my dear."

I looked hard at Sophie; was she affected by Alex in the way that I was? Maybe he wasn't her type. At school, she had dated jocks, and mostly blond, but was that what she liked or just what California offered? I resolved to ask her later. Looking around at Véronique's friends confirmed what I had already seen of French men and how they stacked up to Americans. As with the women, the men were smaller and more delicate than Americans; even their features seemed finer, more carefully crafted. The French had a fierce elegance to them, something sleek and tightly coiled. My gaze wandered over to Thomas, who was now talking to a petite girl with a scarf wrapped many times around her neck. He stole frequent looks in our direction—in Sophie's direction.

"Your poor grandmother," Véronique said, *"quel dommage."*

"Oh, well," Alex said, "at least she's not in any distress at the moment. She's moved past the period where she was so panicked. Now"—he made a *shoop* sound and slid his hand up and away—"she's off down the rabbit hole."

The three of us laughed politely, self-consciously.

"The problem with my mother is that she just cannot take

any kind of intellectual distance from all of this. She's upset that *Mamie* is starting to forget who people are so much of the time. She doesn't understand that what my grandmother requires right now is for people to come and meet her in her world, a world that's of the moment. Which isn't such a bad thing."

He paused and patted his chest pocket for a packet of cigarettes, then extracted one and lit it. "In fact"—he relaxed into a deep drag—"I like her better this way. She is much gentler—she could be quite judgmental when she was lucid."

"Oh, Alex," Véronique said, "what a thing to say. Now what will our new friends think?"

"Ladies, I beg your pardon." Alex now looked directly at me. Suddenly overcome with the urge to touch his face and hair, I shot him a quick smile and looked away until the feeling passed, which it wouldn't no matter how long I examined the lacquer hutch as though it were the most fascinating thing in the room. It felt as though my blood were running backward through my veins. Had I ever felt like this before? I hadn't with Regan. That was a slow burn, a growing affection. This was a shot between the eyes.

"*Alors*, Alex, I have not seen you since June! How was the summer with Marie-Catherine?" Véronique asked.

Ah, I thought. There's a girlfriend. Of *course* there's a girlfriend. My mind conjured her against my will, and to my dismay, the image was a French facsimile of Sophie: golden, glistening skin shimmering in the Mediterranean sun, a chic two-piece in a subdued hue covering only the necessary body parts, sea-salt waves of hair under a wide-brimmed straw hat. I was annoyed at the way Sophie intruded upon this masochistic fantasy. She was now the most immediate image in my mental gallery of the beautiful girl I could never be. But I didn't want to feel these petty longings; I wanted ours to be the kind of perfect friendship I still imagined was possible.

"Well"—Alex made a pained face, leaning in so as to be heard better through the din—"it was mostly wonderful and very relaxing. We took many day trips that were productive for my work. And MC worked quite a lot on her boat series. She is a painter," Alex explained to us as an aside.

Of course she was a painter! I stole a look at Sophie, and indeed, upon hearing this she smiled. One of her own, I thought, a visually perfect visual artist.

"We ate our breakfasts at the Brasserie Galloise every morning, and we saw quite a lot of Paolo and Stephanie, who were getting along well for once."

"*Mon Dieu*, you sound like my parents talking about their visit to the farm in Provence," Véronique said. "You are going to bore our *amies américaines* to death with this story, Alex!"

No, no, Sophie and I protested, we were fine! I for one was glad he was leaving out the romance, as my own images of this girl were enough to make me crazy.

"I know you prefer photographs, but you can tell a story better than this. There is no juice in this list of lovely things you did with MC. I know you, *les deux*, where are the dramatics? Did MC break all your mother's dishes? Cut your clothes up with scissors? Give us something! You see, girls," Véronique continued, turning to Sophie and me, "Alex's Marie-Catherine has quite a flair for the dramatics when she feels she is not being paid enough attention. In fact, before she was a painter she was an actress, which I think suited her."

"Before that she was a dancer and before that a poet. What suits her is novelty. She's completely ridiculous," Alex said.

Véronique let out a mock-horrified, secretly thrilled little gasp. "Such harsh words for your *petite amie.*"

"Ex." *Ix.*

The word sent a tiny frisson of happiness rushing up my spine.

"*Mais oui*, Véronique. If you had any patience at all, I was just arriving at that part in the story."

"Poor Alex, tell us everything!" she said.

Alex laughed. "*Arrête*, Véronique, I know you never liked her."

Véronique pouted to show she was being unfairly judged.

"*Mon chou*, I'm not saying this as a criticism, I am saying that you showed better judgment about her than I did," Alex said.

"Don't be too hard on yourself, Alex. It is easy for me to have a clear head about MC. I'm immune to the charms of her legendary *foufoune.*"

A look of confusion must have passed across my face. Sophie was smiling, which I presumed meant she'd understood.

Alex caught my eye and looked deeply amused. "*Chérie*, I think perhaps they haven't taught you this word yet in your classes at the American institute." He reached out and put his fingertips lightly on my knee.

"Alex would be more than happy to help you expand your vocabulary in this area now that he is an *ix*," Véronique added innocently.

Alex shot her an exasperated look. "Try to be a grown-up,

Véronique." He turned back to me, ostensibly to explain the matter at hand in an *adult* manner. "How do we say this word in English? *Foufoune*. Ah. 'Cunt'?"

I cringed.

"*Ah, non*, that is a harsh word, there is a better word for it. 'Pussy'?"

"*Oui, oui, c'est plutôt ça,*" Véronique confirmed, a tiny, enigmatic smile playing on her lips. Something about her made you feel as though you were in on the joke one minute and the subject of it the next.

"Oh," I said, trying in vain to keep my cheeks from blazing, wanting desperately not to be on either side of the slutty or prudish dichotomy of American girls. Yet it wasn't the language that caused my mind to race and my cheeks to flame. It was the words upon his lips, which made me picture his lips upon the thing itself. I wished to hear him say the two words over and over. That, and to be alone in the room with him.

"Anyway, it's done. Poor me with a broken heart, I have come back to my hometown to nurse it."

Véronique laughed.

"You see this, Brooke and Sophie? You see how she laughs at my suffering?" He placed a hand on my leg and I hoped he didn't sense how my heart rate elevated at his touch. I avoided looking him straight in the face at such close range, imagining my lust and longing would be readily apparent. Instead, I averted my eyes to the top buttons of his shirt, which also proved treacherous, as it revealed just enough of the smooth, brown skin of his chest to make me want to put my lips to it, and seeing the buttons held by their buttonholes made me want nothing more than to separate them from each other.

"*Arrête*. Surely any suffering done in this situation is by poor MC," Véronique said.

Sure enough, his voice indicated no suffering; a play for some sympathy maybe. "Listen to her," he said as he removed his hand from my knee to gesture in exasperation at Véronique. "All of a sudden she and MC are sisters. You always band together as long as men are on the opposing side."

"You are beasts, every one of you. *Les hommes français.* American men are better, less devious."

Alex pantomimed having been stabbed in the heart, and Sophie and I stereoed incredulous laughter.

"Now I have to stop you there, Véronique," a previously silent Sophie said. "American men cannot possibly be better."

"Which is to say *French* men could not possibly be worse," I added.

"Oh, *vraiment*, girls? Please go on!" Alex looked directly at Sophie, and before she spoke again, she paused, and it seemed a private glance was exchanged between her and Alex. Had I missed something?

"At least French men can be romantic," Sophie said.

"Bah!" said Véronique. "French men are bullshit artists, is what they are. They meet you and they are *blinded* by your beauty, your grace, you are like no other woman they have ever met. Until they walk one block from your door and are blinded by some other woman. Infidelity is our national pastime. But you so much as look at another man, and they are furious. No one stands for it in America."

"I don't know about that." I could hear the lack of conviction in my voice. If only she knew that was why I was really here: infidelity and the female American rage that followed it. I felt a sudden flash of desire to blurt it out just to shock them, but I bit my tongue.

"Over there it is a cause for fury, divorce. Here it is met with . . ." Véronique made an apathetic frown and brought her shoulders to her ears, a Gallic shrug.

"But American men," Sophie said, her words tumbling out as though the idea were gaining momentum, "they just want to be let off the hook. The only time you would ever catch them rhapsodizing is when they are trying to get you naked. Even the way they ask for dates"—here, to my amazement, Sophie boldly switched to English, either assuming that Alex could keep up or meaning to leave him behind—"'Do you want to like maybe hang out sometime or whatever? You know, something casual. Or whatever.'"

Véronique howled with laughter, recognizing the lilting California-boy voice.

"*Et puis*"—Sophie returned seamlessly to her perfect French—"they want you to come over and watch a movie, drink some beer, and they think that should be enough to get you on *la bite*."

Without anyone else noticing, Alex leaned over and quickly whispered, "This is our word for 'cock,' *chérie*," his lips grazing my earlobe. I was glad that Alex had taken it upon himself to translate, even though this time it was un-necessary.

"No, I knew that one," I said breathlessly.

"Oh, yes?" Véronique asked, amused.

I recounted the story of Madame Rochet and our intro-duction dinner, the beet salads, and the vivid image of thirty American students all innocently chirping this obscene word.

Véronique and Alex were in stitches. *"Oh la la,"* Alex said, "can you imagine? *C'est délicieux, cette salade verte avec la bite."* This green salad with cock is delicious.

"And it's difficult to avoid," Sophie said. "You do love your beets here."

"C'est vrai?" Alex asked. "You think so? Anyway, Véronique was just going to tell us all about *la bite française* versus *la bite américaine.* Weren't you, *chérie?"*

"Merci, Alex," Véronique said, giving him a little glare, *"en fait,* our dear Sophie has made some excellent points, and I too was subjected to this plot of night phone calls and movie watching. And you are right that Americans can be lazy and charmless."

Were we only speaking of the men still?

"But they have a certain innocence to them all the same. American men always believe themselves to be good inside, or at least capable of redemption. Here the men just revel in their own filth. *Tant pis. Ça n'a pas d'importance,"* she said, giving the shrug again.

"And the women?" Alex asked.

"The women hold themselves to a higher standard, as it is everywhere. Has always been, will always be."

"I won't go near that one. Not while I am here behind enemy lines." Alex smiled as though he secretly knew he could win the argument and so, by letting it go, was, in his way, winning just the same. "And with such beautiful enemies," he added, grinning at Sophie, who rolled her eyes but could surely not be so superhuman as not to be flattered. "Speaking of enemies, Véronique, you have not said a word all night about Grégoire. Which is he this week, friend or foe?"

"Foe."

"But he's over there in the corner. I thought this meant he was surely your friend again and *peut-être un petit peu plus.*"

"Never again," she scoffed. "He's here? He must have come with François. Excuse me, *les filles.* Alex, behave yourself." Véronique stood up and her small figure disappeared into the crowd, her black mane of hair swishing furiously behind her.

Alex moved to where she'd been sitting so as to face Sophie and me. The side of me that he'd been touching suddenly felt exposed and cold. I wished Véronique had not gotten up to leave, not only because I missed the warmth of Alex by my side, but because while she had been here it seemed as if we were the only people in the room, and now that she had gone, it felt as though our group was vulnerable to intrusion. I knew I should try to meet other people at the party, that this was what Sophie probably wanted to do, but I was certain there could not be anyone here more worth knowing than Véronique and Alex.

"Who is Grégoire?" Sophie asked, leaning forward and whispering conspiratorially, resting an elbow on my knee.

"*Le ix,*" Alex said, as though he were telling us something naughty, "although some nights he's not so much of an *ix.*"

"You have such complicated relationships, all of you," Sophie exclaimed, leaning back far enough to take a sip of her wine. "So French."

"And you don't? You seem like a girl who has a few *liaisons compliquées* to your name as well. No? Tell me, Brooke. She does, doesn't she?"

I smiled an empty smile. I wanted to tell him nothing about Sophie.

"No," she said, "not me."

Again I thought of Regan. But would that story even shock Alex or would I simply receive a shrug?

"Allez, not even an *ix*?" Alex pressed her.

"There was a *tout petit ix* from the summer. But he's hardly worth mentioning," she said.

"Cruel woman," he said, his voice delighted.

"And you, Brooke? A *tout petit ix*? Or someone still at home who you will send postcards of the Île de la Cité to?"

"No," I said, "sorry to be disappointing. *Pas de ix.*"

Suddenly, a hand appeared on Alex's shoulder and the squeal of a female voice shattered the intimate circle of our little conversation. A thin girl in a white T-shirt with long waves of pale hair tumbling over her shoulders threw herself into Alex's lap, a jumble of spindly limbs. She spoke too quickly, not taking us into account, and I could only pick up a few words of what she was saying. All I could gather was that she had not seen him in a long time and was excited that he was here.

Sophie raised her eyebrows at me.

"Sophie?" someone called out behind us.

It was Thomas. I was shocked that it had taken him this long to come back and hunt her down. But the circle had been broken when Véronique left, and now he had his chance.

All at once, I felt exhausted. After a few moments of polite conversation with Thomas, it seemed Sophie had either reached her limit as well or had read my mind.

"Brooke, are you ready to go? We have our first round of *traduction* early tomorrow," she said, reminding me of the difficult day ahead.

"Oui."

We stood up and kissed Thomas on the cheek. The girl remained in Alex's lap.

"You're leaving so soon?" Alex asked. He gave the girl a be-seeching look and she sighed and slowly removed herself, still clinging to his side as they both stood up. He didn't bother to introduce her to us. Whether this meant that she didn't matter or that we didn't, I couldn't tell.

"Well, it was lovely to have made your acquaintance," he said, kissing Sophie first. "I'm sure we will all see each other again soon." He smiled, his face close to mine now. He kissed my cheeks. I might have lingered longer if it hadn't been for the girl, who was hovering.

As we made our way back toward the bedroom to find Véronique, I felt disappointment flooding in. No plans had been made to see each other again, no numbers exchanged. What if we never saw Alex again?

I had expected to find Véronique in a heated discussion with her *ix*, but instead she was speaking cheerfully to a boyish-looking guy with his hands dug deep in his pockets. She introduced us to her companion, who was neither Grégoire nor François, and I immediately forgot his name.

Véronique hugged first me and then Sophie, another thing she must have picked up in the States. Then to my great relief, she made sure we all had one another's number.

"Where is Alex?" she asked.

Sophie gestured to where he stood by the couch, the blonde still not giving him an inch of space.

"Ah, *salope*," Véronique said, "my friend. But never mind."

What a strange and delicious little tribe they were with their *liaisons compliquées*. My eyes lingered on Alex again.

He was so beautiful; my eyes clung to his lips, hanging off them helplessly, devastated by the idea of never seeing him again. But then I remembered that he would be here with his sick grandmother and felt a little guilty that the thought cheered me.

"You must come over again," Véronique said. "I'm so glad that you could meet my friends. See you soon, yes?"

We nodded.

"Good," she said.

Sophie and I said nothing as we rode down the creaking elevator together, only smiled at each other and shook our heads a little as if to say, *Can you believe this night? Can you believe these people?*

Being back out on the street again felt surreal.

"That was an interesting evening," I said finally when we were at last at enough of a distance that no one from the party might happen to be walking along behind us.

"I like them," Sophie said a little dreamily.

"I do too." It was a relief to be speaking English again.

Absentmindedly Sophie reached out and took my arm. "I'm so happy that we're here together. I feel like the whole experience will be different because you're here. Better."

I leaned my head against her shoulder. "So am I." Together, we were a force, more than the sum of our parts. *Les Américaines.*

"I need more friends like you. My parents are always telling me that."

"Telling you what?" I laughed, but suddenly felt a little self-conscious. "What's a friend like me exactly?"

"A smart friend. I love my teammates, but all they ever

talk about is boys and parties and they *giggle* so goddamn much." She went on, affecting a stentorian voice, imitating her father, " 'Sophie, you need to surround yourself with people who are serious about their goals.' " She laughed, but it was rueful, and some of the color had drained from her cheeks.

I groaned. "Ha, my mom is the same way. She's always on me about getting perfect grades, having perfect extracurricular activities. Good on paper, even if I'm a mess up here." I tapped my temple with my fingertip.

"Join the club, sister," Sophie said under her breath.

An expansive silence opened between us, a silence I recognized as one that people allow when they'd prefer to be asked what they're thinking instead of offering it, when they want to be certain that their listener is invested and not merely present. So I asked her.

"Just thinking about my parents," she said, looking down the street as though she'd suddenly lost track of where she was going even though we were heading in the same direction we always walked together. "I wish they wouldn't worry about me so much."

"Do they? That surprises me. You seem like you have everything so together. I would think that most parents would kill to have a daughter like you."

"I should amend that to say my *mother* worries, my dad mostly criticizes. He doesn't like to encourage feminine emotions."

"Yikes."

Crossing her arms, she said nothing. I'd only met her father once, at the volleyball game I'd gone to. He was tall with a full head of gunmetal-gray hair that must once have been blond like Sophie's. He was slightly terrifying, like a fearsome, gracefully aging Viking. As I remembered him now, it seemed that Sophie's mother did cower a bit beside him. But I didn't know much about fathers, after all.

Sophie's expression had turned stormy and I couldn't tell what had just happened. This sensation had become familiar; half the time I didn't quite know how my French phrases were received by native ears, but I wasn't normally worried about having this tone-deaf feeling when I was with Sophie and speaking in English.

"Do you remember how I left school last year?"

"Yes," I said, thinking we were moving away from the subject back to talking about travels.

"I wasn't volunteering abroad with my cousin, I was in a treatment facility."

"Oh. What kind of—I mean, rehab or something?"

"No." She smiled wryly, as though the idea of her being a drug addict was funny, and indeed it was far-fetched. "I have these episodes sometimes. Not often. Just spells where I go up and down. It can get a little extreme."

"I'm sorry." I wanted to ask her more but it didn't seem respectful.

"I've never told anyone outside my family. It's not really the way I want people to see me, you know?"

"I understand."

For a moment we were quiet. Her arm had stiffened in mine and I wondered if she felt she'd said too much. I wanted to say the right thing; to show her the admission didn't make me think less of her; that, if anything, it made me feel closer to her.

"Lots of people struggle with stuff like that, depression or whatever," I said. "It's nothing to be ashamed of."

"It's not that I'm ashamed. I just worry that people will treat me differently even if they don't mean to. If everyone thinks I'm happy-go-lucky, then it makes it easier to believe that I actually *am* that way. You know?"

I had a million questions but I didn't want to grill her. "Honestly, Sophie, it's sort of a relief to know that you're not completely perfect."

Sophie turned and looked at me at close range, disbelieving. "Perfect?"

"Utterly. Perfect face, perfect body. Smart, confident, funny, charming—shall I go on?"

"Why would I stop you?" She smiled now, to my relief.

"Then let's not forget athletic. Oh, yes, and your superior language skills. Add to that the fact that no one can even hate you because you're a sweetheart."

"You're full of shit. I'm a disaster," she said, but her voice and the tiny smile that broke through her pout said otherwise. Somewhere beneath any neuroses she might have, she must know what she was, how others admired her, but nonetheless I felt it my duty to convince her.

I halted abruptly in the street. "Sophie, I won't take one more step until you admit that I'm right."

"Brooke!" She stood a few yards down the deserted sidewalk, far enough away that I had to raise my voice a little.

I stayed put. The giddiness of the evening had reached a crescendo, and I felt myself happily atop it. Crossing my arms over my chest, I stared her down with pursed lips, waiting for her to take me up on my dare. "I mean it! I will accept that you are not *perfect* as such, and I believe your claim that you are in fact from this planet despite all evidence pointing to the contrary. However, I will not stand here and listen to you call yourself a disaster. It flies in the face of everything we mere mortals hold dear. Admit you're a goddess!"

She hung her shoulders as though in defeat. When she looked up at me, her eyes were shining and it was all I had wanted, to replace the look that had been in them a few moments before.

"You're on quite a roll," she said quietly. She walked toward me and put her hands on my shoulders. "Tell me how anyone ever resists you."

She put her arms around my neck and pulled me tightly to her. After standing like this for a moment longer than an ordinary embrace, she took my arm again and we continued on down the street toward our homes as before, only now I could feel her arm relaxed in mine. Somehow I knew that if I hadn't responded to this confession in the right way, the door to Sophie's inner self would have been closed to me forever, as I now realized it remained to so many who knew her. So I felt no regrets about my effusive display of admiration. It had never occurred to me that she would need this kind of reassurance, much less from me. Perhaps anyone's worshipping at her altar would have satisfied her, but I hoped it was somehow better coming from me, that she'd meant what she said about me. I hoped wildly, though I realized it wasn't likely, that she saw some of herself when she looked at me; saw if not an equal, then at least something of a similar species.

We continued on for a quiet moment and I watched her from the corner of my eye as she gazed contentedly at the town houses along the street. I felt the girl beside me had solidified, become more human. It made her even more beautiful, but as she looked back at me and smiled, I felt a tiny hint of worry creep up my spine.

We reached her door before mine and she hugged me again. She then kissed me three times on the cheek.

"Trois."

"Trois bisous," I echoed back, *"pour les Américaines!"* She threw in a kiss on my lips. I wanted to devour her.

Making my way down the small hill back to my family's house, I let the decline carry me with its momentum. My feet flew underneath me and it felt glorious until I nearly tripped. I was exhausted, I reminded myself, and still a little drunk from the party.

When at last I was in my bed, my spinning mind and my exhausted body did battle with each other. I worried we'd never see Véronique again, that we'd somehow made a bad impression on her or, worse, bored her. Sophie hadn't been quite her usual self for the earlier part of the evening—sitting there in near silence all that time—and I realized it had strained me a bit to hold up the conversation for both of us. But then, maybe I'd fared better with Alex without Sophie's being turned up to her usual wattage. I felt guilty the moment this thought crossed my mind; it was hard to reconcile the image I had of Sophie with what she'd told me tonight since she had always seemed to simply radiate health and happiness. I tried to wrap my head around the idea that "Peru" had been a treatment facility, a rather different kind of adventure. But she was fine now, wasn't she? Her family wouldn't have let her come here if she wasn't.

Though it seems obvious now that I should have been jealous of Sophie from the beginning, I didn't even know enough to properly envy her. At least at first. Instead, I assumed that because she was drawn to me, I could become like her: bright and brave and teeth-kickingly gorgeous. Even her troubles seemed sexy, the imperfect in her making her only more complex and alluring.

At last I let sleep cloud my brain. I tried with my last shred of consciousness to spirit myself onward to only good dreams by thinking of the triumphs of the day. Véronique. Sophie.

Alex.

SOPHIE AND I soon discovered that the best bars in town were all located in a neighborhood called Saint-Félix. We stayed out late talking to anyone who would talk to us, about anything they wanted to talk about, drinking and laughing about nothing. We laughed with relief when we could understand the words our companions were saying, with abandon when we could not. I crept back into the house in the wee hours many nights, feeling certain that the ancient wood creaking under my feet would give me away to my host family. We went to school bleary-eyed and drank instant coffee until our nerves stood on end.

Some British and Irish expats, and the French people who wished to make their acquaintance, hung around one particular pub. The inside was a cross between a Bavarian beer hall and a sports bar, with a pastiche of European soccer paraphernalia covering the walls. Soon enough Sophie and I would be known there, but in the beginning it was just an easygoing place to sit and talk without drawing as many stares as we did elsewhere.

One Tuesday, we met there after one of Sophie's later classes at the university. Because she'd done well on the placement exams, she took most of her classes at the university rather than at the institute, where I took nearly all of mine.

I was used to being at the top of the class and it still rankled me to be remedial.

"Doesn't it already feel like we've been here a long time?"

"In a way," I said, though it had only been weeks.

Sophie pulled a pack of cigarettes out of her purse and extracted one with her delicate fingers. She put the cigarette to her lips, lit it, and inhaled.

"I'm sorry, you *smoke*?"

She shrugged. "Only once in a while at home, but I decided I ought to pick up a vice while I'm abroad, you know? Since I don't have to worry about volleyball. I don't suppose you'd like one?" She proffered the pack as an afterthought as she went to tuck it back in her bag.

"Only when I'm drunk."

"That can be arranged." She took a drag and sighed. "Truthfully, I smoked kind of a lot with Jason this summer."

"Ah, so this is the fault of the epic summer fling, is it? What do we hear from him these days?"

Sophie shrugged. "A couple of the most boring e-mails I've ever had the misfortune of reading. That's about it. God, what is it with guys who just write the most bland laundry lists of things they've done? Everything is always 'cool' or 'chill,' or if not, then 'lame.' I mean, learn to write a narrative sentence, Neanderthals."

"So we've moved on from Mr. Summer Fling, then?"

"Since all he really had going for him was a hot body and gorgeous green eyes, yes. Those things don't translate well to e-mail. Not that I don't still dream of the hot body."

"You could always ask him to send you some shirtless photos. I'm just jealous that you spent the summer having hot sex with a beach god. I spent it trying to cook *coq au vin* recipes with my mother."

Sophie sighed. "Don't be too jealous."

"Ha, tell it to my dry spell, sister." My last interlude with Regan felt far away indeed.

The waiter came by and I ordered us each another *bière blanche*. I hadn't really been exposed to quality Hefeweizens at home and I couldn't get enough of them here.

Sophie smiled into her lap and shook her head.

"Oh, sorry, did you not want another one?"

"Of *course* I want another one. It's not that."

"Then what are you smirking about over there?"

"It's just a little ironic." She leaned her head back and shook her hair over her shoulders. "I mean, I happen to know a thing or two about dry spells. Self-imposed, but still."

"I don't get it."

"Nothing, nothing, ugh, never mind."

"Oh my God, *what*? You can't say something cryptic like that and then take it back. Not fair, completely against the arbitrary full-disclosure clause of our friendship that I've just now imposed."

"Oh, well, in that case," Sophie said.

"I mean it. Spill!"

"All right, all right. But you can't laugh at me, it's kind of embarrassing. Thing is, my summer was sadly not a nonstop humpfest, more of a heavy-petting-fest. Because I am, in fact, a virgin." She smacked the heel of her palm to her forehead.

"Oh." My head spun as I tried to absorb this. But why had I just assumed otherwise? It seemed a little incredible that sexy Sophie was not in fact doing the deed itself. A cloud of sex seemed to sort of hover around her at all times; it seemed almost cruel that it was a fake-out.

Stubbing the butt of her cigarette out in the ashtray, she immediately dipped back into her purse for another.

"I'll have one of those after all."

She gave me a grateful look.

"That's good. I mean it's good that you're doing that if that's what you want. Can I ask why you decided to, um, abstain?"

"*Abstinent* sounds better, doesn't it? *Virgin* sounds parochial. So anyway"—she shifted in her seat—"sorry, I know I'm being awkward; it's just that I don't talk about it much."

"You're not being awkward," I said with what I hoped was a comforting smile. "Nobody else's business anyway. Me included, if you want."

"No, no. I trust you. It's not religious or anything. It's just that it's gonna be a big moment no matter what, you know? Like you'll always remember it, good, bad, or ugly. It will always be a touchstone. I guess I've just never met anyone whose face I want to think of for the rest of my life. 'Cause you're going to no matter what."

The cigarette burned my lungs, but the nicotine was already having a soothing effect and I luxuriated in it, taking another long sip of my beer while I contemplated what she'd said.

"And I know this is going to sound lame and rom-comy, but I want my first time to be with someone I love, you know?"

"That doesn't sound lame at all." I nodded, a little thrown by how self-conscious she suddenly seemed. "God, I'd forgotten I like cigarettes, drunk me must know best. She knows she likes a smoke but sober me always wants to deny her."

"Sober you is only looking out for your health, after all."

"Okay, well, since we're sharing, and drinking"—with that we clinked glasses—"I'm going to tell *you* something."

"Oh, do it!" She settled into her seat and gave me her full attention.

I hesitated for a moment, staring into the amber abyss of my beer. It wasn't a lack of trust in Sophie that was holding me back. Instead, I had suddenly realized what it meant to have never said aloud or even written down what had happened. It had the effect of making it seem made up, as if it were a fanciful, fictional story that I had been writing and revising for so long that I had forgotten it wasn't real. Yet I had kept it defiantly to myself, since to talk about it would make it matter in some way that I couldn't quite yet own up to. It all felt so far away now, though, it would feel like spinning a campfire story. I had a memory of the emotional impact of the affair, the breakup—if that's what our ending could reasonably be called—but I didn't seem to exactly *feel* any of it any longer. I had a thrilling sense of detachment from my former self, felt I could somehow both take credit for her actions and not take responsibility for them.

So I told Sophie everything, and she listened wide-eyed with an occasional little gasp. I focused on maintaining a cool distance from the story, something I had been trying hard to cultivate since the denouement of the disastrous affair. For the first time, it felt effortless, the story was somehow now under my complete control. My calm felt authentic, as Regan and his pitiful wife and the slick surface of his oak desk seemed far away. So my indifference wasn't a charade after all.

"Holy *shit*," she said after a long silence, then continued delightedly, "I never would have suspected you! I know lots of girls have crushes on him."

"Regan? Really?"

"Professor Douglas? Oh, yeah. Nerd hot."

Just like that, I was more seductress than sucker, someone who had captured a desirable older man in a story of sexual conquest rather than submission. Somehow the story flipped from making me look weak and even a little silly to letting me be triumphant and naughty. Suddenly, it all amounted to bragging rights instead of a sob story. Sophie's admiration made it so.

I slept better that night than I had in a long time.

WHAT DOES it mean, this sneeze?"

My cheeks burned. A sparkle of quiet, terrified laughter came from around me, and I let a cautious smile creep onto my face. Surely the professor must be kidding. His eyebrows knitted together yet more furiously, and I quickly tried to set my face back to neutral. Not a joke, then, it would seem.

"Mademoiselle, quelle est l'histoire de cet éternuement? Vous êtes Française ou Américaine? Presumably you should be one or the other, as you are in this class, but I have now asked you the question in both of the languages which we are here to master—a *wild* ambition, I readily admit—and yet you sit here mute. *Silent. Alors, vous êtes portugaise, néerlandaise, colombienne?"*

"No, I'm American."

"Ah! Mais bien sûr. Elle est Américaine." Some of the French students giggled and smiled in collusion, though they had surely missed much of his rapid-fire English. I could hardly blame them for their relief that they were not the ones being singled out by our terrifying professor of translation, Monsieur Boulu. He had been pacing before a giant whiteboard for the last half hour on a diatribe that leaped from one tangent to another in wholly inexplicable ways, pointing an index finger at cowering students as he said a word in one

language and demanded to know its equivalent in the other. What meager translations were offered were mostly shot down, although Sophie had scored a point by identifying *la bougeotte* as "wanderlust." And then I had sneezed. Loudly.

"I will ask you yet again, *Mademoiselle États-Unis*. What is the meaning of this sneeze?"

I looked around as though I might find some information or encouragement on the faces of my classmates, but no such luck. Even Sophie's face was blank, if sympathetic.

"The sneeze has no meaning, *monsieur*," I said, trying to keep my voice as respectful as possible. "It's just a noise."

"Wrong!" he said, slamming an open hand against his desk and then addressing one of the more persistent gigglers. "Perhaps you can tell us why this has meaning? Why it is relevant?" The student was sitting in the front row, and Monsieur Boulu leaned forward across his desk, looming from his towering height.

Sheepishly, the student shook his head.

"Non? Alors, arrêtez avec les rires bébêtes! Stop with the giggles!"

The poor kid nodded and obediently scribbled something on his notepad as we had all been feverishly doing throughout class.

"Alors, Mademoiselle États-Unis. Now that you have had a moment to reflect on the question, perhaps you can enlighten us on this issue which you have so helpfully brought to light."

I took a deep breath. "I'm sorry, *monsieur*, but I cannot see where an involuntary noise fits into our discussion of language. It's just a noise I made. A-choo."

"Aha! Now we are getting somewhere. *Mademoiselle États-Unis* said 'a-choo' because she is American. *Mais Monsieur* Giggles *là veut dire 'atchoum' parce qu'il est Français.* Do you see now where I am going? The phones in America *ring* and the phones here in France *dring*; the dogs there say 'woof,' the dogs here say *'abois.'* Now I will trust that you have encountered *un chien français* during your time here?"

I nodded.

"And did he sound any different than an American dog?"

I shook my head.

"You see"—blessedly he turned his laserlike focus from me and back onto the class—"language is deeper than what we are conscious of. It is not just a way of speaking but a whole way of communicating with the world. It is not only about what comes out of your little mouths, but also about what goes into your little heads. That is assuming of course that anything permeates at all." He smiled pointedly at Monsieur Giggles, who grinned back dumbly.

"You must begin to look beyond everything that you've taken for granted about language. You must begin to see that one sneezes in French or in English depending on who hears the sneeze, that the sound of a dog's bark is meaningless to us unless we can interpret the sound into our language, and not just the language of humans but the language of French or American humans, who will disagree about what the dog has said because they do not hear it in the same language. You must move beyond the laziness that makes you think that this is simple onomatopoeia, because onomatopoeia is a mirage! Let us not be lazy students of language."

The students, despite their confusion (or terror), were

riveted by the passionate speech. He took in our faces with a satisfied smile and appeared content for a moment.

"Many thanks to *Mademoiselle États-Unis* for bringing this noteworthy aspect of language to the forefront of our discussion today."

As much as the class terrified me, I'd fought for my place in it. Sophie and Adam were approved to take his class already, but because of my low test scores I had had to petition both him and Madame Rochet, and I did so fervently. My French verbal skills were improving in leaps and bounds thanks to my long nights at the pub with Sophie. Plus, I suspected somehow that Madame Rochet was developing something of a soft spot for me; she seemed to respect my devotion to the language, at least.

"Brooke," Adam said to me as we went into the hallway now flooded with students, "you were the star today!" Putting his arm around me, he pulled me to his perfectly laundered side.

I rolled my eyes with a groan and collapsed into him. "Can you even believe that happened? So mortifying."

We were getting slightly wary glances from the French students following us out of the class. I couldn't tell if they were appalled or impressed with us, but if we hadn't brought attention to ourselves before then, we certainly had now.

"No," Sophie said, appearing at my other side, unconcerned about how much room we took up across the hallway, "not at all. You held your own. At least you didn't burst into tears!"

"You're right," I said, glowing from their warmth. "A *traduction* class during which I do not break down crying may be called a success."

"Go on, Brooke," Sophie said, leaning into my ear, "admit you're a goddess."

"What's going on there, *les filles?* Inside jokes? *Les blagues intimes?* Tell me or I will start calling you *Mademoiselle États-Unis.*"

"We do have to tell you about our new French friends at some point," Sophie said, giving me a look that I read as *Not about the street, not about what happened there.* "And you must tell us about your *liaisons dangereuses* with your Internet friend."

"Oh, God, *him.* I will fill you in later, *les filles,* but right now I'm off to class."

"Me too," said Sophie.

I had nothing until later that afternoon, so I said my good-byes.

"We'll meet later for *un pot,*" Adam said, almost as an afterthought, as he and Sophie walked away hand in hand. I hoped my envy didn't show and that my desire to always be with Sophie wasn't blatant. Groups of three are always difficult, like a stool that's never quite on balance.

I made my way up the austere concrete corridor. The university was not quite as I'd imagined when I'd been dreaming of coming here over the summer. I had pictured it looking like the university I attended in California but more romantic and rustic. But the University of Nantes was utilitarian looking, much more reminiscent of American public high schools than any universities I had seen in the States. Maybe this wasn't accidental. They didn't bother with artifice or professors who pretended to care about your opinion here.

I had two hours before my next class and I sat in a sunny

patch in the park down the street from the institute and called my mother on my prepaid cell phone. This was the early era of cell phones and I didn't even own one back home, so I still marveled at the novelty of being able to call my mother while sitting on a park bench. She was an early riser and would just be waking up.

"Hello?" The connection was fuzzy and it sounded a little as though I were listening to her from underwater.

"Hi, Mom, can you hear me okay?"

"Brooke! I'm glad you finally called. I was getting worried."

"Sorry, Mom. They've been keeping us really busy here."

A few yards away, two construction workers were sitting on the grass eating a late lunch, and a little farther away, a couple were kissing on a blanket, the girl straddled across the boy's lap. It reminded me how long it had been since I had kissed someone; it only made it worse that the last time had been under such unfortunate circumstances.

"Tell me everything! I want to know about your host family and your classes and the people you've met, the things you've seen!" My mother's words ran together in excitement.

I suddenly felt exhausted at the prospect of even beginning to relate these details, much as I did when I sat down occasionally to take notes in the purple moleskin journal my mom had given me as a going-away present, in which I had sworn to myself I would make careful entries every day. But every time I sat down to write—my mind spilling over with the observations I had amassed about the food, the buildings, the French students, my fellow Americans—I was overwhelmed. Instead of the lovely, linear entries I had composed in my head, details came scrawled out at random and I was left with accounts that would later seem hieroglyphic: *Remember those strawberries, Americans: well-meaning colonists*, and of course *Sophie . . . ???* And later *Alex. Alex. Alex.*

I told my mother I couldn't talk long and offered some cursory information. *My host family is nice. Three kids. Only one class at the university.* I related the story of the sneeze, and my mother said the professor sounded like a pompous jerk, and I told her a little nastily that she had missed the point of the story. Even though Monsieur Boulu *was* a pompous jerk, I wanted her to understand how exciting it all was. It was perhaps then that I realized my mother might never quite be capable of understanding me again.

The construction workers got up to leave, and now that no one else was around, I unabashedly stared at the couple under the tree. The girl's skirt was hiked up around her hips, and the man's hands were entwined in her hair, though he frequently removed one to caress a thigh or fondle a breast. I began to wonder what would happen if they actually started to make love under the tree. Would I be compelled to leave? Would it be rude to stay? It sent a thrilling shiver up my spine to think that they might have noticed me here and were hoping I would stay to watch them. After all, they must be exhibitionists to be so openly groping each other in public. Or maybe they were simply so caught up in their mutual passion that they were impervious to anyone else.

"I have to go, Mom, I have class."

"All right, sweetheart. Have a good time and be safe. Oh! And say hello to Sophie for me. How is she doing?"

"She's doing great, this whole thing is a breeze for her."

"Well, she seems very bright," my mother said with something like pride in her voice, as though Sophie were her daughter as well. I felt a twisting inside me. Faint, and then gone.

I stayed there for a few moments after hanging up, but without the prop of the phone conversation I began to feel too conspicuous sitting there. I headed back to the institute feeling hollowed out and wishing I'd never gone to the park at all.

⁓

That afternoon I checked my e-mail in the computer room—the one and only place most students had access to the Internet, unless they wanted to pay to use a café—and was surprised to see an e-mail from Sophie's mother, Rebecca.

Hi Brooke,

I hope you girls are having a great time in France! I'm so sorry to bother you but we haven't heard from Sophie in a couple of weeks and we're getting very worried. Could you please tell her to contact us right away? I'm sure everything is fine! We just worry, as parents. You girls will understand when you're older (-:

I hope you're both enjoying your French sojourn!

Hugs and kisses,
Rebecca (Sophie's mom)

I wrote her back hurriedly, telling her that both Sophie and I were doing well, adding in a white lie that the program had been keeping us busy with schoolwork and organized outings (there were organized outings, but Sophie and I avoided them like the plague), and that I was sure that Sophie just hadn't been able to get any time in the computer room to e-mail them.

I found Sophie in one of the rooms, curled up in one of the decrepit institute armchairs, an abandoned novel in her lap as she snoozed.

"Soph"—I shook her shoulder—"wake up for a second." When she finally roused herself, I told her about the e-mail.

She rolled her eyes. "Oh, God, how mortifying."

"I told her you were fine and that we'd just been busy with school."

"So you lied"—she smiled—"good instincts. They made me promise to e-mail them every other day. I mean, how ridiculous is that?"

I shrugged, wondering if there wasn't a reason for it. "Parents."

"They make me never want to go home."

T HE WEATHER seemed to get cold over-
night in Nantes and the days shortened
dramatically. The initial shock, cultural and otherwise, of entering the country had worn off by late October, and most of
us were settling in. The other Americans hung out only with
each other and had their little power struggles and allegiances
among themselves. Sophie and I stuck together. We still spent
some time with Adam and Lindsay, traveling with them to
Munich for Oktoberfest and to Dublin for a long, incredibly
drunken weekend, but we mostly kept to ourselves, continu-
ing our adventures as a twosome.

We saw Véronique and her friends occasionally after that
miraculous first night with them, but we didn't see Alex.
Much to my dismay, I couldn't stop thinking about him. It
became hard to recall precisely what he looked like, and I
found the more I tried, the hazier his image became, until
I remembered more the feeling of being near him than the
details of his appearance.

One night at conversation club, I resolved to ask Véronique where Alex was. She came in a few minutes late with
a somewhat doleful-seeming Thomas by her side, and taking
him by the arm, she headed for us as soon as she saw us.

The four of us helped ourselves to wine and sat down
together. The young teacher who was supervising the session

immediately came over and separated us, officiously explaining that there were to be partnerships of only two, lest some talkative member of the group dominate the conversation. Secretly, I was glad to have Véronique to myself so that I could gossip with her.

"This wine is really pretty good," I said.

"Of course, it's the wine of the region. What we always drink."

"That's a difference between the U.S. and France. No one would bother serving good wine at something meant for college students in the U.S. There would be some awful boxed wine if there was any at all."

Véronique pursed her lips and nodded in agreement, perhaps remembering some horrifying boxed-wine experience during her time in the States. "But there are also some very nice wines in California," she said generously.

I leaned over the desk and lowered my voice. "Véronique."

"Oui?"

"I was just thinking the other day about the first time we hung out at your apartment. Whatever happened to your cousin?"

"Alex?" She smiled.

"Yeah, I thought he was in Nantes but we haven't seen him again."

"He went back to Paris for a bit for work; he booked a couple of good jobs there."

"Oh. Okay. I was just wondering." I hoped it wasn't completely obvious how crestfallen I was.

Véronique studied me for a moment before giving me a wry smile. "He'll be back, though, for the holidays. Hopefully he'll stay for a while, but you never know with him."

I nodded. "Being a photographer must be like that."

"Should I bring him around again next time he's in town?"

"Oh, only if you want."

"Of course I do. He's my cousin, I love him." She took a sip of her wine. "But then, don't we all?"

"Oh, no," I said too quickly, "I mean, I only met him once."

"Sometimes that's all it takes," she said playfully.

"Oh, well, I'm American. We don't really do things that way."

She laughed out loud and rolled her eyes. "I forgot how scared Americans are of that word. It's nothing to be ashamed of; lots of girls fall in love with my cousin the moment they lay eyes on him."

I bristled defensively. I wanted nothing less than to be one of these many girls. "I just thought he was interesting. I like photography," I blurted out helplessly.

"Oh, yes? I didn't know this. Do you want to be a photographer?"

"Well, no, I want to be a writer. I'm just always fascinated by other art forms. How they come to be." I hoped I'd finessed the phrase in French accurately enough to at least make sense.

She looked at me a little quizzically. "I didn't know that you were a writer."

"I don't talk about it much."

"Why not?"

I shrugged, not sure how to explain—let alone in French—the horrible feeling that I would be called a liar if I said things like this out loud or, even worse, secretly considered a fraud.

She nodded. "Maybe I do understand. I'm an actress but I never want to talk about it."

"That's right. Can we see you in a show while we're here?"

"Perhaps"—her smile looked a little wary—"but why are we talking about me when I know you want to be talking about Alex?"

I sighed. Was I surprised that she saw right through me? Had I been hoping she would? I gave up. "How old is he anyway?"

"I believe twenty-five?" She ticked off years on her long fingers. I had noticed that she always had perfect fingernails, smooth little ovals in an array of shades. It seemed to me that she must change the polish weekly, and today they were eggplant. "Yes, because he finished at the École des Beaux-Arts four years ago now."

Twenty-five still seemed far off and remote, the other side of some gateway to adulthood that was only barely coming into my line of sight.

"And he normally lives in Paris?"

"Yes, you would love his place there. It's a large apartment on the Left Bank that his father's family owns. He has parties there all the time. I used to go up there on the train when I was sixteen, and my mother would get so angry with me."

"It's your mother's family that's related?"

"Yes, our mothers are sisters. Virginie, who lives in Nantes, is Alex's paternal grandmother."

I wondered why someone who was living in a grand, family-owned apartment on the Left Bank would *need* to leave town for work, but I took it for granted that—this being France and involving both money and family—there were innumerable nuances I wasn't privy to.

"So is she very close to her mother-in-law?" I asked. "It sounded like she was pretty upset about her decline." I hoped it wasn't obvious how fervently I'd listened to Alex's every word.

"With Virginie? No, no. Not close so much, just locked into this stubborn dynamic, I suppose. I think they enjoyed resenting each other, but you can't keep hating a sick, old woman. Anyway, Alex will be back soon to help, as he said. He has always been her favorite, and he is a good grandson to come home. It is a sacrifice for him, to be back here. I cannot imagine coming back to Nantes after Paris and with all of that with his mother . . ." She didn't finish the thought.

"But I like Nantes," I said, although having only seen a glimpse of Paris while traveling from the airport to the train station, it was all simply enchanted France to me.

"Yes, but it's provincial. Particularly when you've grown up here, it feels very small. Our family has been here for no one knows how many generations. Our other grandmother hated Virginie; she was the beauty of her time and I think she was nasty to everyone. You come to know everyone in Nantes who is more or less your age, you see. Like with Thomas, I don't remember a time when I didn't know him."

We glanced over to where Sophie and Thomas were sitting. Sophie was staring down at her hands as she spoke, perhaps to avoid the intensity of Thomas's gaze, which was trained on her unabashedly.

"He looks like he might eat her," I said without thinking,

then briefly panicked that my comment would offend Véronique, but she only laughed.

"Poor Thomas, your friend is so beautiful and he doesn't know quite how to talk to beautiful women. He was very small when we were growing up," she said as though it explained everything.

"He looks normal-size to me." I stole another surreptitious glance. My caution was unnecessary, though, since a bonfire could have sprung up next to him and it wouldn't have distracted him from Sophie.

"Yes, fortunately. But in his head he is still the same tiny boy. Maybe he will get past it someday. I hope he's not making your friend uncomfortable."

"No, I don't think so." I didn't add that I thought Sophie liked the attention, regardless of what she thought of Thomas. It would have made *me* uncomfortable, but then I wasn't gorgeous like Sophie. When people stared at me, it only made me worry that I had something in my teeth or hair. I had known Sophie for long enough to know that there had likely never been a time when she wouldn't have known why people were looking at her. She lived in a parallel universe.

"You are good friends with Sophie, *non*?"

I nodded.

"She is indeed lovely, and she speaks French so perfectly," Véronique said. Her words had a tone of suspicion, and I felt sure that she was used to being one of the prettiest girls in the room, perhaps even in town. She didn't extend her compliment to include me, as an American girl would automatically have felt compelled to do, which I found refreshing; let's not pretend we're all equal. And yet . . .

"She's like that with everything," I said.

Véronique smiled. "How nice for her."

I didn't want her to dislike Sophie. I feared that we came as a package deal.

"Does all of your family still live in Nantes?" I asked after a pause to change the subject. Véronique ran her fingers through her hair, tossing it over her shoulder absentmindedly.

"*Ah, oui.* My parents, all my aunts, my brothers and sister. So many of them never left and they don't want me to either. I don't how people can do that, stay in one town their whole lives."

"I could never stay where I grew up. I'll go back to visit my mom but never to live."

"You're going to move somewhere wonderful, like New York, or maybe Paris?"

"Maybe."

Véronique and I were kindred spirits. We were both just waiting for our real lives to begin, fully formed and waiting for us just over the horizon.

THE HOLIDAYS came and went. Those who could afford to, including Sophie, flew home for Christmas, and those of us who couldn't were at the mercy of our *nantais* families. Sad as I was not to be with my mother—whom I was starting to really miss after the several months I'd been gone—I was happy to be staying. I didn't want to leave and risk breaking the spell of being abroad.

I was rewarded with the opulent spectacle of Nantes at Christmastime. The place du Commerce and the place Royale, city squares that had been the backdrop of my time in France, were transformed into the largest Christmas market in the region. Dozens and dozens of small wooden cottages took over the city, featuring handmade toys, intricate decorations, and exotic treats from Morocco to Madagascar. On Christmas Eve we attended a somber midnight Mass in the Roman cathedral in the city center. I was awestruck to be taking part in a service there; I had previously seen it only through the eyes of a visitor. Members of the Dubois family packed every corner of their house, and we ate roasted chestnuts and drank copious amounts of wine over the several days of celebration. I was shocked to discover that I loved pâté.

Christmas was just as magical for children in France as it was in the United States. Max was eager to inform me about all of their traditions—leaving shoes by the fireplace, the *bûche de Noël,* a sweet roulade fashioned to look like a yule log—and asked me what Christmas was like where I was from. When I told him about stockings and letters to Santa Claus, he seemed vindicated to know that Santa appeared in such a far-flung place as California. The Duboises had insisted I not buy them anything but had purchased several gifts for me, including a purple scarf and a notebook that Max was quick to point out had been his idea. "For your stories," he said conspiratorially. Max and I had occasionally chatted in the kitchen in the mornings, and one day when he had asked what I wanted to be when I grew up, I mentioned my dreams of becoming a writer. I was so touched by these gifts I found myself fighting back tears.

Sophie returned a few days into the New Year. I met her at the train station, and when she stepped off the train from Paris, she threw her arms around me as if I were a long-lost love.

"It's so good to see you." Relief was palpable in her voice, as though she'd been worried that I might not be here when she arrived. I was just as glad to see her. In America I'd barely known her, but in France I wasn't whole without her.

"How was your trip?" I asked as we went to board the local tram to the city center. There had been a light snowfall the day before—the first we'd seen in Nantes—and the city looked enchanted as we passed through, both subdued in the hush of fresh snow and festive with the leftover decorations from the Christmas and New Year's celebrations.

Sophie let out a long sigh. "It was fine," she said, switching to English.

"Just fine? Was it strange to go back?"

"Honestly, I wish I'd stayed here with you. My parents were stressing me out the whole time."

"About what?"

"About everything!" She closed her eyes as though trying to forget the whole episode. I let it lie for a moment.

"Grades," she said finally. I nodded. My grades hadn't been good during my first term in France either. My spoken-language skills had greatly improved and I had aced my grammar class, given how easy it was, but any other schoolwork that required effort hardly seemed worth doing.

"And they want me to go back on this medication I was taking before, try to hook up with a therapist here." Sophie stared out the window.

"Do you think you should?" I asked cautiously. I was alarmed by her parents' reaction. French Sophie was the only Sophie I'd really known; what if I was missing the signs that she was backsliding?

She looked at me and I worried she was angry, but then her face softened. "They just worry too much. I'm doing fine, better than fine. I'm having the experience of a lifetime here." She smiled at me in a way that was meant to be reassuring. But the mention of medication worried me and the way she was brushing it off even more so. Still, I sensed that the conversation was over. I told her about my holidays and let her know that we were meeting Véronique for *un pot* later. She brightened at that news.

Strangely, considering that it was a Saturday night, the bar was deserted when we arrived, save for a group of loud Irishmen in the corner and a couple furiously kissing and groping by the window.

Sophie and I ordered chardonnay.

"God, it's so nice to be able to order a glass of wine like a goddamn grown-up," Sophie said. "It was so awkward whenever I was out to eat with my parents; it just seemed so unreasonable that I couldn't drink."

"Well, not too long until we're twenty-one."

"It's not that." Sophie took her hair down from her ponytail and shook it out, then wound it around her fingers with an agitated, nervous energy as she talked. "Or it's not *just* that. Being back in the States, you realize how fucking *puritanical* everything is. All the prissiness about booze and sex, all the low-fat cheese, it's just bullshit."

I laughed. "Low-fat cheese is kind of an abomination."

"I'm serious. And it only gets worse. Imagine having two weeks of vacation a year. Imagine living like that! Here they barely *go* to work in the summer."

I nodded. I did understand. Before this we had never fully realized that there was any way but our own to live; there were bound to be some consequences. It was hard to imagine Sophie wanting to get out of her life back home as much as I did, but that understanding only made me feel closer to her.

"All the more reason to enjoy our time here," I said.

"I don't think we should leave." She took a swift sip from her wine as soon as the bartender put it down in front of her. "I'm not kidding."

Before I had a chance to respond, Véronique appeared in the doorway. *"Coucou!"* She was wearing a bright red wool coat that I hadn't seen before, her dark hair splashed across her shoulders and dramatically silhouetted against the vivid color.

We said enthusiastic hellos as though we were old friends

greeting each other after a long absence. As we told stories of our holidays, I noticed that Sophie's story of her trip home included no echoes of what she'd said to me earlier. But this was understandable, I supposed.

When Sophie went to the bathroom for a moment, Véronique leaned over and grasped my arm excitedly. "I have a surprise for you, *chérie*."

"What is it?"

She shrugged and took a sip of her water. Her nails were a glossy, candy-apple red.

I asked again, persisting. But of course I suspected. Nonetheless, when he walked through the door, I had to stop myself from swooning.

He had a scarf bundled so completely around his neck that only his nose and eyes peeked above it. I felt as if I were seeing someone recognizable but not exactly someone I knew. It was as though he were a celebrity that I was trying to place.

Véronique beamed at him and kissed him three times on the cheek. "*Mon cher cousin,* I've missed you."

"What a nice surprise," he said, coming over to kiss me. "I didn't know that you would still be here."

We chatted for a few moments about our Christmas holidays. Sophie returned from the bathroom and said her hellos.

"I was sorry I couldn't make it home to celebrate with you," Alex said, making a pleading face at Véronique, "I had so much going on in Paris."

"But you're back now, Alex," Véronique said with a tinge of admonishment.

"Yes, I want to work on my new project. No more fashion bullshit in Paris for a while."

"It must be hard on you," Sophie said teasingly, "spending time with all those models."

Alex made a sound of disgust. "I hate being around models. They are barely humans. It's what happens when you turn people into commodities, they neglect the rest of themselves so completely that they begin to disappear. They are lifeless facsimiles of women."

Véronique laughed. "And yet you've managed to bring yourself to date a few of them somehow."

"Exactly," Alex said, not smiling, "that's how I know. It's a temptation a man has to face down in his life; he must have it and reject it to know it's not worth having. And then he will be free to search for real beauty in the world."

With this his eyes flickered over—certainly unintentionally—to meet mine. My heart almost stopped.

"I don't know, Alex," I said, smiling, "you're saying you don't find models sexy? I'm incredulous."

"Ah, sexy least of all. You see," he continued, addressing our confusion, "sexy isn't a question of looks."

"Oh, no?" I asked. "What is it a question of?"

"It's a question of mastery of oneself, mastery of one's instruments. And most of these girls don't have an ounce of that. They're like marionettes; people just pull their poor strings all day long."

"People like you," Sophie said, "the photographers who work with them, photographers who dehumanize them for their own ends."

At long last Alex smiled. "You weren't listening, *chérie*, it isn't me who dehumanizes them."

"So it's their own fault? You have no part in it?" Sophie asked.

What was happening? I wanted them to get along, I didn't want the dynamic to be disrupted by the tension I could suddenly feel between the two of them.

"Perhaps I'm not completely innocent, as you say," Alex said, a tiny smirk playing at the corner of his mouth, "but I'm an artist trying to make a living. Anyway, it's behind me, I'm done with it. I can now focus on my real work for a while."

"So are you going to tell us about your new project?" Véronique asked brightly, turning the attention away from a peeved-looking Sophie. "Or are you going to make us beg?"

"No begging, but I can't tell you. I only barely know myself."

The waitress meandered over to ask if we wanted anything else to drink. Véronique ordered chinon for her and for Alex.

"I can't stay too long, *les filles*," Alex said. "I have to get settled back in at the house."

"One drink," Véronique said. "Don't be so boring, Alex!"

"It's this cold. It makes me want to stay in bed until it's warm again."

"You're so spoiled—too many years of being able to run off to the south whenever you want. It's made you soft."

"This could be true." He took a sip of the wine that had just arrived, then leaned his back onto the bar so that he was between Sophie and me. "So, girls, your French is much improved since I saw you last. You have been studying hard, *non*?"

"Don't know about that," I said, "but thank you anyway."

"It's marvelous to learn another language, isn't it? Then you can start to really be yourself again. It's important to be able to speak your mind." As he said this, he smiled pointedly at Sophie, who made a frustrated little grimace, though I could see she was barely concealing a smile. She was not immune to his charms, I thought, however she pretended.

"So what will you do now that you're back?" I asked.

"Well, tomorrow I am spending the day with my grandmother. That reminds me, Véronique, will you please come over for tea? Virginie loves you." It seemed odd that he would refer to her by her first name.

"Of course," Véronique said, "with pleasure. We should bring Sophie and Brooke as well!"

Alex looked at us thoughtfully. He seemed amused by the suggestion, perhaps encouraged by Sophie's lively debate skills.

"Not if it's an imposition," I said quickly.

"Of course it's not," Alex said. "No, that would be wonderful. What a novelty that would be for her, two young American girls in her salon. *Alors, toutes les filles.* Tomorrow at four o'clock *ça marche?*"

He took Véronique's face in his hands and pulled her in for his usual three kisses, then repeated this with Sophie and me. I took a deep breath at the opportune moment. His scent was now in my memory from the first night, and it brought with it an automatic rush of desire.

Soon after, I left to meet up with my host family for dinner. Nicole had asked whether I would be joining them that morning and I had impulsively said yes. I had renewed my dedication to spending more time with them after the holidays. I was growing especially attached to little Max, and his face flooded with delight whenever I joined them at the table.

Nicole's cooking was tasty, and this night she served a roasted chicken with leeks and asparagus. I told them that they would be horrified at the way most American families eat dinner every night, grabbing something microwaved, eaten over the sink or in the car. The kind of meals they had each night here most Americans had at best once a week on Sundays. They were predictably and gleefully aghast at this— all except for Max, who thought this would give him more chances at the frozen fish fingers that Nicole served him once a month when she had dinner with her book group.

And how were my studies? they asked. Was I reading good French writers?

"Well," I confessed, "I am taking a wonderful theater class at the institute where we are reading Ionesco, Corneille, and Molière, but on my own I'm afraid what I have been reading is a bit shameful: translations of Danielle Steel and Nora Roberts."

Nicole gamely let out a mock gasp. "Who are these writers?" Monsieur asked, and Nicole explained. *"Alors,"* he said, his broad, smiling face making me think of all fathers everywhere, of what I might have missed, *"pas Baudelaire ou Flaubert, ma chère?"*

The kids all groaned in unison at the rhyme. Dad humor was the same everywhere.

"But you'll be happy to hear that I am reading *The Stranger* in English and that I plan to read it in French afterward."

They nodded approvingly.

The cheese-and-yogurt course lasted longer than usual as Max performed a version of "Oh My Darling Clementine" that he was learning for school, sending me into such hysterics that I could hardly explain to the family where the song had come from. I thought of my first few nights with them, how I was terrified to answer a simple question, much less tell a story or a joke. How far I had come.

At last I went up to bed with a tisane and the feeling that I could not have lived this day any better than I had done. I pulled back the curtain on my bedroom window so that I could look out and up into the night sky from where I lay in my bed.

But I couldn't settle down. I had not only seen Alex at last after all this time, but would have to prepare to see him again tomorrow. It brought me some relief to see that Alex and Sophie didn't seem to get along well. But was I mistaking sexual tension for dislike? I needed to say something to Sophie about my debilitating little crush on the Frenchman. Then he would become off-limits, wasn't that the rule? But what if Sophie wanted him too? What would I say then, that I saw him first? The thought of competing with Sophie over a man made me ill. I would sleep on it, I decided. Everything would be clearer in the morning.

I HAD A sense of my options unfurling, becoming limitless. I was aware of things inside of me shifting and taking new shape.

That Sunday, I woke up early to finish a paper for my theater class before I met with Sophie for lunch and some shopping in the town center. I didn't want to be preoccupied with schoolwork later when we saw Alex and Véronique. Yet it was difficult to focus on my paper with the afternoon that loomed ahead. The day was sunny despite the cold, with the sort of clear air that sharpens the senses, makes you think something exciting could happen.

At last I was free and joined Sophie at our favorite sandwich shop near the school. I hated to meet so close to the institute on a Sunday, but we had both developed something of an addiction to the *sandwich au jambon* there, with the ham served on warm, fresh sliced minibaguettes slathered on both sides with butter, and the location was close enough to the shops we wanted to visit that we could justify going there.

"Oh, these are so good," Sophie said. "Why don't we have sandwiches like this in the States? I suddenly feel like everything we do to our sandwiches is ridiculous! Lettuce! Mayonnaise! Pickles! They're done up like cheap whores."

"Sandwich putain américaine!"

"And the bread! The bread is a goddamned disaster. It doesn't belong to the same species as what they've got here. Can you imagine if we introduced them to Wonder bread?"

I cringed. "We'll have to ask Véronique if she had any such horrifying encounter when she was there. Last night I got a kick out of telling my host family about microwave dinners and people eating in their cars. They were appalled. It's like they've heard about these odd things but don't quite really believe we do them. Much like I never really believed they could eat the way they do every night here—all around the table with the cheese plate and everything—until I saw it with my own eyes."

"How sad." Sophie finished the last bite of her sandwich, which she had put away with impressive speed. Brushing crumbs from her mouth, she pulled her scarf tighter around her neck. "They're more sophisticated than we could fathom, and we're even lazier than they could imagine."

"On second thought, maybe we shouldn't say anything to Véronique about the Wonder bread, in case she doesn't already know. It might ruin what's left of our American mystique."

"Good point." Sophie took my gloved hand in hers. We walked a couple of blocks before she stopped abruptly. "Oh! We have to stop in here."

I had walked by the Sonia Rykiel boutique several times and stopped to admire the mannequins in the window that towered several feet above street level—as if the general air of luxury and glamour of the place were not enough to make you feel small and overwhelmed—but I had never dreamed of going in.

The clothes were quirky and luxe in a particularly French way; the shapes were a bit boyish with stripes and small florals, whimsical girlie accoutrements of lace and bows.

"Bonjour," a saleswoman said from a corner, where she appeared to be adjusting a few hangers that already hung perfectly spaced. She did not ask if she could help us with anything. I hadn't done enough high-end shopping to know if her seeming indifference could be accounted for by our being in France or our being two twenty-year-old girls—me carrying my ugly canvas shoulder bag—in a fancy store.

Sophie either didn't notice the saleswoman's icy demeanor or didn't care. She went through the store fingering the delicate striped sweaters and the intricate ruffles of the dresses. I wondered if she was bold enough to try something on.

I recalled my late-night reverie and my conviction that I should tell her about my attraction to Alex to make sure she kept her distance. But suddenly in this well-lit, posh store watching Sophie model a beautiful gray purse in the mirror—face thoughtful as though actually considering it for purchase—the whole thing seemed ridiculous. We didn't even know Alex that well, and I felt better about my chances in the light of day. After all, attraction was a mysterious and mercurial thing. I wouldn't say anything, I decided, I didn't want to jinx it. I couldn't imagine why I'd felt so strongly about it the night before.

"What do you think?" she asked me in English. We tended now to switch back and forth between the two languages, sometimes without even meaning to or knowing we'd done so. I thought fondly of how lovely it was to be the sort of person who did that.

"So gorgeous." I tentatively stroked the buttery leather with my fingertips. *"Et plus chère que ma voiture,"* I said in French for the benefit of the saleswoman, as though its probably costing more than my Honda were somehow her doing.

"I think I have to have it," Sophie said with a dramatic sigh. "I first saw it weeks ago." She then lowered her voice as if she were telling me something naughty. "I've been back to visit it since."

I looked again at the saleswoman; had she been a witness to the beginning stages of this illicit affair of *le sac à main* as well?

This completely perfect bag was a sound argument for the transformative power of fashion. Without it, Sophie was a beautiful student, but with it, she was made over as French Sophie, adult Sophie, some future Sophie yet unrealized. Isn't this why we buy what we don't need? Not to *have* something new but to be made into something new?

"Let me see." I took the bag from her and took a long look at myself in the mirror. On me the bag had a slightly different effect, demanding different hair and shoes and the addition of accessories completely foreign to me, like bangles or a scarf. Still, the effect was miraculous, the bag suggesting that I might be capable of being transformed, that owning it would give the rest of me something to live up to. I gave it back to Sophie before I could fall deeper under its spell, feel the pain of not owning it.

"Oui," Sophie said, "I have to have it."

I laughed and sighed; if only. Then to my astonishment she caught the attention of the saleswoman and repeated herself: *I must have it.* A little ghost of a smile crossed the saleswoman's lips as she went to the back to get a newer one to replace the floor model Sophie was holding, although it looked pristine to me.

"Sophie," I hissed in a tight whisper.

"What?" she asked cheerfully, not at all defensively. I looked her in the eye and saw no fear. A moment before I had thought she was kidding, but now I realized that she was completely set on buying the bag.

An older woman with a small terrier came into the shop and began a slow lap around the floor.

"J'arrive tout de suite, Madame Voulu, veuillez patienter un tout petit moment." The saleswoman had reappeared and welcomed the regular patron with a few degrees more warmth than she had managed for us.

"Alors, mademoiselle," the saleswoman said to Sophie, pulling the bag from its plastic wrapping and displaying it on the soft dust bag for Sophie to inspect.

"Ça marche," said Sophie, *"c'est parfait."*

The actual purchase seemed to take place in some sort of suspended animation; the bag was placed tenderly in its dust bag and then into a sleek, glossy carrier bag. Sophie calmly produced a credit card from her wallet—this was surely the "for emergencies only" credit card ubiquitous among American students—and paid the woman, who thanked her and told her to enjoy her *joli sac à main.*

Sophie took my arm as we left the store, brimming with delight and babbling somewhat disjointedly about her purchase. "I've always wanted a bag just like this; it reminds me of one that my mother had when I was little."

The sun warmed our shoulders and I dug my sunglasses out of my canvas bag, now seeming more decrepit than ever.

Were we the kind of friends who could get on each other's case about a thing such as this? If it had been a modestly indulgent purchase, something that cost the equivalent of a month or so's *bière et sandwich* money, then I would have scolded her handily, but this went beyond that into more serious territory. I knew Sophie's family was well-off, but purchasing a bag that costly surely wasn't wise. Even though she'd described her weeks of longing for the bag, the purchase itself had seemed to happen on a whim. But it was done. My stomach turned over with horror at the realization that the time to have said something, to have been the good friend and voice of reason, had passed me by when the saleswoman had disappeared to go get the bag; that had been my moment to speak up. But perhaps it could be returned, we were only blocks away. "Sophie . . ."

"Oui, chérie?" Her eyes sparkled. She looked so happy I suddenly didn't want to ruin it. After all, this was Sophie, she knew what she was doing. What did I know about how rich girls lived? She was spontaneous, she was *fun*. I should keep my nerves to myself and go along for the ride.

"I'm dying over that bag, it's *so* gorgeous," I said.

There was no sign that the outrageous purchase she'd just made disturbed her, no indication that her heart was racing or that she regretted what she'd done. She just *had* to have it. My concern twisted into something else, an appalled envy that echoed in my head: *You are not the same.* I batted the thought away.

"You can borrow it anytime you want, *mon amour.*"

And perhaps I could, perhaps I could buy bangles and a scarf and some sleeker shoes and borrow the bag and feel its magic. So later, in a less pricey store, I let Sophie convince me to buy not only a scarf but a little floppy hat that looked like, but wasn't quite, a beret. *A beret? In France? You cannot be serious. But this is not some cartoonish mime's beret, this is* très moderne, très jeune, très chic. In the face of *le sac* they seemed like a bargain, so I bought both items and left wearing them with my black T-shirt and dark jeans, draping the scarf over the lapels of my overcoat.

"We should get some chocolates for Alex's grandmother," Sophie said as we made our way down to the place de Transportation. I hadn't thought of this and was glad that Sophie had, as it would be gauche to come to tea empty-handed.

We went into a shop tucked in a little alley; I had walked by before and looked longingly into its windows but had never had a reason to go in. This was nothing like an American chocolate shop with its waxy squares of milk chocolate and gaudy bows. These window displays were so opulent that they seemed pulled from a children's story. There were all shapes of chocolate—sports cars, animals—truffle balls piled impossibly high and dusted with ultrafine cocoa, small squares of dark chocolate with miniature paintings on their faces.

Walking in, we shut the door swiftly, the frigid air blowing down the shadowy alleyway behind us. The older couple inside owned the shop and displayed none of the *froideur* of the *vendeuse chez Sonia Rykiel*. They seemed to take seriously the task of helping us select our chocolates, asking Sophie and me a dozen questions about our plan for the chocolates and the intended recipient. They made certain to impart upon us the dire importance of getting these chocolates to

Madame *tout de suite,* as they would only be good for a few days: these were serious, fragile French chocolates.

The box cost us nearly fifty euros. I handed Sophie my cash as she stood at the register, but she waved it away. "Next time," she said as though this were as regular a purchase for the two of us as our *sandwichs au jambon.* Meekly, I tried again, but she couldn't be dissuaded. I winced with shame; she *knew* I couldn't afford it.

By the time we left the chocolate shop we had just enough time to walk to the de Persauds' house at a leisurely pace. Our purchases served to make us slightly different girls from those we'd been before, adding to the feeling that this day was somehow momentous. Instead of just imagining a future Brooke and Sophie, we now *embodied* future Brooke and Sophie. We were clearing the way for them. Their unspoken, shared conviction was that these future selves would never lose touch with each other. I thought the future would be a more level playing field. Sophie had begun the race ahead of me, but she didn't have to remain there.

During this afternoon I began to understand what I found so seductive about Sophie: the possibility of seeing the world as she saw it, as an alternate universe where life was above all else an adventure. I thought again about what she called her "bad periods," then looked at her, radiating happiness. How could it be? Maybe her parents were just worriers, overprotective. Parents could be that way. Yet here she was next to me, swinging her expensive new bag, gleefully pointing out children in the street who were bundled up to their ears in scarves with only their eyes visible, peeking out from under their caps. Ever the golden girl.

When we finally reached the house, we stood in front of a large, elegant town house with gladiolas in the window boxes.

"This looks fancy," I whispered to Sophie. We had double-checked the address and were hesitating as if to have one last moment to ourselves before entering. If nothing else, the cold would eventually have driven us to ring the doorbell, as the abbreviated winter day had already left half the city in shadows.

"Well, you knew they'd be posh. *De Persaud*. Anything with a *de* in it is a dead giveaway."

"Like *'de Sade'*?"

We both faced forward as though we'd already rung the door chime and were waiting for it to open.

"Ooh, dark! But, yes, he was a marquis, after all." Sophie finally leaned forward and rapped gently on the door.

When we heard no signs of life from within, I located a not-very-functional-looking gilded doorbell and pressed it. Sophie and I both startled as a thunderous chime resounded from within, then struggled to stifle our giggles before someone opened the door.

A petite but intimidating dark-eyed woman in a house-keeper's uniform appeared and looked at us suspiciously. We gave our names and explained quickly—afraid she might actually shut the door in our faces if we didn't convince her—that we were friends of Alex de Persaud's and had been invited this afternoon for tea.

"*Bon*," she said in an accent that did not sound French, and we followed her into the foyer. The house was lavish, and somehow much larger than had seemed possible from the street. The foyer was decorated with the sort of Louis XIV furniture that would have appeared ridiculous and effete in any American home I had seen but looked perfect here.

Sophie and I remained hushed and humbled in the foyer waiting for someone to come and get us. At last Véronique and Alex appeared at the top of the staircase and came down to where we were standing, their feet hitting the steps nearly in tandem.

"*Salut, les filles!*" Véronique said.

They looked like a couple welcoming guests into their home. I had the impression that Véronique had not just arrived but had been here awhile. She seemed at ease in the house, sliding her hand down the banister as she walked. The four of us exchanged kisses and hellos.

"And what is this?" Véronique exclaimed upon seeing the carrier bag from Sonia Rykiel. Gleaming and huge as it was, it was rather impossible to miss.

"*Un peu de shopping,*" Sophie said, her eyes shining.

"Just a little bit, no?" Véronique delicately fingered the top of the bag and peered into the lip. Sophie set the shopping bag down gently, extracting from it the dust bag and then the purse itself. Gasping, Véronique reached out to touch the bag, which Sophie gladly handed over as though it were a remarkably attractive and well-behaved child of whom she was proud. I was taken aback upon seeing the bag again, the luxurious leather, the gleaming silver hardware. How long would you have to own something like this before it would look to you like a simple thing of quotidian life? Or worse, would you come to hate it and regard it with remorse, wishing you had taken a trip to India with the money? What dilemmas to have, not something I'd need to worry about. And maybe those who had either option didn't have to choose. Sophie didn't have to choose.

As Véronique admired the bag, I could see the wheels turning behind her eyes, the sizing up of not only the bag but also the girl who'd purchased it. But Véronique knew so little of Sophie that she was much freer than I to make sweeping assumptions, to simply think *rich girl*.

"It's a classic," pronounced Véronique, *"c'est très cool."*

"Oui," said Alex, showing an interest in the bag that no straight American boy would have volunteered in a million years. *"C'est si soigné."*

At length Véronique handed the bag back to Sophie.

"Oh," I said finally, "we brought these as well." I handed the gold box with the thick maroon ribbon to Alex, feeling like a fraud for not having contributed to the purchase of the chocolates and yet being the one to present them.

"Thank you, I will give them to Magdalena to serve after tea. I'm so glad you're here," Alex said. "I told my grandmother that we had two American guests. She's forgotten by now, but she was very excited at the time, so I am confident that it will be a very pleasant surprise." He was wearing a fine cashmere sweater in a deep eggplant color and looked clean shaven for the first time since I'd met him. When he kissed my cheeks, he smelled fresh and slightly perfumed as though he had just awoken and showered before we'd arrived. I felt reassured that I'd done the right thing in not hastily mentioning my crush to Sophie, which would only have increased the tension I felt around Alex. Furthermore it could upset the delicate international group dynamics to have knowing looks being passed back and forth. They would know immediately something was up; I was still counting on continued exposure to his presence to acclimate me to it and temper my attraction. Until I could be on more even footing, part of me didn't want him to know the hand he held in case he might play it or, worse, *not* play it.

We followed them upstairs to a sun-drenched, enclosed patio. As we made our way across the neat, faded blue tile, I took in the wondrous flora that covered the perimeter of the room—bougainvillea and lavender—and marveled at how these plants thrived so well in the city. I remembered then that Alex had said his grandmother Virginie's most beloved place was the family house in Cap Ferrat, and I wondered if this was an attempt to re-create that for her, as she must be too frail now to make the trip there. With the clear, late-afternoon sun shining through the glass dome that covered the patio, the Mediterranean effect was especially convincing.

I was so blown away by the surroundings, it took me a second to notice that Virginie was in the garden already, taking the four of us in with a look of mild confusion. As Alex approached her, he seemed to come into focus and her face registered delight. *"Alex, mon petit chou!"* It occurred to me that she might have been sitting there in solitude for quite some time. The idea that Alex and Véronique had left her there alone struck me as ineffably sad.

"Bonjour," she said to the three of us. Her voice was stiff, but her cloudy-blue eyes twinkled and a smile seemed to be lurking at her lips.

"Mamie, je vous présente Sophie et Brooke."

"Et quelle des deux filles est votre femme?" she asked, allowing a tiny grin to slip over her face. She spoke softly but mercifully

slowly, meaning she would not have to be asked to speak *un peu plus lentement* for the slower of the two Americans.

Alex laughed and looked at her affectionately. "No, *Mamie*, neither of them is my wife. They are friends."

She made a harrumphing sound and pulled him in close. *"Pas encore."*

Not yet. At this we all giggled, which seemed to thrill her, and she gently commanded us to sit. Sophie sat closest to her at the edge of the rattan bench with me at the other end and Alex in between. Véronique took the chair across the table from her.

"Thank you so much for having us today, Madame de Persaud," Sophie said. As she spoke, a look of recognition crossed the older woman's face.

"Katherine?" she said, even more quietly, as though her voice had escaped her in her surprise.

"Oh, no. Actually my name is Sophie?"

Madame de Persaud looked at Alex, her face suddenly distressed.

"What's wrong, *Mamie*? This is Sophie, one of my American friends who has come for a visit."

"Mais non," Virginie said defiantly. "This is my sister Katherine." With this, she reached for Sophie's hand, which Sophie offered with trepidation, looking at Alex nervously.

Alex looked at Sophie as though suddenly equally uncertain who she actually was. "My God," he said under his breath as a broad smile came to his lips. "She does look just like Great-Aunt Katherine when she was young, doesn't she?" He added a little more soberly, "But this is not Katherine. This is my friend Sophie, she's American."

"Then where is Katherine?" Virginie asked impatiently.

"She's not here, *Mamie*," Alex said, a tired frustration revealing itself in his voice. I understood from his tone that Katherine was not only "not here in the house" but also "not here among the living."

"Indeed," Virginie said, at last releasing Sophie's hand and patting her on the arm. Virginie smiled to herself as though she was onto this little trick and had decided to humor us and go along with it. "So you're American. Are you from New York City?"

"No," Sophie said, "the other side, California."

"I might move to New York when I finish school," I said, desperate to add something to the conversation. I was disappearing beneath the waves.

"Oh, yes? I lived there just after the war and I had a fine time. I used to know that writer. Who is that writer I knew back then, *chéri*?" she said to Alex.

"Henry Miller, *Mamie*."

"*Ah, oui. C'est ça.*" She looked pleased.

The housekeeper reemerged carrying a full tea service. She was so quiet and conservative in her movements that you forgot she was there even as the delicate china and impossibly perfect little pastries and tea sandwiches appeared before us.

"He was a very strange man. But you know they all are."

"Writers?" I asked.

"Americans."

At this we all laughed without anyone noting the faux pas.

"Brooke is a writer," Véronique said.

Virginie's head swiveled between Sophie and me, as though trying to determine who Véronique was referring to. "Novels?" she said to the space in between us.

"Short stories," I said, "but hopefully someday a novel."

She nodded. "I knew a writer once. An American, what was his name, Alex?"

The conversation went on like this for another hour or so, going in circles, looping back around, full of sharp turns and non sequiturs. The effort of trying to both keep up but also to not react to the surreal nature of the conversation was exhausting. Madame de Persaud drank several cups of tea but left the food untouched. When Alex urged her to eat something, she scolded him and told him she was watching her figure.

"Well, I think I shall go and take a little rest," she said to Alex. "Katherine, walk with me to my room."

Sophie looked at Alex with surprise, and he smiled apologetically.

"Why don't I go with you as well?" Véronique offered, at least knowing where Madame de Persaud's room was and perhaps some other vital protocol.

"You're Alex's wife?" Madame questioned Véronique as Alex helped her to her feet and Sophie came around her other side to take her arm.

"*Oui, Mamie. C'est ma femme,*" Alex said quietly, grinning at Véronique, who beamed back in collusion. I sat stiffly, again the only person lacking a vital role. I was glad for the prop of my teacup to occupy me, even though the tea in it had become cold.

Alex stood until his grandmother and the two girls had left the room, then sat down with a long sigh and turned to me. He was smiling. "Some days she is much worse. I had hoped she'd be a little more lucid for your visit, but we never know these days."

"It's okay, it's not necessary to apologize." My words tumbled out one after another. It caught me off guard to suddenly be alone with him after imagining it so many times.

"I'm not apologizing." His smile grew wider as he extracted a silver cigarette case and pulled from it an unusually long cigarette. He offered me the case and I took a moment to study it before handing it back to him, explaining that I didn't smoke, though I wasn't certain if this was true anymore. It had become Sophie's and my shared vice, but I couldn't imagine doing it in front of him; I was too afraid it would make me appear unappealing, that I would somehow do it wrong.

"*Bien sûr, les Américains.* The case is charming, though, no? I have to special-order cigarettes for it." This seemed both indulgent and in keeping with my idea of him. He took two deep drags. "I do appreciate that you came today. And the two of you showed such grace. The woman Virginie once was would have appreciated your composure in the face of such lunacy."

"Happy to be here." This sounded wrong somehow.

"My mother can't bear to be around her. It's ironic because they fought all the time before the dementia, and now it would seem my mother wants nothing more than to go back to that. I think seeing her foe so disarmed is deeply disturbing to her. You women are strange creatures."

"It seems that all of my associations today are damning. Women, writers, Americans . . ."

Alex laughed. "You're so clever. Why can I never meet clever girls like you, mmm?" He inched now just a bit closer to me on the bench.

But you have met me, I wanted to say. I feared he meant

that he could never meet clever girls whom he also wanted to sleep with. So instead I only shrugged and stared into the remaining few drops of my now-cold tea. Alex took the teacup gently from my hands and set it on the table. My gaze, robbed of its diversion, returned to Alex.

"Tell me, then, how is your writing going? Have you written many stories while you have been here in France? Does this place inspire you?"

I wanted to say that this place—meaning this splendid garden room and furthermore the inhabitant I shared it with right at this moment—inspired me very much. "A change of scene is always good for creativity, I suppose," I said instead.

"Do you suppose?" he asked playfully. "This is what I'm hoping for, coming back here. I think Paris has dulled my senses. The city of too many lights."

"And what do you take pictures of?"

"What do I take pictures of?" he parroted.

I felt we were in some precarious sparring match that I hadn't meant to enter into. "Yes, well, *en fait* still lifes or landscapes or . . . ?"

"*Ben, non,*" he said as if these mundane suggestions left a bad taste on his tongue, "people." *Les gens.*

"Right. Models."

"No, not if I can help it. As I said the other night, I prefer to shoot a regular girl. More interesting." He smiled gently and I wondered if this was supposed to somehow flatter me. What a useless word *interesting* was, conveying both multitudes and nothing at all.

"Not much money in regular girls, though, is there?"

"My other work is art, and I'm afraid that, as you say, the

intersection of art and commerce is usually poverty. You will see once you have left school whether or not you really want to keep writing your 'little stories.'" He said the last two words in English.

I blanched. "My 'little stories'?"

He thought for a moment, taking a drag on his cigarette. "Excuse me, your *short* stories. I forget the difference in English from time to time. You have more words than we do, which is lucky for you, my writer bird. I only mean that you will know what is really in your heart when you have to worry about paying the rent, buying food, that sort of thing."

It seemed unlikely to me that he knew much about struggling to live off his art, or poverty of any kind. He seemed rather relaxed for someone on the ragged edge. There was a hungry gleam in his eye, but not in that way.

"Isn't it scary to live like that? From one project to the next? With that uncertainty?"

"Sometimes yes, it is." He smiled and leaned in, whispering now as though he didn't wish anyone to overhear him, the smell of smoke and of him overwhelming me. "But with fear you must learn to not only face it but to make yourself its master. Otherwise, *chérie*"—his face was so close now that I couldn't look him directly in the eye—"it will always be yours." With this he kissed me on my jawbone right below my ear, nearly on my neck. I breathed in sharply, and before I could stop myself, my fingers flew to where his lips had touched, to capture the fleeting sensation of the kiss.

He had returned to his chair and was leaning back with one foot crossed over his knee. He regarded me as though gauging how well I was absorbing what had just happened. I called upon my remaining reserves of will to seem detached or to somehow emulate the look of slight amusement that he and Véronique always wore.

Finishing his cigarette—the smoke from which still burned my eyes—he stubbed it out in the elegant ivory ashtray next to him on the seat cushion.

A thousand questions thundered through my brain all at once. Was he trying to sleep with me? Was it possible that he didn't know the effects of what he'd just done? Or did he not care? He was watching me as if he knew exactly what I would do next and was just waiting for me to get around to it.

"So you are not afraid," I said.

"No, that is not what I said."

Magdalena reappeared to clear away the remains of the tea service. I had no idea how to behave around a servant and folded my hands in my lap like a child in a church pew. Alex said something to her in what sounded like German, a request she acknowledged with a grunt without bothering to make eye contact with him. He remained silent until she was well out of the room.

"If you knew me better, you would know that I am always afraid," Alex said.

"I don't believe you."

A look of irritation crossed his face. "It's true, but people see what they want to see. You will see what you want to see."

I found myself staring into the chasm of hostile silence that had opened up between us. I wanted to dismiss it as pouting, but I could see in his face that something had unsettled him, and all I wanted was to make it right. Where were Sophie and Véronique? What was taking them so long? But maybe it was better that I had a few more moments left to undo the damage.

"I didn't mean to upset you," I said at last, futilely searching for the word for "offend." Now was not a moment for the ubiquitous *comment dit-on.*

"Upset me?" He gave me a measured smile. "Never."

The chasm had closed, but so too had some important window. I felt the fatigue of trying to keep up with someone who was not only speaking in another language but speaking enigmatically at that.

"It's just hard to imagine someone like you being afraid. That's what I meant. You seem so confident. But it's always a mistake to think you know everything or really anything at all about someone. Especially someone you've just met. Thank you for reminding me."

I was again at a disadvantage; when the words themselves take so much energy, the tone can so easily get lost.

"Actually, I have the feeling"—he leaned forward just a bit—"that you are a girl who can know a person just by looking at them."

"Maybe so." I smiled as though he'd guessed a secret of mine. "But still, you have to be careful." *Il faut faire attention.*

Magdalena reappeared with a bottle of wine and four glasses. She put them down on the table and opened the bottle of wine. I noticed that she didn't bother to be quiet when Madame de Persaud was gone from the room.

Alex thanked her in German as she left the room, and again she left without acknowledgment.

He smiled coldly and shook his head. I looked at him questioningly. "Magdalena doesn't like me, or my mother.

If it was her choice, they never would have left that ugly old château in the Loire Valley. She doesn't like 'the city,' as she calls it, and she knows she's out as soon as my *chère grand-mère* leaves us. She thinks we're after the old woman's money."

"Well, are you?"

To my relief, he laughed. Before he could say anything more, Sophie and Véronique came back into the room.

"Ah, génial! Du vin," Véronique said.

"Bien sûr." Alex leaned forward and filled our glasses with a crisp sauvignon blanc, then turned to Sophie. "I cannot believe my poor demented grandmother thought you were her sister. You're a good sport."

"Did you know your aunt Katherine well?" Sophie asked. "Do I actually look like her?"

"I never met her, she died young. But from photos it does seem that you look a lot like her, yes. In fact"—he finished the bit of wine that was still in his glass—"I think I know where there are some photos upstairs. I will show you." Standing, he reached out a hand to Sophie, which she took and followed him. I felt the spotlight of his attention shift onto her, watched her settle into it.

Since Véronique remained rooted where she sat, I surmised that we were not invited to come along and watched as Sophie and Alex left the garden room hand in hand.

Maybe they would be right back with a photo album and we would all look at it together, I told myself. But then why did Alex take Sophie with him and not simply go fetch it and bring it back?

Véronique smiled at me as she refilled first my glass and

then hers. For a moment I was worried that she had somehow read my thoughts. "I told you they were a complicated family," she said, reclining and taking a long sip.

I had so many questions I wanted to ask her, and none of them seemed appropriate. For starters, did she know which of us—presuming it was one or the other—Alex preferred? What had he said about us? Surely they'd spoken about *les filles américaines* when we weren't around. Or if he had said nothing, what was she inclined to believe? And what *was* the deal with the grandmother? Did some vast Astor-like fortune hang in the balance?

"They seem fascinating," I said distractedly. Sophie and Alex weren't coming back, at least not right away.

"You will meet Alex's mother at some point. I will be curious to know what you think of her." I liked this reference to a future time when we would all be together here again, implying that Sophie and I had passed the test.

Eventually Véronique went for another bottle of wine. I sat quietly alone in the room wishing with every fiber of my being that Sophie and Alex would reappear. What was taking so long, looking at the pictures? I wanted them sitting in front of me so that I could banish the images that were racing through my head of the two of them alone together.

"*Voilà!*" said Véronique, appearing with another bottle of the wine we'd just been drinking. No sooner had she filled our glasses than Alex materialized behind her with a different bottle of wine and the gold box of chocolates.

He laughed when he saw that Véronique had already produced a second bottle. "*Mais c'est un rouge*"—he gestured to the red wine he carried, brushing a bit of dust off the decrepit-looking label with its peeling corners. "We will open it and let it breathe then, that will be better, *non*?"

"You should see this cellar," Sophie said quietly to me in English as she sat down beside me, her eyes wide.

"And the chocolates." Alex pulled the ribbon gingerly away and opened the box. "So lovely of you girls to bring these." I had forgotten about them, that we were meant to have them with the tea. "Tomorrow we'll tell *Mamie* that she was very bad and had three of them at tea," he said playfully.

Since Sophie and Véronique laughed, I decided I was being uptight in thinking that this comment was cruel. I couldn't be upset that we'd decided to eat the chocolates, though, they were too divine. I silently swore to myself that I would never subject my taste buds to a waxy See's or Russell Stover again as long as I lived.

"So you must really tell me now," Alex said, looking at Sophie and me, "what you think of France. You have been here several months now. Have you learned all of our secrets?"

"We love it," Sophie and I said nearly in unison, which made us giggle.

"And you don't miss the U.S.?"

I shrugged. Sophie said, *"Non, pas du tout."*

It seemed unimaginable that we'd be leaving in a few months. I knew I wouldn't be ready then, if ever, to go back to what I'd known.

"But it's your home," Alex said.

I did miss my mother, but didn't want to sound childish saying so.

"Home is an overrated concept," Sophie said, "we just might never go back."

We all laughed a little, though it seemed she wasn't joking.

"Wouldn't that be something," Véronique said evenly. "So, how was your little treasure hunt?"

"Hmmm?" Alex asked.

"Did you manage to find any decent pictures of your great-aunt Katherine to show Sophie before you began pillaging the wine cellar?"

"Oh, yes! I brought one to show you." Alex pulled an old black-and-white photo from his back pants pocket, then reached across the table to hand it to Véronique.

She took it from him and examined it, shaking her head. "*Extraordinaire*, really just like you, Sophie."

Véronique passed me the photo. In it, two young women in their twenties were standing by the seashore. The brunette was apparently Virginie, as lovely in her youth as I'd been told. Next to her a lithe blonde was smiling, holding her pinned-up hair in place with her hand. The resemblance to Sophie was undeniable. The back of the photo read, *Cap Ferrat 1938*.

"Incredible," I said dutifully. My heart sank; it was as though Sophie had always been here, so much did she belong. She took the picture for a moment, staring at it a little wistfully as though the memory actually belonged to her before returning the photo to Alex. I watched them closely and saw again that something seemed to flicker between them, some secret exchange. It could easily have been my imagination—or so I told myself. Ever since they'd returned to the room, I had been hyperaware of the space between them, searching for an afterglow of what I imagined had taken place while I'd been sitting with Véronique. It took me considerable energy and another glass of wine to let it go.

"I think *Mamie* has a soft spot for you now. All the better," Alex said, gazing away as though no longer speaking to the three of us.

Eventually several more people, including Véronique's friend from the first party who had thrown herself at Alex, showed up at the house and helped us to finish off the bottle of wine along with a couple more. The friend flirted mercilessly, but in light of the day we'd had, she suddenly seemed harmless.

When it was at last time to leave, Alex walked Sophie and me back down the stairs and kissed us goodbye in the foyer. Véronique stayed behind.

"You must come over anytime you like," Alex said. "You have no idea how happy I am to have such interesting company around. This can be your second home in Nantes, *non*? Sophie, you could come and paint here, and, Brooke, you could write in your journals. *Ça serait formidable.*"

The invitation felt so genuine in the glow of Alex's presence. But once Sophie and I were out in the street, it was as if we'd gone through a portal and the house had disappeared the moment we'd left it. I didn't express this sentiment aloud to Sophie for fear that saying it would somehow make it true.

It was late by the time I got home and I fell into a slumber that gave me no sense of having actually rested, a sleep from which I would not remember any of my dreams but would leave me with the sense that I had sweat out fear and desire in the night like a fever. In the morning I felt empty and wrecked.

As WE pulled up from the depths of the winter into March and the days began to grow longer, much to my horror time seemed to speed up. The sun stayed up later into the evening and the air during my morning walks became less and less frigid, and I was reminded that summer was approaching, that my days in France were numbered.

My contempt for my fellow American students had only deepened as I'd grown closer to Alex and Véronique, and also as I'd grown closer to Sophie. It felt increasingly as if Sophie and I were from a different country than the other students. The longer we were all here, the more tightly drawn into each other they seemed to become.

I found myself becoming smug toward them, and the boys in particular were the subjects of my ire. They reminded me too much of the boys at home, the boys to whom I knew I had to return when this was over. I held them accountable for the sins of all those frat boys whose inattention had in part driven me to the disastrous relationship with Regan. Those boys who blindly worshipped Sophie because she fit their narrow view of beauty, not because of the person she was, the person that I saw, that I believed myself alone in seeing.

Sophie remained in preternaturally good spirits, and we were now spending much of our free time at Alex's mother's house. Though Alex's mother was still absent, his grandmother was always glad to see us if she was awake and feeling well—especially Sophie, whom she continued to regularly mistake for her sister. Sophie, despite her initial uneasiness with this, had adapted to playing the role and had eventually seemed to almost believe that she was somehow there on behalf of the erstwhile Katherine.

Just as Alex had said we would, we spent long afternoons in the garden room, drinking and chatting and supposedly working on our artistic pursuits. Sophie did indeed paint and I did bring my journals. I was occasionally productive but was open to any distraction that presented itself, such as when Véronique came in wanting help running lines for *Le Cid*, in which she was going to be performing the lead role with a small underground theater troupe.

Alex often wouldn't be there with us. He would welcome us at the door, help us to get settled, then disappear into his darkroom, though he would sporadically emerge with mysterious questions about women.

"Les filles," he would say to us, "tell me, does a woman want her hand held or to have the man's hand on the small of her back when she walks into a room? Does a woman prefer to make love in the evening after drinking or in the morning after dreaming? Does a woman like her hair stroked or pulled?"

We would answer enthusiastically, bicker amiably. We were willing participants in his personal laboratory.

"Hand held. It shows he thinks of her as an equal!"

"But you hold a child's hand; the small of her back makes her feel like a woman."

"At night—who wants sex before coffee?"

"In the morning—best way to start the day."

"Pulled."

"Pulled."

"Tiré. Absolument."

Sometimes I would find myself dreamily watching over Sophie as she painted. It wasn't her work that interested me—she kept the easel turned away and was secretive about her paintings—but Sophie herself while she was working. Facing her canvas, her focus was immutable. After working for a while she would often pull back from her canvas, surveying it with a range of emotions displayed on her face, from confusion to mild disgust to a manic, grinning wonderment. She never seemed aware that I was looking at her, and since no one else was there, I watched unabashedly, occasionally recording her reactions in my journal as though studying an opponent in a chess match. When she almost had something just right, she would stick her tongue out just a little. I knew because this expression seemed to always precede a big smile.

One day as I was watching her, Alex called to me from the doorway in a stage whisper: "Brooke."

I worried for a moment that he had been there and seen me staring at Sophie paint, but he was lingering in the doorway out of her sight line. He beckoned me over.

I got up quietly, apprehensively laying my journal down and walking toward him. Sophie was in a trancelike state and didn't seem aware of either of us.

"I want to show you something." He took my hand, loosely at first and then interlacing his fingers with mine as we walked. We walked down a set of stairs off the kitchen.

"Where are we going?"

He squeezed my hand in return and said nothing. My imagination reeled and I could feel my blood crashing through my veins as we wound down the increasingly narrow stairway.

For the amount of time I had spent with Alex—to say nothing of the amount of time I spent thinking about him—he remained utterly mysterious to me. I felt he would open one door only to reveal yet another door. Infinite doors stretched before me like an image in a fun-house mirror.

I followed him into the dark, humid room. I gasped, overpowered by the scent of chemicals.

"Sorry, darling." Alex turned and placed his hands on my shoulders. "I'm so used to the smell, I completely forget."

I shook my head and smiled to indicate that I was fine. That it had just taken me by surprise.

Several shallow bins of chemicals were laid out before us, and numerous photos were drying on clothespins.

"I was just developing these photos from the other night and I wanted to show you."

I hadn't even realized that Alex had been taking photos of us. How formidable his talent must be for him to have gone unnoticed by someone who practically chronicled his every move.

He pulled me by the hand to the corner of the room, where a series of four photographs of me and Sophie sitting on the bench in the garden room hung in a row. The images were like a stop-motion film of her telling me something and my incredulous face, her whispering something in my ear, the two of us laughing, and then the two of us a little more composed and exchanging a knowing look.

I let out an astonished giggle and clamped a hand over my mouth.

I looked at Alex; he appeared to be glowing under the intense red light of the darkroom and was watching me intently. What an odd thing it must be to see someone absorb a piece of your art of which he or she is also the subject.

I looked more closely at the photos; Alex had captured something. Would a stranger see it, I wondered, the bond between Sophie and me? That we were having the time of our lives? It seemed so plain in the photos, so evident. Even as I gazed at the images, I saw them as separate from myself and felt envious of the two girls in the photo. My doppelgänger looked happier than I believed I had ever been.

This feeling of seeing myself from an appealing distance was something entirely new and almost unsettling. I didn't normally like looking at pictures of myself. Photos always seemed to do nothing but highlight the flaws that I saw in the mirror and preserve them at a higher resolution. The ones that occasionally came out well seemed to be lovely only by some serendipity of accidental shadows and angles.

But these shots were different. I couldn't ever remember a photo of me where I had looked better. Was this the way the world saw me? Was this the way that Alex saw me? As long as the latter was true, I supposed I didn't care too much about the former.

"You are blushing. How charming."

"I wonder what she was telling me. I can't remember."

"I don't think it matters. It might have been nothing at all. But I love the way the two of you are so unguarded here. *Sans défense.*"

He moved closer to me to point to one of the middle photos, and I could smell his skin, a musk of sweat and a twinge of the chemicals from the photo. I'd never smell these things again without thinking of him.

"You are very special to each other, you and Sophie." He cocked his head to one side. "Almost like sisters."

"It feels that way." I longed to know how he felt about Sophie, about me. "It's been good to be here with her."

"And good to have you here. Here in Nantes, here in my family's home. My friends in Paris are quite intrigued when I tell them about you two. *Les deux belles filles américaines* who spend so much of their time with me."

I blushed and turned away. "Sophie is very beautiful."

"And you. You are too."

I shook my head. I wished I hadn't said anything.

"Regarde celle-là." Alex pulled another photo from a clothesline farther back. I studied the sepia print of me in the garden, alone on the bench clutching my teacup. "I snuck back when we left you to find the photos of Katherine the first time you were here."

My face in the photo appeared vaguely anguished. I'd been worried about where Alex and Sophie were, what they were doing. What relief it would have been to know that he was in the corridor with his lens focused on me, not thinking of Sophie at all. I wanted to go back and whisper in the ear of the girl with her teacup, tell her the truth. But then I thought of Alex observing me unnoticed and knew that to tell her would be to take this moment away.

"I don't know what they say about this girl in America," he said, standing behind me with his head on my shoulder, looking down at the picture, "but here she is beautiful. And you cannot argue with the French about these things; we are renowned all over the world for our aestheticism." After a moment's pause, he continued, his voice unnervingly serene, "Tell me how you feel when you see these photos."

I shrugged, wishing we could move on. He pulled away to gaze at me, smiling and folding his arms across his chest as if he could wait all day.

"I guess in some ways," I said cautiously, "I feel like it's not me."

He gave me a quizzical look.

"I mean, I know it *is* me, but it's just that seeing myself *captured* like this, I know I won't ever be quite that same person again. Someday in the future I'll take out this picture and I'll be completely different. I'll look different, have a different life. And I know I'm already heading towards that moment, my future self. When someone's taking your picture, it seems like they're capturing the present, but really they're turning it into the past, they're making it an illusion because you can't go back to when the photo was taken and know exactly how you felt. You just know it's gone: the moment, whatever you were feeling, whatever you had with the other people in the room with you, all gone."

When I finally had the courage to look back up at Alex, a strange expression had crossed his face. The air in the room seemed to have thinned and he seemed knocked off-balance.

"Sorry," I muttered, "that probably doesn't make any sense. You're a great photographer, I really like the photos, I'm sorry—"

"Stop!" he said. *Arrête!*

I bit down on my lip, feeling as if I might cry.

Reaching out abruptly, Alex grasped me by the shoulders. "No one understands. People, they think what I do is superficial, and it is! It is superficial when I am taking pictures of models and handbags. It's so manufactured! None of it's real." He was working himself up now, nearly yelling. He released my shoulders and began to gesture wildly in the small space of the darkroom.

"But you understand. You see how *sad* it all is."

I nodded. The moment felt surreal. My nerves were frayed.

"You should see, Brooke. You should see what these photo shoots are like: all the makeup, the lighting, the *artifice*. All to create a false moment! But here"—he came up behind me now so that we both faced the pictures that hung on the clothesline—"these moments are real, they *were* real. As you said, we can *capture* them, save them from the erosion of time. Virginie was beautiful once as well, remember?"

I let myself lean back into him and he nuzzled my cheek with his head and put his arms around my waist. My skin felt hot and my pulse erratic. I wanted to stay until something happened. Stay until I felt his lips on my neck. Stay until I felt his hands underneath my clothing. Stay. Just stay.

But reaching up to the clothesline, he took down the photo of me with my teacup. "You won't always be her," he said softly, "but I want you to remember her. Even when you've lost what she had and found something to replace it. Don't let her go. Not completely."

I was light-headed.

"Back to the garden? Back to watching our Sophie paint?"

He took my hand, and I nodded weakly. If Sophie was *ours*, was he as well? Was there simply no separating any of us?

My stomach sank in despair as I realized that if nothing had happened with me alone with Alex in his darkroom, it never would. I was glad that I was in front of him on the stairs so that he couldn't see my face.

As we reached the landing at the top of the stairs, just as we were about to step out of the gloom, Alex stopped me. "Ah, wait one moment, you have some ink." Crouching down, he licked his thumb and rubbed a spot on the bare skin of my thigh just below the hem of my skirt. I froze.

"There," he said once the spot had been erased. He looked back up at me and laughed. I knew I was blushing.

"Don't laugh," I said helplessly. But he wasn't listening. He pulled me into him and kissed me. My head spun. He wove one of his hands into my hair and tugged it. I let out an involuntary little gasp.

"You like that," he whispered in my ear, letting his tongue follow his words. "I know because you told me." The hand that wasn't wrapped in my hair, he plunged between my thighs. "You've told me everything I need to know."

I gasped for breath and he kissed me again.

Then, just as suddenly, he stopped. Leaning against the wall with one hand over my shoulder, he smacked the wall with the other with a little burst of laughter, then sharply drew in his breath as if steeling himself. He looked at me as if he might kiss me again but instead walked away, leaving me there to catch my breath.

⤜⤛

Later that evening, Alex's mother finally returned from the countryside. Sophie had already put away her canvas and paints in the studio where Alex let her keep them, and I had abandoned even the pretense of writing. Alex had joined us in the garden and I was furiously trying to catch his eye when he mentioned wine; I offered to fetch it myself if he would tell me where to look. He relaxed back into his chair. The wine cellar was right next to his darkroom, he explained. I could pick anything I liked.

"You just relax," I said, cheerful now, unconcerned about leaving him alone with Sophie.

I happily trotted down the stairs. It felt so wonderful, so luxurious, to be allowed free rein of the house like this. It seemed to me that Sophie, knowing me as she did, must have an inkling that something had happened with Alex. I imagined that when I finally told her, she would roll her eyes and tease me for telling her what she already knew. But not just yet; I wanted it to be my secret for a while.

The wine cellar was dark and had a hard, dry, musty smell that assaulted my nose. It was small and cramped but well stocked, and as I made my way through the racks, I laughed at my previous vision of Alex and Sophie caught in an embrace here. That hadn't happened, I told myself. Wouldn't happen now. He had declared himself. As I picked up bottles one by one, I realized that I hadn't the slightest idea what to choose. I was a novice in the face of what I could only assume was a fairly impressive collection. Some bottles looked ancient and I feared I would defile them even by removing them from their racks. Toward the end of the room was a case of Côtes du Rhône that looked newer and had only a few bottles missing from it. As it seemed like the safest option, I grabbed a bottle and headed upstairs.

As I made my way through the kitchen, I heard a small commotion in the foyer and slowed my steps, suddenly rigid with fear. Was this only Magdalena back from the market? Even if it was her, I didn't relish the idea of encountering her alone after having raided the de Persauds' wine cellar. It was not Madame de Persaud, I knew she was upstairs in her room napping because Sophie had been to check on her when she'd put her paintings away in the studio.

I froze in the wide-open foyer when I saw Magdalena with several pieces of monogrammed luggage and behind her an elegant middle-aged woman who was removing her hat. They both stopped in their tracks when they saw me, standing in my denim skirt and sweater, my hair bunched on the top of my head, holding what was—for all I knew—an expensive bottle of wine pillaged from their cellar.

"Hello," the woman said. This, of course, was Alex's mother, the other Madame de Persaud.

In my rush to explain myself I bungled my French so badly that I might as well have been speaking Greek.

"Excuse me?" she said. Upon closer inspection, she appeared a little frailer than she had at first glance, like someone who had smoked since birth and didn't eat enough protein.

More slowly this time, I tried again to explain that I was a friend of Alex's, that he was in the garden and had asked me to bring up a bottle of wine. I heard myself botch several tenses, but at least these rudimentary facts seemed to register with her. She looked to Magdalena for confirmation, and she grunted in response.

"I was not planning on having company for dinner this evening," Madame said.

I told her we didn't need to stay, that we could leave soon. I apologized again and again—for what I didn't know—but it felt necessary.

"No, no. I want to know Alex's friends. You must stay." It was an order, not an invitation. She smiled now and I could see traces of Alex in her face; the eyes in particular were the same, although his dark complexion must have come from his father, as her skin was pale and her face was pulled a little tight.

I smiled back and stumbled out my thanks: *"Oui, d'accord. Er, avec plaisir."*

What should I do now? I wanted to tell Alex and Sophie that she was here—she seemed like a person you might like to be forewarned about—but it felt rude to scurry out of the room while she was still standing in the foyer.

She said something to Magdalena too quiet and too low for me to hear, and they headed toward the kitchen. As she passed by me, I saw Madame de Persaud's eyes swoop over me and take in what I was wearing with a hint of disdain. Stopping when she was right next to me, she glanced at the label of the bottle of wine that I was still clutching like contraband.

"Ah, the Domaine Saint-Martin that *le maire* sent us this Christmas." She looked me square in the eyes with a gaze both warm and terrifying. "What excellent taste you have."

I traced the word *le maire* in my head; shit, I thought, the mayor? I wondered if she might take it from my hands as if I were a child who had mistakenly gotten hold of something valuable, but she continued past me and then I was alone in the foyer. I decided the only thing to do was to take the bottle to Alex and let him deal with it. Heading toward the stairs, I wondered how I had the misfortune of selecting what had looked to me like the most innocuous bottle in the wine cellar and having it turn out to be a gift from a local dignitary.

"*Ah, non,*" Alex said, sounding more disappointed than angry when I told him about the return of his mother. "Was she horrible to you, Brooke?"

"Not at all," I said, unsure whether that was the truth but feeling that it was the safest answer, that if she had been a little bit horrible, it would be more polite to pretend I hadn't noticed.

"She wants us to stay for dinner," I added quietly. Sophie sat silently, her eyes flicking back and forth between Alex and me. I was suddenly struck by the notion that I was interrupting something.

"Of course she does." Alex's tone was more exasperated than at the initial news of her presence. "She wants to figure out what the two of you are doing here." He laughed caustically. "Imagine. My mother comes home to find an American girl standing in the foyer with a bottle of her precious Domaine Saint-Martin!"

"I . . . I'm sorry. I didn't realize that this was expensive, I just saw that there was a whole case of it and thought it would be okay."

"Oh, *chérie*, no, it's absolutely fine. I told you to take what you wanted." He snatched the bottle from my hands and carried it to the hutch that held the clean glasses, where he expertly plunged the corkscrew in and popped the cork out in one smooth motion. "In fact it's marvelous that this is what you chose."

I took a seat next to Sophie, and Alex handed us both a glass of the deep red *vin extraordinaire*. "Marvelous," he repeated again under his breath as he poured himself a glass. "I will go talk to her." He touched Sophie's shoulder as he passed. "You *should* stay, though, unless you've got someplace else to be."

I had told my host family I would be back that night for dinner. "No, I would love to stay."

When he had disappeared, I turned to Sophie, resisting the urge to ask her what they'd been talking about while I'd been gone.

"This wine is wonderful," Sophie said with a devious little grin. "You have good taste."

I shook my head. "I can't believe that just happened. And look at me."

"What about you? You look fine." Of course, Sophie was wearing one of the fetching little floral dresses she seemed to have a dozen of with a light cream cashmere sweater. The outfit managed to be both demure and show off her long, golden legs at the same time.

"Not for meeting Alex's mother."

"Well, me neither in that case." I looked at her incredulously but she didn't react. "Anyway, how were we supposed to know she was coming by? I was beginning to think she didn't exist!"

"I can assure you that she does and that she is everything you would imagine."

"I wonder what his father was like," Sophie said. "I get the sense he was the nicer one."

"Why the past tense? Where is his father?"

"He passed away. I thought you were here the other day when Alex was talking about it but I guess you weren't. It sounds like they were close."

"Interesting," I said, trying to find a word that might mask my bitterness that she'd known this essential Alex information before I had. "What happened to him?"

"I don't know. Alex didn't really say and I didn't want to press him about it."

Of course not!

"A mystery," she said to my silence, then leaned in toward me, smiling mischievously. "These people are full of them."

I nodded and drank more wine.

I had expected Alex and his mother to be a little cold with each other from the way he spoke about her while she wasn't around. But to my surprise, when mother and son were face-to-face, she seemed quite loving with him, offering gratitude that he'd looked after her mother-in-law. And Alex was solicitous and made inquiries about his mother's time in the Loire Valley, which he referred to as *la campagne,* with no mention made of "an ugly old château." So Alex was capable of a certain duplicity—but weren't we all with our families? Who has not had the experience of simultaneously complaining about a family member but still loving the person deeply? I assumed that whatever differences existed between French and American families, one rule held true for both: that we may say whatever nasty things we like about our own family but become enraged when anyone on the outside does so. I decided to try to see the best in Alex's mother.

This didn't prove to be difficult, as she was charming and

seemed pleasantly amused to have Sophie and me there. We ate dinner on an enclosed outdoor patio where we could appreciate the cool evening breezes. I was sure she could tell that I was nervous to be there, and I hoped that this wasn't communicating any bad intentions on my part. I wanted to amend her first impression of me as the grubby American girl helping herself to her treasured wine collection. Every so often she smiled at me in a way that was more incisive than reassuring, as if I were some kind of rare species that she was trying to identify.

Sophie smoothly recounted a story of a winery trip through the Loire Valley that her parents had taken when she was in high school, of how the gems they'd brought back were some of the first wines she'd ever tasted. I could tell that Alex's mother was impressed with her. Sophie seemed rather relaxed in the company of the intimidating Frenchwoman, and as usual Sophie had perfect control of the language and was fluidly explaining how she was finding life at the university. I was at a disadvantage for how unsettled I was feeling after the kiss; the scene kept flashing through my mind, obliterating my ability to focus on anything else. I stole looks at Alex throughout dinner, trying to gauge whether he was similarly preoccupied, but he never seemed to be looking in my direction.

"Will you be staying the summer?" Madame de Persaud asked.

"No," I replied, "we're only here until the end of May."

"Only a couple more months, *quel dommage.*" I thought I heard in her voice an undercurrent of relief that we would not be permanent fixtures in her courtyard, in her son's life.

"We may come back," Sophie said. "That is, Brooke and I love France. We might look for work here after we're finished with school."

Madame de Persaud seemed surprised by this, as though Sophie had just announced that we would be moving into her house. "Well, that's marvelous. So what sort of work would you like to pursue? Perhaps work as teachers or with an American company? So wonderful all that you girls can do these days. Not like when I was young. Then it was always about *le mariage.*"

"Actually, Mother, they're artists. Sophie is a painter and Brooke is a writer," Alex said, smiling.

"Oh, girls, you mustn't listen to Alex too much." Madame de Persaud turned away from her son as though he had been responsible for putting in our heads the notion of who and what we were. "He's very bright, but he's not terribly sensible about work. That is, on the rare occasion that he encounters it. *La vie bohème*, it's the French disease, you must be careful not to catch it."

She took a sip of her wine and a fraught silence engulfed the table. I watched for Alex's reaction, for an explosion or harsh words, braced for the moment when he would do something dramatic like crash his plate to the ground and storm away from the table. But to my surprise, he was simply smirking. I looked at his mother, who still had her air of relaxed contemplation, and then back at Alex and his slightly menacing expression.

"You must listen to my mother, girls," Alex said finally. "She knows so very much about hard work."

"But she did work hard," I said, unable to stop the words

before they came out of my mouth. "I mean, it's hard work raising a family."

The three of them looked at me as though stunned. Madame's face wore a frozen, slightly horrified smile. I sensed I had said something deeply inappropriate.

Alex at last began to snicker. "It is hard work indeed!" I looked helplessly at Sophie but she was staring at her plate as Alex spoke. She was embarrassed for me. "Just ask our nanny, Marie-Louise."

Now Madame de Persaud laughed and turned to us. "You always love your children when you are a mother, girls. It's a blessing and a curse." But her hands shook a little as she put her fork down on her plate. Unsurprisingly she had hardly touched her food.

Sophie and I smiled uneasily. The conversation went on calmly. Madame de Persaud asked us questions about the United States. I felt the edge of my deepening sadness that though it felt as if my experience in France was just beginning, in reality it was speeding toward a conclusion, and that—despite what Sophie and I said to each other in our giddy moments of invincibility—I would forget my French, my bond with Sophie would slowly loosen and eventually evaporate, and I would never see or hear from Alex ever again. Almost unconsciously I slipped my hand into the pocket of my sweater and ran my finger over the edge of the photograph. The memoires wouldn't be enough. I couldn't bear the thought of Alex and Sophie going on without me. There had to be another way.

THE PREMIERE of Véronique's play was on a Friday night. The theater was little more than a basement room with dingy rows of seats and a low ceiling. Sophie and I brought Adam along. We hadn't seen much of him outside of school for the past few months; he had a French boyfriend whom we'd never met. He wasn't out, according to Adam, but given how conservative and Catholic Nantes was, that wasn't too surprising.

"So, will Alex be here?" Adam asked as we hurried along the side street to the theater.

Despite the fact that it was now late March, there was still the occasional very brisk day, and I pulled my coat more tightly around myself. "Yes, he should be," I said. I still hadn't told anyone about the kiss. The longer I went without saying anything, the harder it became to speak up, and I began to wonder if it had actually happened.

"Can't wait to meet this mystery man," Adam said as we joined the back of the small queue outside the door to the theater.

"You're one to talk about mystery men, Adam," Sophie said, punching him lightly on the arm.

"True," he said with a grin, "but not my fault."

Following each other down the narrow staircase, we sat

down in the third row. I didn't have to look to know that Alex wasn't in the room.

"We'll save him a seat," I said, pulling off my coat and draping it over the chair closest to the aisle. We'd brought flowers for Véronique, and the cellophane around them crinkled loudly in my lap.

Just as the lights were dimming, Alex materialized beside me as if out of thin air. He murmured his hellos and then turned his attention to the stage, where Véronique had appeared dressed in a white nightgown, sitting on the edge of a bed combing her long hair and looking lovely as Chimène. It was oddly thrilling to see her onstage, even in such a small theater.

She gave a stirring performance despite having to play opposite a meek and unconvincing Rodrigue. Was I surprised that she was a good actress? I wasn't sure. Something about her was malleable but at the same time opaque; you could know her in one sense but not in another.

After the show we went to meet her backstage. Alex looked calmer than when he'd arrived, and he greeted Adam with a hearty handshake that someone must have told him to use with American men. As we wound around the stage to the tiny area behind the curtain, Alex fell behind with Sophie, slinking an arm around her shoulders, asking her what she'd thought of the show.

"Oh, baby"—Adam leaned in to whisper in my ear—"you better watch out for that one."

I looked at the two of them together. She looked a little sullen, and then Alex whispered something to her that made her laugh.

I turned back to Adam.

"Alex, he seems like *trouble*." Adam winked at me and I smiled.

Véronique saw us and ran over. "You came!" Her stage makeup was still on, making her look hyperreal, like a caricature of herself.

"Of course we came!" I handed her the flowers. "Véronique, this is our friend Adam from the institute."

Véronique squealed with delight and kissed him on both cheeks. "Of course, I've heard all about you. You're the only one of the Americans that the girls still like. We've turned them, you know!"

"I know it," Adam said. "I've been dying to meet you two."

Still on a high from the performance, she threw her arms around Sophie and Alex as they joined us. "Let me get this stuff off my face and put my clothes back on and we'll get a drink."

⁕

"To Véronique!" Alex said. We clinked glasses.

"To Chimène!" I said.

We drank a couple of rounds together at the bar next door to the theater. I was filled with the warmth of having brought two separate groups of people together and having them like each other. About an hour after we'd arrived, Adam's mobile phone started buzzing incessantly.

"Goodness me, I forgot the time." He handed me some euros for the bill and began his goodbyes. "Off to meet my own Rodrigue." He gave Véronique a wink. After he left, she and Alex said how much they'd liked him, and Sophie and I beamed as though he were ours.

A bit later when the bar got crowded and our waitress seemed to have abandoned us, Sophie and Alex went up to the bar to get us another bottle of wine, looking conspiratorial again.

"What's with those two tonight?" I said out loud, barely meaning to.

"What do you mean?" Véronique lit a cigarette for herself and then handed me one. I was becoming less concerned about my new smoking habit by the day.

"I don't know," I said, forcing a bright, casual tone. "They're acting like two kids who have a secret."

"Maybe they do." Véronique smiled slyly.

I gulped and took a long drag on the cigarette to hide my expression; they were such helpful little props that way.

"I like your friend Sophie," Véronique said, sounding as though she meant the opposite, "but I was hoping you and Alex would get together. What a shame you're not interested." She took a drag from her cigarette; her nails, despite the improbability of their being painted that color in the seventeenth century, were royal blue. She looked at me and held my gaze until I cracked.

I sighed. "How did you know?"

She gave a little chirp of laughter. "Because you are a woman and Alex is Alex."

I nodded. I hated to be such a cliché. It was a hopeless and tiresome choice, and I felt both unrealistic and unoriginal. Of course she should laugh.

"He talks about you. Often."

I felt a stirring in the pit of my stomach. "He does?"

Véronique rolled her eyes. *"Tout le temps. 'Les Américaines'!"*

"So he talks about *us*," I said, hoping I didn't sound as disappointed as I felt.

"I don't think Sophie is right for him," she said, both ignoring and addressing my comment in a way that seemed particularly French. "She reminds me too much of Marie-Catherine."

"In what way?"

"Beautiful and crazy." *Belle et folle.*

"Sophie? Beautiful, yes, but not crazy." As much as I warmed to the idea that Véronique thought that I was the one who belonged with Alex instead of Sophie, I had no desire to rake her over the coals and felt suddenly defensive of her.

"Maybe you're right, you know her better than I do. Just some of the things that Alex has told me. But anyway, Alex is so dramatic."

What had Sophie told him? Something noteworthy enough for Alex to, in turn, pass it on to Véronique, obviously. This, along with Sophie's having known about his father's death, were nascent signs of an intimacy that I felt left out of.

"And you know Alex much better than I do," I said.

"Which is why I am shocked that he has not made a move yet. It is very unlike him."

I could feel my face turning red.

"Ahhh. I see. When?"

"Two weeks ago. We were coming up from his darkroom. We had been having a kind of intense discussion."

"Vraiment? About what?"

"About photography. Well, sort of. I think it was also about something else. What is this new project he's working on in Nantes, do you know?"

"Haven't a clue. He's very secretive about his work." She smiled, but I had the tiniest flash that I had caught her off guard somehow. "He must trust you if he talked to you about it at all. And then what happened?"

"We were heading back to the garden, and then just as we reached the top of the stairs, he pushed me against the wall and kissed me. I was shocked. He took my breath away."

"*Très sexy!*"

"Then he just walked away and we haven't spoken about it since. I'm so confused."

"Ah, well, not to give my cousin away, but he's a true seducer, you know? He would leave you wanting more. Not like an American boy, who acts all at once. You must enjoy it."

Did that mean that there would be more?

She looked pleased as she took another sip of her drink. "And I heard you met my aunt? Madame de Persaud the younger."

"Yes," I said, quickly checking that Alex and Sophie were still at the bar, "we had a very strange dinner with her."

Véronique nodded. "There is no other kind of dinner with Alex and his mother, trust me."

"I'm fairly sure she thought I was robbing the wine cellar when I first ran into her."

"Oh, no!" Véronique said with delight. "That is so perfect. Alex will love you for it."

I smiled and looked down at my lap, unable to keep from thinking, If only.

"The truth about Alex and his mother?" she asked.

"Please!"

"Well, no one knows the truth, but Alex will joke—or perhaps he's not joking, one never knows—that his mother poisoned his father."

I gasped.

"I don't know if he says it because he really thinks it might have happened or because he hates her. He has other reasons to hate her, so again, who knows?"

Was Véronique being serious? This family was unlike any other I'd ever met. I felt a surge of delight that I had access to the dark, secret suspicion before Sophie did. I knew how childish this was but I couldn't help it.

"She doesn't seem very respectful about his chosen career path," I said.

"Ah, no, to say the least. She wanted him to work for the government. She is always trying to convince him to give up on the photography. He thinks that she's trying to make sure that Virginie doesn't leave him any money. He's probably right on that count. His mother would say she's doing it out of love, to keep him from becoming idle, and no one would question her."

"That's not right," I said, feeling defensive on his behalf, then adding quietly, "he's so talented."

Véronique looked up from her glass and studied me for a long moment. "But, yes, he is, isn't he?"

Before the conversation could go any further, Sophie and Alex reappeared.

"We have the best idea," Sophie said, looking conspiratorially at Alex.

"Can you believe, Véronique, that *les filles* have not yet been to Paris? It's a complete tragedy! Since my mother is back in town and crowding the house, I thought we should all go this weekend. What do you think? Say yes."

"D'accord. Oui!" Véronique said, mimicking Alex's enthusiasm.

I chafed at the idea that Alex and Sophie had planned this on their own and I was only now being included, not to mention the money, which I did not have. Later, as Sophie and I were walking home, I attempted to raise the concern of cost, but Sophie swatted it away.

"It'll only cost us the train ticket since we're staying at Alex's apartment, and I'll buy yours if you're out of cash."

"I can't let you do that." For Sophie, money was nothing, an unimportant detail. In her life it had always just been present, like background noise. In my house, we'd been hypervigilant of every dollar; it wasn't something I could just turn off. The awareness of it coated me in a thin layer of shame.

"Why not? Who cares?"

"I do."

"You're good for it; I'm not letting you say no to this. Why are you being this way all of a sudden?" Sophie's eyes were sparkling, almost manic.

"I'm not. I've just spent a lot of money while I've been here and it's making me anxious."

I looked at Sophie, who was regarding me incredulously, swinging her beautiful gray bag as though she didn't have a care in the world. My protestations tasted like tin coming off my tongue. Sophie had slipped right into their privileged world; I was the odd woman out, the spoilsport.

"Okay, we'll go."

She threw her arms around me.

I wanted to ask her what she'd been talking to Alex about, but I sensed with a sharp pang that it wasn't my business. For as much as we'd been having a shared experience here, we'd also been having separate experiences—and being experienced separately by the people we'd met.

You understand. No one understands, but you understand.

I had secrets of my own.

SOPHIE AND I arrived late by train into Paris; Véronique had blown off her Friday classes and gone down the night before. I'd been tempted to suggest that we do the same, but I was starting to panic about my abysmal grades. My experimental laissez-faire attitude about schoolwork wasn't seeming like such a good idea anymore as March rolled along. I did still care, more so when I reminded myself that I did, in fact, have to go back to school in California at some point. Real school where things like grades would once again matter to me.

The Gare Montparnasse train station was the only part of Paris that I'd seen before, and I was struck immediately with an intense sense of déjà vu. I could almost see the imprint of a past Brooke through the gaps in the crowds as they crisscrossed in front of me, her worried eyes darting across the platform, unable to appreciate that she was in Paris because she was so nervous about catching the train to Nantes. She didn't know Alex or Véronique yet and couldn't have dreamed how much things would have changed by the next time she'd be here.

It seemed to me that from the moment we set foot there, Paris conformed to my expectations in an almost uncanny way. It was as if the city were bending toward me to give me what I had imagined. The whole feel of the place—the wicker chairs on the pavement, the red awnings, the cobblestones—you couldn't take a step without knowing you were in Paris. The city seemed lit up from within.

Compared to Nantes, the Paris metro was fairly easy to figure out, and we made it to Alex's apartment in the sixth arrondissement without any trouble. Whatever I had been expecting from the de Persauds' apartment on the bank of the Seine, the reality was even more exquisite. The apartment was in a building that took up the entire corner of the city block, with an elegant café at its triangular point. I gazed up at the narrow windows, the tiny wrought-iron balconies, the detailed stonework; it was dizzying. The doorman smiled and let us up. The smile threw us. We laughed in the elevator—had he thought we were French? Had he thought we belonged here?

Véronique answered the door. "Hi, girls. Come in." She was wearing a long black silk robe, knotted tightly around her waist, and her slick black hair was coiled around the top of her head in an intricate knot. It seemed as though we'd caught her off guard, even though she'd known when we were scheduled to arrive. She seemed weary and a little preoccupied. Alex was out. "I think he's working" was all she would say. Then, just as quickly, she switched on her charm again and was anxious to hear what we wanted to do the next day. She went into the kitchen, a large room with an impressive display of copper pots suspended around a central island.

The apartment was chic, much more modern than the house in Nantes, and in cooler colors, blues and grays. We sat down on a plush white couch.

"You mustn't be afraid to be tourists while you're here. We

all secretly love to show off the city, and it gives us an excuse when we have visitors. So the Louvre, the tour Eiffel, Montmartre, whatever you want!" Véronique said.

Sophie wanted to go to the Louvre to see *Winged Victory* and also to see the *Mona Lisa* "so that I can be one of those smug people who tells you it's not worth seeing," she said. I wanted to see Sacré-Cœur. But that was all, we said, we wanted to enjoy the day.

"*Parfait*," Véronique said, "and Alex is having a party here tomorrow so you will be able to meet lots of *vrais Parisiens*."

Sophie yawned and I involuntarily mimicked her.

Véronique laughed. "You are exhausted, no?"

"Yes," Sophie said, "this week was long."

"We don't want to go to bed before Alex gets home, though," I added quickly. I had prepared myself to see Alex that night; in my imagination this was when we would continue what we'd begun.

But Véronique shook her head. "You won't want to wait up for him, trust me. He could be gone all night. You've had a long day. Just come see one thing before I put you to bed."

We followed her and she gingerly unlatched and pulled back the French doors, revealing a balcony I hadn't seen until then. As a gust of brisk early-April air blew in, Véronique held her robe closed as the wind sent the silk fluttering around her. We followed her onto the balcony.

"If you lean out a little and look to the left, you can see it."

We did as she said, and we both let out a little gasp as the tower came into view, glittering and unbelievably close. The Eiffel Tower was something I'd expected to be disappointed by. A certain kind of person, even some students, even some

French, loved to let you know it was overrated. But I couldn't be disappointed. What you don't understand until you've seen it is how well the rest of the city gathers around it, stooping at its feet. No buildings for miles and miles were allowed to be taller than six floors. The only one that ever broke this rule was the Montparnasse Tower, which people liked to joke was the box the Eiffel Tower came in.

"That always impresses visitors," Véronique said with a little laugh. It was strange at times like this to think that she was the same age we were.

It almost hurt to imagine living here, that's how much I wanted it. Knowing the people who owned this place, being allowed to sleep here as an invited guest, gave me the illusion that it might be possible. Even though some deep, gnawing place inside me still told me it wasn't. Paris didn't feel like a place you could just *go* to the way you could move to any American city. Its money and glamour were ancient and inherited, as inaccessible as the stars.

Véronique pointed us in the direction of the guest room, wishing us a good night and sweet dreams, her voice cheerful. As we walked away, I glanced back at her. She was standing next to the French doors, gazing out into the night, the same unsettled look on her face as when we'd arrived.

Sophie and I slept together in the guest room. When she came to bed, she had on what looked like a new nightgown, a light lavender color and silky, meant for someone to see.

"Where did that come from?"

"Oh, I've had this." She pulled back the covers and wriggled in next to me, then whispered, as though afraid Véronique would hear her, "Feel." She took my fingers and traced them over the silk that clung to her hips. It was buttery soft. "Can you believe this place?"

"It's amazing. I don't want to say it's like a fairy tale, because you know I'd have to kill myself if I said something like that, but, well . . ."

"It's like a fairy tale?"

We both laughed.

"It's about as far-fetched," I said.

Sophie pulled herself up on her elbow and looked down at me, her hair falling over her shoulder, her face suddenly serious. "Don't say that."

"What?" I asked, confused.

"That it's far-fetched. We could get here, we could come back."

I laughed a little sadly. "I know we can. Aren't you a little excited to get back to the States? I'm not, but I would think you would be."

She looked down at me annoyed. "Why would you say that?"

"Easy, tiger, it's not a criticism. It's just that, you know, you have volleyball and everything to go back to."

"So that's all you think I am, huh? Like everything is so perfect."

I sat up now to be able to look her in the face. "No, Sophie, that isn't what I mean, but you have to admit that from the outside your life doesn't look so bad."

She swung her legs off the bed and was suddenly on her feet as though intending to leave. "Wow, you too, huh? Everyone thinks I'm not allowed to have any problems. Do you have any idea how alone that makes me feel? That's exactly why I want to stay—I can be new in France. People here understand me."

That we were having this argument in bed made it feel as though we were a couple. I would have laughed if it wouldn't have incensed her more. Something clicked just then. "Alex?"

"What?"

"Alex. He understands you. That's what you mean by 'people here.'"

She looked flustered. "No, I didn't mean Alex. Not just Alex anyway. Actually I was talking more about Adam and you, or at least I thought you."

"Of course me. I don't judge you. Talk about unfair. I had an *affair* with a *professor*, that's what I'm going back to!" My voice was raised now and I was up on my knees on the bed. "I have no real friends and I come from a piece-of-shit town that I'm terrified will suck me back in the moment I'm back on American soil. Fucking sue me for being a little envious of your circumstances, Sophie."

"Look," she said, backing off a little now, "I recognize that from the outside, it looks like I have a lot to go back to. But I don't want any of it anymore."

"Then what do you want?" Which was more preposterous, that she wanted me to sympathize with her, or that I did?

"This." She came back to the bed, taking my hands in hers. "We should stay. We could have this." She gestured to the room around us, meaning not only the room but the apartment or one like it, Véronique and Alex, Paris, France, the world.

"I just don't want to get my hopes up. We still need to finish college, you know."

"We have choices," Sophie said, lying back with a deep sigh, "that's all I'm saying. You need to recognize that. Promise me you'll think about it."

"Okay, I will," I said, not even knowing what exactly I was agreeing to think about.

She leaned up and kissed me on the cheek. "Let's get some sleep." She turned off the lamp. I could feel her fall asleep next to me, leaving me alone in the darkness with my thoughts.

⤙⤚

The next morning I woke up with the uneasiness of being in an unfamiliar bed. I looked around for Sophie but she wasn't next to me. What time was it? I put on my cotton robe and walked cautiously out the door. I could hear voices and laughter coming from the kitchen. Sophie was on a stool by the center island, still in her nightgown, covered with only a sheer robe, sitting kitty-corner to Alex, who was in jeans and a black T-shirt. A day or two's worth of scruff covered his chin.

"There you are," Véronique said, appearing before me, nearly running into me as she zipped from one end of the kitchen to the other. It's always surprising to see people in the morning for the first time. "Did you sleep well?"

I nodded, pulling up a stool next to Sophie.

Véronique had dark circles under her eyes despite her chipper demeanor. "Have some coffee." She poured me a cup from a nearby French press.

"Mmmmmm," I said, looking at her gratefully.

"So good, right?" Sophie said. "And Alex got croissants!"

"Hello, *chérie*," he said, coming around to kiss my cheek.

Véronique whipped out a plate and he pulled a croissant from the white paper bag.

"*Merci.*"

The croissant was so flaky and perfect that it came apart in my hands and my stomach growled. I snuck a look at Alex as he poured himself another cup of coffee. He looked disheveled. Had he not come home last night? I didn't want to ask.

The day was bright and warm and cheerful, and I soon forgot my uneasiness, forgot my tense conversation with Sophie, forgot that Alex had been gone all night, forgot that I ever had to go back home. We took it easy on the sightseeing, blowing off the Louvre at the sight of the long line and opting instead for a ride on the carousel and sandwiches on the steps of Sacré-Cœur. I found myself looking up into windows as we walked around Montmartre, past brightly colored shutters, in through gauzy curtains to the lives within, allowing myself for the briefest moment to imagine them as my own.

"I will show you my favorite place to observe the Eiffel Tower," Alex said. "It is just far enough away to see the whole thing but close enough to really appreciate the lights."

We exited the Trocadéro metro station just as the sun was getting low in the sky. Sophie and I stood there, unabashedly awed by the tower looming in front of us. Véronique and Alex stayed back, and Alex took some pictures. I had become so accustomed to his lens that I barely noticed anymore when he pulled his camera out.

"Wow, there's a reason this thing is world famous," I said. The grass stretching between the tower and us was manicured and brilliant green; people lay right on it or had arranged themselves on picnic blankets.

"No kidding." Sophie reached out and took my hand, "I'm glad we're here together." Click. Click.

Alex gave us a little tour on the way home of his favorite wine store, his favorite *fromagerie*, his favorite *boulangerie*, and we picked up supplies for the party that evening.

Sometime after nine o'clock Alex's friends began to arrive. I tried not to be intimidated but found it challenging. The girls were, without exception, beautiful and gamine as though they were off-duty ballerinas and models, which, it turned out, some of them actually were. They were standoffish for the most part, and though I caught them occasionally peering at me with what appeared to be great interest, they didn't seem especially keen on talking to me. I escaped several times to the kitchen to refill my wineglass, which resulted in my drinking much faster than I meant to.

Later I went out on the balcony for fresh air. Just as I was feeling a bit of peace, Alex stepped out to join me. At last I was alone with him. He had come to find me.

"Are you enjoying yourself?"

"Of course! Your friends seem nice," I said, lying through my teeth and feeling a little woozy.

Alex laughed. "No, they don't, because they're not. And most of them aren't really my friends." He didn't even bother to lower his voice much, which I found both audacious and admirable.

"Then why are they here?"

"I wanted you to see what my life is like, and sadly it is full of these people."

"And who are they? *These* people." My head was spinning from the wine; I wished I hadn't drunk so much. Before, all

I'd wanted was for my senses to be dulled, but now I wanted them sharp again.

"Models, some other photographers, some musicians, those two old guys talking to Sophie own a magazine and a fashion label." I followed his gaze to two men in the corner, both well built with graying hair. It felt strange to be at a party where real adults were in the mix, adults who were closer to my parents' age than mine. Sophie was flirting with them, her head tilted back in laughter, her hand coming to rest on one of the men's arms. They were enraptured. It was like a sport for her.

"Why are they in your life if you don't like them?"

"Because they are necessary. You will understand some-day." He reached out and traced a finger across my cheek. "And because in truth I like to be with people, even people I don't like. You see? You can learn so much by watching them."

"That I think I understand, and if you don't care, they can't hurt you."

Alex turned his head slowly—or perhaps it was only my vision, my responses, that were slow—and gave me a wide, languid smile. He would kiss me again, I felt certain.

"Can you see how afraid they are?" He leaned in. "Look closely. They're afraid because they know they're beautiful now but they're losing it even as we speak. It's just seeping out of them, evaporating and floating up into the night."

"I think you give them too much credit." I fixed my slightly unsteady gaze on a blond girl with a green silk scarf wrapped several times around her neck. She was also stand-ing with the two older men, twisting a glass of champagne between her fingers and staring off into space. "I don't think they know anything."

"They couldn't articulate it, but they know. Trust me, I work with these people. Behind the self-assured exterior there's nothing but panic. What I really do is bottle time, intercept beauty as it's leaving the world."

Alex suddenly leaned over and kissed me on the mouth. I started but then let myself ease into it. Just as quickly, he pulled away.

"There you are!" Véronique said, appearing suddenly in front of me. "Come, come back to the party!"

I giggled and followed her, sneaking a look over my shoulder at Alex as I went. He was smiling at me, feet planted, his eyes full of something I couldn't quite read.

Many of the guests were headed to another party after our get-together. To my relief, Alex declined to join them, and we stayed back drinking wine among the picked-over cheese plates and party debris.

"Who was the one with the green eyes, Alex?" Véronique said, draping her leg lazily over the arm of the chair she was sitting in. "Frederique maybe?"

"Ah, no," Alex said, settling into the corner of the couch, "Franck. *Mais fais attention.* He's married to that girl he was with."

I sat on the floor with my back against the couch; it seemed the closer to the ground I could be at the moment, the better.

Véronique shrugged. "Well, he was not acting married."

Alex laughed.

"So it's not really my problem, is it?" she said cheekily, leaning forward to refill her wineglass.

"Oh, no," I said without thinking, "trust me, Véronique, you don't want to go there."

"*Vraiment?*" she said. "Is there a story here, Brooke?"

I looked up at their expectant faces, then glanced back at Sophie, who sat opposite me on the couch. She raised her eyebrows and smiled as if to say, *May as well*. My cheeks burned.

"Go on, *chérie*," Alex said, leaning forward to run his fingers through my hair, which was pooled on the couch behind me. "Tell us. We're your friends."

"Okay. Yes. I do know from personal experience. A professor of mine."

They squealed with delight, approval.

"But it all went wrong."

More squealing from Véronique. *Mais bien sûr!* "Did the wife find out?" she asked in a hushed voice.

"Yes. And then they fired him. And they sent me here."

"Really?" Alex said. "As punishment?"

"No. What sort of punishment would that be? Just to get me out of the way. So maybe it was a good idea after all, the affair. I don't know if I'd be here otherwise; the school paid for my trip."

"I didn't know *that* part," Sophie said to no one in particular.

I looked back up at her and shrugged. "I was embarrassed, I guess."

"Glad you got over that," she said, her voice inscrutable.

"And what about you, Sophie, any affairs?" Véronique asked. "Ah, no, of course not. Too pristine."

"My best friend's boyfriend, actually," she said suddenly, her face turning steely. "My freshman year."

I looked at her, aghast. Véronique's smile was wicked,

impressed. Alex's expression was unreadable. Who was this girl? I must know of her; our school was too small for me not to. My mind riffled through the series of interchangeable blondes who'd served as Sophie's sidekicks.

"She found out. She was furious, but"—Sophie's shrug was pulled directly from Véronique's playbook—"I was interested in him first, so it wasn't really quite that simple."

"What a scandal!" Véronique said.

I looked at Alex; he was watching Sophie intently.

"Anyway," Sophie said, "I'm exhausted. It's been a long day."

Were we ending the night so soon? But then, Sophie could go to bed without me.

"Yes," Alex said, finishing his wine, "let's get to sleep so you can see some more of Paris tomorrow before you have to leave." I stared up at him, waiting, but he threw me an empty smile before heading to his bedroom.

❦

In the guest room, Sophie seemed to be avoiding eye contact as she prepared for bed.

"So what was that all about?" I finally asked her.

"What was what about?" I'd never seen her like this: quietly seething.

"You told me you'd never slept with anyone, at the pub, you told me that." I was stumbling over my words, not wanting to blurt out what was threatening to bubble up: *You* lied *to me! How could you?* "So that wasn't true?"

"It was a certain truth."

I stopped where I stood. She wound an elastic around her

hair, which she'd been busily braiding, and perched on the bed, patting the edge for me to sit down beside her. "Look, I'm sorry. We had only just started to get close then. And I thought you would think I was this awful person. It's not exactly something I'm proud of."

"I would never think that; people make mistakes. But why tell Alex and Véronique just now then?"

"Because Véronique was making me feel ridiculous. She thinks I'm a joke, I can tell. She loves you, but I always feel like she's laughing at me behind my back."

"I'm sorry that you feel like that," I said cautiously, "but I don't think it's true. How could anyone think that about you?"

"Because she's so knowing, so cool, so, so . . . goddamn French!"

Sophie looked up at me and we both burst out laughing.

"Maybe I'm being too sensitive," she said, climbing into the bed with me and turning off the light.

"Anything is possible."

For a moment we were both quiet.

"Still want to stay forever?" I whispered.

"Bien sûr."

⁓

I woke several hours later with a dry throat and an urgent need for the bathroom. Creeping back toward the bedroom, I noticed a soft glow coming from the sitting room. I walked carefully down the hallway and peered around the corner, finding Alex sitting in the corner of the couch. He wore only his pajama pants and his knees were splayed open, an elbow propped against the armrest as he read a novel. Why was he here and not in his bedroom?

He didn't notice when I came into the room, and for a moment I stood there helplessly, wondering if I should go back to my room but unable to tear my eyes away from him. A moment later, he looked up at me. He didn't seem startled but I apologized anyway, a nervous laugh squeaking out of me.

He continued to stare up at me as though I hadn't spoken, as though he weren't sure I was really there. He put his book down slowly on the end table. And now he smiled, still not speaking. His expression charged me with boldness. It was a standoff and the choice was mine. I let my mind go blank and summoned an otherworldly courage that I knew I had to wrap my hands around before it left me.

I walked over to him and slid onto his lap and into his arms. He put his hands on my hips but otherwise did not move until I leaned down to kiss him, my hair falling around my face and brushing against his collarbone. Once our tongues touched, it was as if he was alive again and I felt his whole body respond, his mouth and his muscles moving beneath me as he became hard between my legs, his hands digging into my skin. Filled with heady longing, I kissed down his torso, pulling at his pants to take him in my mouth. The solidness of him between my lips was a grounding force, and as I moved my head up and down, I let the rhythm of the movement soothe my fraying nerves. How satisfying to control him, if only for a moment.

Time passed in dizzy circles as I heard him moan above me, felt him tense beneath me, felt the fingers of his right hand twist into my hair. When it was over, I settled onto my heels. His head was leaned back on the couch, his eyes were closed, and he was panting to catch his breath. I felt frozen where I was, as though just as quickly as he'd belonged to me, he'd become untouchable. At last he sighed, then stirred. He got up off the couch, knelt to where I was, tenderly moved the hair off my shoulder and kissed my cheek. Then he left me there, crouched on my knees in the lamplight where I'd found him.

I WAS CERTAIN it would change things. I was still naively entranced by the effect of a blow job, mistaking the fleeting power for something more enduring. But the next day it was as if nothing had happened. As with the previous interlude in the stairwell, it was as though these moments were such an expected part of Alex's life that they changed nothing. The four of us walked around the city in sleepy, companionable quiet the next day, finding one of the few cafés open on a Sunday to have a late lunch before returning to Nantes.

As I'd predicted, time seemed to go faster and faster until we had only four weeks on the calendar left between us and the date on our return tickets to California. We had one last extended weekend, and we'd taken Alex up on an invitation I had begun to sincerely worry would never come: Cap Ferrat.

Alex left a day early to get the house ready for our three-day visit. I offered to join him but he told me not to miss my classes. I felt a now-familiar pang that I had humiliated myself but tried to push it away. Sophie and I were heading down by train on Thursday night, and the three of us would spend the day together on Friday before Véronique's arrival first thing Saturday morning.

Waiting for Sophie at the train station, I sat watching commuters heading back and forth, women corralling children toward the trains that were headed for La Baule and Paris, and remembered the first time I had seen the station on that chilly day in September, a lifetime ago. I couldn't avoid the fact that in a short time I would be passing through this train station on my way back to California. What could life there have to offer me now? I knew the feeling would fade and that made me even sadder still, to know that someday soon I would look back at this time in my life with the nostalgia of the remote, of the impossible to recapture. As harried travelers clicked and clacked by me, scurrying to their platforms, I could suddenly see the rest of my life spinning out before me. And it all seemed horribly mundane: job, better job, husband, kids, dinners in front of the television.

"Bonjour!" Sophie said from beside me. I had been watching in the direction I'd been sure she would come from and so was startled. She was wearing a white linen dress and had a large straw hat on her head.

I hugged her, shocked with the relief I felt to see her, bringing me back to the present. Her skin was warm and just the tiniest bit damp from the heat. "Nice hat!"

"I ran to Galeries Lafayette between my morning classes and bought it. It was too expensive but I've always had a fantasy of wearing a hat like this on the French Riviera, and I thought, if not now, then when?" She grinned. It was nearly midday and we were catching the last train to Paris that would get us there in time to catch a same-day train to Nice.

"You mean aside from all of the other times we're going to be spending long weekends on the Riviera when we move to Paris?"

"Of course! Well, then I'll already have the hat, won't I? Oh!

Then I'll have to get a hat*box* to carry it in. And some steamer trunks!" She took my arm as we headed for the platform.

"Oh, yes, in my previous life as an heiress at the turn of the century, I had a matching set!" I said as we boarded the train. "I think you need servants to have that kind of luggage."

"Does this mean you aren't planning for a future where you have a staff? I know I am. Just a modest one, four or five." She tipped her bag into the overhead compartment and we sat down across from each other by the window.

"Oh, yes," I said, settling in, "because you know, short-story writing is quite lucrative."

"You're going to write a novel that wins the National Book Award and gets a big fat movie deal with a Hollywood ending that is henceforth known as one of the greatest love stories of all time."

"Wow, future me is a huge sellout."

"Don't worry, I am too. It was all those years we struggled living together in Paris and eating cheap *croque-monsieurs*. It made us hard. It's okay, though, because we made a pact to sell out and live in adjoining penthouses with our gorgeous husbands."

"Ooh. Tell me about them." I lowered my voice a little. The train was pulling out of the station and two people had sat down next to Sophie and me.

"Well, you married the leading man from your movie. He's *much* younger than you. We're in our forties now. In the States everyone would make a big deal about it, but we're in France, so no one cares."

"So we became permanent expats?" I smiled. "If I'm a cradle robber, what about you?"

"Married to a Frenchman. We have a very tempestuous love affair. Sometimes Jean-Claude and I even throw plates on the floor."

I felt an absurd stab of relief to hear the name of her fictional French husband, to hear that it was not Alex that she was imagining herself married to.

"You really like Jean-Claude most of the time, though. He's very charming and we've all known each other for many years. He jokes constantly that you and I should just be married to each other because you always take my side. But really he should be thanking me because you always convince me not to leave him."

"And what does this Jean-Claude do?"

She looked out the window and an enigmatic smile crossed her face. The sun was still high. "He's a graffiti artist. Though he's finally being accepted by the fine-art community and has been selling murals for big bucks. He feels very conflicted about it."

"He sounds much more interesting than this boy toy I'm shacked up with, I have to say."

"You thought so until you saw the boy toy naked, then you were very interested."

I laughed. "I think maybe you should have been the fiction writer, Sophie."

"What fiction?" She nudged me with her bare toe, having slipped her feet out of her delicate metallic sandals the moment we'd sat down. "This is clairvoyance."

I smiled and leaned back to close my eyes. I hadn't slept at all the night before, unable to shake my anxiety about this trip and the roulette wheel of possible outcomes that it presented—though now that I was with Sophie, I couldn't remember what I'd been nervous about. Her way of talking about our future together seemed so authoritative; she had the certainty of someone who knows she'll go on to do something special. How much we didn't want to imagine ourselves in ordinary lives! We couldn't take the idea of being funneled onto the conveyor belt of diligent workers that filled the cities. After the tests, after the homework, there was *life*, and this didn't, *couldn't*, mean two weeks of vacation plus sick days.

I felt myself drifting to sleep. In the throes of my late-night insomnia I had promised myself I would talk to Sophie about Alex. Yet now, in the light of day, discussing it seemed terrifying. Our liaisons had happened in such a secret way, and I worried I'd somehow killed it in Paris, that if questioned, he might deny it all.

When we got off the train in Paris, the memory of that night came back to me, rising up my spine and making my cheeks flush. If Sophie noticed how quiet I became as we ate our sandwiches during the layover, she didn't say anything. She seemed equally lost in her own thoughts.

"So tell me," I said, resuming our earlier conversation as we settled into our train seats for the second leg of the journey, "do we still know Alex and Véronique in this future life? We are in France, after all."

Sophie smiled and ran her fingers over her head. "Véronique lives in Paris and we run into her at parties sometimes," Sophie said thoughtfully. "And Alex gets very famous actually."

"Well, he's so talented, after all."

"He becomes a big-shot celebrity and fashion photographer."

"So he sells out like us?"

"It's inevitable really. But he doesn't have the excuse of having been a starving artist. You see, his grandmother leaves him all her money *and* the house in Cap Ferrat."

"Well, that's good."

"But we lose touch with Alex."

"Until one day when you run into him at the *boucherie* of course."

"Yes. I decided to go myself instead of sending my cook, Corinne, because it was such a nice day, and then there's Alex, who doesn't trust anyone else to choose his meat for him."

"And you'd know him anywhere," I said, "he looks just the same."

"He's aged well, it's true. Though between you and me, I think he's had some work done. He spent some years in America and I think it made him vain. But, anyway, we reunite. And decide to come again for a weekend in Cap Ferrat."

"Do we bring our husbands?"

Sophie shook her head. "No, the three musketeers, like old times."

It was now or never, I decided. Here in the safety of the story, I could let it be known. "Of course. And then one night after a little too much wine, Alex and I realize the truth."

"Ri-ight," Sophie said slowly as though trying to guess a pantomime in a game of charades, "the *truth*."

"That we've been in love with each other all these years," I said quietly, "ever since we met."

Sophie craned her neck to face me. For a long time her expression was inscrutable. I silently pleaded with her to understand. I hoped that even in the context of this game, my words had been blunt enough. At long last she smiled a big, wide smile and let out a satisfied little laugh as though to say, *Ha, I knew it!* And maybe she *had* known all along. Maybe I'd never been hiding it well.

"You'll have to get rid of the boy toy now, I suppose," Sophie said, finally unlocking me from her gaze and leaning over to take a sip of her sparkling water, "although it would be very French of you to just keep sleeping with both of them for as long as possible."

"Oui." Relief travels up my spine and I smile. "But in the end, I'm an American. So I choose true love."

Sophie laughs. "The Hollywood ending."

Did Sophie believe in this future? Did I? Could I?

"What do you think, *chérie*?" She reached out to stroke my hair. "A glass of wine in the club car?"

I nodded and felt a wave of relief wash over me. The truth was out now and it wouldn't divide us after all; Sophie and I were, in fact, indivisible.

We had a couple of glasses of wine and stayed on in the club car for dinner. When we finally returned to our seats, we were nearly at our destination, and I drifted off. I woke up not long after with my body aching from the odd position it had contorted into. Normally I could never sleep sitting up, but sheer exhaustion from the night before aided by the peace of mind I felt after finally unburdening my soul had put me out. Sophie was still sleeping when they announced that we were approaching the station in Nice. She looked so young when she slept, the picture of innocence and loveliness.

I leaned over and jostled her knee. "Soph."

For a moment she didn't stir. She always slept soundly, even on trains apparently.

Finally her eyelids fluttered awake. She looked around for a minute and then smiled. "Tell me we're in Cap Ferrat," she whispered, her voice raspy with sleep.

"Only partly, we're in Nice. Alex is coming to get us to drive us there, remember?"

I didn't know much about Cap Ferrat. Back then, I could scarcely imagine such a place; the most glamorous beach I'd ever been to was in Santa Monica. I knew that Cap Ferrat was on the seashore and that you couldn't reach it by train. I had asked Nicole about it, and though she had not said so outright, I got the impression that it was the exclusive territory of the very wealthy.

Sophie held my hand as we crossed the platform. After what felt like the perpetual chilliness of Nantes, the warm evening breezes seemed to announce that we were somewhere more welcoming.

I could see people looking at Sophie and me. I felt rumpled but Sophie still looked perfect, her long hair tucked under her wide hat. In front of the station a long parade of gleaming luxury cars jockeyed with one another for position. Every few seconds, someone gave a cry of recognition and trotted toward one of them, their luggage tumbling along behind them. As I stood perusing the chaos, Sophie pulled her phone out of her gray purse.

"Were we supposed to call him when we arrived?"

"He said he would be here," she said quietly. I could feel the same thought crossing both our minds in that instant. What if he didn't come? Almost against my will, I imagined

Sophie and me calling and calling him, waiting a couple of hours at the train station while the crowd of happy travelers on holiday and weary commuters around us thinned as the day's final train came and went. Then finally, without another option, we would take a train back to Nantes and wait for an explanation. I would have this fantasy again many times in retrospect, no longer with a sense of dread, but with a sense of possibility, a blind wish that everything might still somehow be saved.

But, of course, he did come. After a quarter hour that seemed to go on for half a day, Alex pulled up in a gleaming blue convertible with its rich, cream-colored soft top pulled back. It occurred to me that men like Alex knew how to make their entrances, knew to make you wait just long enough that you found yourself in touch with the exact despair you'd feel if they were to abandon you, then they'd show up to save the day a moment later and fill you with the joy of their presence, the relief of having been rescued from their absence.

Seconds ago I'd been standing there with an inexplicable but gnawing certainty that he wouldn't show, but then he had appeared, coming around the car to kiss us and to swing our bags into the tiny trunk. He was sorry he was late and he would have called or sent an SMS but the streets of Nice confounded him and he had to keep his eyes on the road.

Sophie climbed into the backseat without discussion— she knew now, after all—and I took a seat next to Alex.

"Ready?" He turned to smile back at Sophie and then at me, leaning over to squeeze my bare knee as he did so. I nodded, almost delirious with happiness as we pulled away from the train station.

"There is a quicker way through the back roads," Alex explained, his voice nearly disappearing in the wind. "But I thought we should take the long way that goes along the ocean. You have never seen the Mediterranean before, isn't that right?"

As if on cue, I gasped as the breathtaking expanse of dark ocean came into view as we rounded the corner. A full moon was rising, its reflection flooding the stirring waves. Sophie put her hand on my shoulder and shook it as if to say, *Do you see this? Can you believe it?*

"You know Somerset Maugham had a house here," Alex said, looking over at me. "*Of Human Bondage*. Do you know him?"

I marveled at the perfect symmetry of things. "I do, yes."

As we made our way past the harbor, where the yachts ranged from big to aircraft carrier, and smaller sailboats swayed and knocked against one another, I had the sensation that we were on our way to our new home, instead of somewhere we would only be spending a few days. It suddenly felt as though the future that Sophie and I had laid out in such detail during our train ride was real and that we were heading toward it now, were already in it. I felt released from time, sure that anything was possible, that perhaps I would turn around and see not only Sophie sitting there but the fictional Jean-Claude in the backseat beside her. We were not our present selves but our future selves, with twenty years of history and friendship behind us. The days ahead were to become a jewel in our common past, something we would reminisce about for many years to come.

When I think of it now, I see us hurtling toward our doom; there'd be no going back from what happened at that house. The moonlight, intensified by the sparkling sea and the gleaming white boats that swayed atop it, seemed to obliterate whatever we'd left behind us and illuminate all that might be before us. There were no bumps in the road, not a cloud in the sky, not a harbinger of trouble for miles and miles.

I T TOOK us about forty minutes to get to Cap Ferrat from Nice. The town jutted out on a peninsula that was a short distance from Monaco; the landscape was dense with trees and surrounded on all sides by inky water, barely visible beneath the moon.

The house was stark white and sharply modern with windows that encompassed entire walls and with massive arched doorways. Inside, a grand foyer opened up to a vast kitchen and living room. Alex continued on through the house as Sophie and I stood there gaping. Sophie reached out for my hand and squeezed it and we exchanged a wide-eyed glance.

Alex laughed. "Don't be shy, girls. Please, make yourselves at home!"

I gazed at him standing there in his loose tan trousers and linen shirt that appeared fresh even after the long drive and thought that he never seemed quite so at home when he was in Nantes. This was clearly his natural habitat. I felt a longing to fit so neatly in a place like this, to appear like someone who belonged in a mansion by the sea. Most of all I longed to look right next to Alex, to look as if I belonged with him. I felt a blossoming joy as I let the idea enter my head that maybe I *did* look as if I belonged, that maybe it was how I saw *myself* that had been askew all along, and that the version that Alex and his lens saw was the real thing, which had been beyond my grasp until now.

We sat on the patio, which stretched across the entire side of the house, and had a glass of wine before bed. Blue Grecian pots with forsythia crawling out the sides lined the railing at intervals. All that lay between the house and the ocean was a steep hill covered in greenery through which I could see a footpath leading down to the beach.

"Is the beach private?" Sophie asked. The cove of pale sand below us was surrounded on either side by rocks and was completely deserted; it looked haunting in the waxing moonlight.

"*Plus ou moins.* There is a hotel a ways down and the occasional intrepid tourist wanders through. But there will be no families with beach umbrellas and screaming children, if that's what you're asking."

I had never seen such an enchanted-looking place; it seemed impossible that the outside world could bother us while we were here. Though what happened there would spark the series of events that would seal our three fates.

"I will take you to your bedroom," Alex said as we drained the last of the bottle. "You both look exhausted and you must be well rested to enjoy your first real day of vacation tomorrow, yes?"

We let ourselves be led to the bedroom, and Alex tucked us in and kissed us on the foreheads like sleepy children. I had never slept more soundly.

❧

"What would you girls like to do today?" Alex asked when we emerged the next morning. "*Simplement aller à la plage?*

If you're not in the mood for the beach, we could visit the Ephrussi de Rothschild museum or just relax awhile and go into town. Your wish is my command," he said with a courtly little bow. "But right now you must come out onto the patio"—he pushed open a sliding glass door—"see it in the sunlight."

Sophie and I followed him, smiling. Our footsteps echoed in the expanse of the house and added to the pleasant sensation of our own smallness, a feeling augmented by the high ceilings and the light flooding in from the windows facing the Mediterranean. The brilliance of the sun over the sea made everything blend together; you could no longer tell where the ocean ended and the sky began.

Though the house was spotless, it had an abandoned feel to it. I sensed that the fridge and cupboards would either be completely empty or freshly and very deliberately stocked. There'd be no condiments and salad dressings left over from recent meals, no steaks in the freezer. The house was opulent but strangely anonymous. There were pictures on the walls that I assumed were of various members of the de Persaud clan, but I didn't recognize any faces.

We opted to go to the beach since possible showers were predicted for later that afternoon and we wanted to take full advantage of the sunny weather while we had it. Sophie and I returned to "our" bedroom to change. I would have preferred to be assigned a bed with Alex, but since that wasn't an option, I was happy to sleep next to Sophie. The room was spacious, done up in a tasteful nautical theme, and it appeared to be meant for children. Sophie and I hurriedly began taking off our clothes.

"This place is amazing," Sophie said quietly as she adjusted the triangles of her bathing-suit top and tied it securely in back. "I can't believe we're here."

"I know." I instinctually turned away from her as I removed my top. "It's already making me sad to think about leaving."

"Don't say it, don't even think about it."

We were both quiet for a moment. The windows in our room faced the sparse forest behind the house. There was no evidence of life in that direction; the sea lay on the opposite side.

"Okay, I won't." I pulled a swimsuit cover over my head and dug out my sunglasses and a tattered novel. We then ventured down the hall and called out to Alex.

"In here!" his voice echoed from a set of double doors.

Sophie opened the door slowly, and again we were taken aback by the brilliant sunshine coming through the windows and over the ocean. This was obviously the master suite, done up in vivid Mediterranean whites and blues with a giant, pristine white bed in the center.

Without warning, Sophie dropped the beach bag she was carrying and with a running start threw herself facedown onto the middle of the bed.

I laughed. "Sophie!"

Alex's head protruded from the giant expanse of a marble bathroom. He was smiling.

"You said to make ourselves at home," Sophie said to Alex with a mock-sheepish tone. "Come on, Brooke!"

I looked at Alex, who grinned at me indulgently and shrugged. Slipping my sandals off, I tiptoed toward the bed and plopped down next to Sophie.

"This is the best bed in the history of beds," I said. Sophie reached out and squeezed my hand.

"You two are welcome to sleep here instead of in your room," Alex said, reemerging from the bathroom closet with three thick, blue-and-white-striped beach towels in his arms. "Of course, on the condition that I sleep in between you," he added jokingly, or perhaps, I realized, not so jokingly. Sophie cocked an eyebrow at me suggestively.

"We could sleep half the university in this bed comfortably," Sophie said.

"*Allez, les filles*, let's get to the beach while the sun is still in the sky; there's plenty of time for lounging in bed later."

We gathered up some fruit and beer and headed down the narrow, overgrown path that led from the house to the beach. I had the excited energy of a kid sneaking onto someone else's property; it seemed we couldn't possibly be allowed to be in this paradise unsupervised. At twenty we were not quite used to the idea of having free rein over ourselves, though we would never have admitted this at the time.

We fanned our towels next to each other three in a row, and no sooner were we completely settled than Sophie leaped up again. "*Merde*, I forgot sunscreen. Did anyone bring any down?"

I hadn't and Alex was unconvinced of its necessity.

"I'll be right back. Do we need anything else?"

"A few more beers maybe?" Alex said, lying flat on his back and pulling his hat down over his eyes.

Then Sophie was gone back up the trail and Alex and I were alone with the ocean as our backdrop, the exact landscape of my fantasies.

I leaned back on my elbows and stared at the sea. As usual, I hoped he would leap on me the moment we were alone, and as usual, he did not.

"How long do you think you'll be in Nantes? Are you anxious to get back to Paris?"

Alex sighed and shrugged. "It's true that I miss Paris, but I don't know when I will be able to go back for good. And it has been useful for my work to have some quiet and to have come across a couple of interesting new subjects." I could see the curve of a smile cross his face from beneath the rim of his straw fedora. It was unsettling not being able to see his eyes.

"Interesting new subjects? Care to elaborate?" I hoped he meant me, I hoped he would say so.

But he just sighed as though my question had been rhetorical.

I sensed that if I asked further questions, they wouldn't be answered. "I hope Sophie and I come back here someday."

"To Cap Ferrat?"

"I meant to France, but yes, to Cap Ferrat if we're invited." I settled myself on my stomach with my face turned toward Alex.

"You are always invited."

"I can't believe it will be time to go back to California soon." *Tell me not to go,* I didn't say.

"You mustn't think about it yet." Alex propped himself up on his elbows and tipped his hat back to look at me. "You have to learn to live in the moment, *chérie,* or you are not even really living at all. Don't you know that?"

Would it be now that he came toward me? "I know you're right, but I can't help it. I try to be present, but my mind just won't cooperate. Sometimes when I'm enjoying myself, the only thing I can really feel is time passing by me too quickly."

"It's a trap to think that way. You will always be simply planning and anticipating or reminiscing and regretting. You have to savor the moment, the day you are in. You cannot think about where you will soon be or you might as well already be there instead of here."

"I don't want to be anywhere but here," I said, never having desired anything more. He smiled at me and lay back down on the sand, pulling his hat over his eyes as if to imply that the problem had been solved.

A short time later, both of us turned when we heard Sophie approaching, and Alex eyed Sophie's bare torso with blatant admiration. And who could blame him? Sophie had the kind of body that health-club marketers and women's magazines wanted to make us all believe we could achieve if we worked hard enough, but the truth was, it was a gift of blind fate. I couldn't help but wonder how my whole life might have been different if I could have removed my clothes, stood before a mirror, and been faced with that instead of my own body.

I closed my eyes and tried to regain the serenity I had just felt, to remind myself that I did not need to compare myself to Sophie all the time, that she was a friend, not a rival. Sophie—perhaps assuming that I was sleeping and not wanting to disturb me—asked Alex to spread sunscreen on her back. I opened my eyes and for an excruciating moment caught a glimpse of Alex's hands caressing the space between Sophie's shoulder blades, his fingers sliding underneath the straps of her bikini top.

We lingered on the beach for hours, drinking beer and lapsing into a comfortable stupor in the warm sun. Eventually clouds came in—seemingly from nowhere—and the winds that sprang up from the ocean chilled us.

"It probably won't last long," Alex said, shaking the sand out of his beach towel and rolling it up. "But why don't we go into town while it's cloudy, then maybe we can head down here again this afternoon."

My head spun as I stood up; I felt myself sway back and forth as I made my way up the path once again behind Sophie and Alex. Once we were sheltered from the breezes of the ocean, the air felt dense and humid, as though the molecules were pressed up against each other.

We changed back into our clothes and got into Alex's car to drive the short distance into Saint-Jean-Cap-Ferrat. I let Sophie take the front seat this time. It seemed only right since I had been in it the whole drive from Nice, but seeing them together laughing and chatting in the front of the car, their words mostly getting lost in the wind, I had the unpleasant sensation that I was suddenly invisible.

We had lunch in a small café near the harbor where Alex seemed to know all of the employees. The maître d' welcomed him and spirited us to a choice spot on the patio despite the small crowd of tourists who had obviously been waiting for a table. A German woman openly scowled at us, and I smiled back at her as if I were totally oblivious. How good it felt to be the person for whom the rules were different, if only momentarily and by proxy. It occurred to me that both Alex and Sophie were probably familiar with the sensation.

Soon after we sat down, a short, portly man came tumbling out from the kitchen and threw his arms around Alex. Judging by the deference of the attendant waiters and bus-boys, I figured him to be the chef or owner or both. Between the lilt of his regional accent and the speed at which he spoke to Alex, I could barely understand him but gleaned that he planned to bring us something special. A moment later a bottle of crisp, delicious sparkling wine appeared unbidden.

"I've been coming here since I was a little boy. The de Persauds have been good customers for many generations," Alex said.

"You never talk much about growing up," Sophie said. "What were you like when you were a kid?"

Alex looked out to the harbor for a moment. "A pain in the ass mostly," he said just as the waiters appeared with salads.

We laughed. "I bet that's not true," I lied. I could imagine young Alex as a terror, ruling over the other children—and the occasional adult—the way that the bright and somewhat spoiled always do in the kingdom of childhood.

"I could see you being a bit mischievous. Torturing a nanny or two," Sophie said.

"I could be guilty of that. In fact we even had an American au pair one summer. I was twelve at the time, completely in love with her. I think she was the last American in the house until the two of you."

"Your first love," I said, smiling, "what illustrious company to be in."

"Not my first." Alex speared a beet on the end of his fork and put it in his mouth. "That happened when I was five or so. But certainly one of the great loves of my early life. There is nothing like an unrequited passion to stoke the flames of your imagination. It's the fantasy of her that's lasted so long, not so much the memory of the girl herself, whoever she was."

"What did she look like?"

"Tall, I think. But maybe she was only tall to me at the time because I was *tout petit* for my age. She was blond."

"Naturally!"

"We have something against blondes now?" Sophie asked, a sparkle in her voice.

"Oh, no," I said, my voice laden with what I hoped was cheerful sarcasm, "gentlemen prefer them. Even young gentlemen, apparently."

"I have no preference," Alex said magnanimously. "Beautiful. That is my only preference."

"How generous of you," I said. In my heart, that distinction, even the word, belonged to Sophie.

"And what do we think our Brooke was like as a child?" Alex said. "Sophie, did you know her then?"

Two busboys came from either side and discreetly cleared our plates, readjusting place settings so meticulously that it looked as though nothing had touched our table to begin with. It occurred to me that I had never been in a restaurant quite like this one. I kept smiling nervously at the staff, while Sophie and Alex looked perfectly at ease.

"No, we didn't know each other until college, so your guess is as good as mine, Alex."

"Not very exciting I'm afraid," I said, "what we refer to in the States as a late bloomer. I was very quiet and spent a lot of time reading."

"A late bloomer? Well," Alex said, "some things are worth waiting for."

I blushed.

"And, Sophie?" he asked. "Were you also a late bloomer?"

"Bet not," I said, "bet you were born in bloom."

Sophie gave me a wry little smile and I remembered the conversation we'd had in Paris, that it upset her that everyone thought things came so easily to her.

"I'm certain," Alex said, smiling appreciatively at Sophie, "and she probably drove all the poor boys crazy."

It seemed like a long time until anyone said anything else.

"A mixed blessing if there ever was one," Sophie said quietly, "boys being what they are when they're young. Though you, I'm sure, were lovely," she added to Alex. I closed my eyes so I wouldn't roll them.

"I was an animal," Alex said, "you wouldn't have wanted to know me then. I wish *I* hadn't known me then."

"Good thing we're all so grown-up now," I said, "like all of this was *so* long ago."

"In a way it was, though, *non?*" Alex said. "Years are not simply measured in minutes and days, Brooke. Not all years are equal, and the ones that take us away from childhood are so crucial."

"I just think it's funny that we're sitting around talking like we're so very old and sage when we'll look back a couple of years from now and feel like we were so young and stupid." *Sage* was a convenient word, a cognate.

"But that's exactly my point! In two years you will feel as though you are a decade older than you are now, and yet it will only be some seven hundred days, eight seasons, that will have gone by. You will see, you can tell me if I'm wrong then. When you get back from France—worldly and unfamiliar in your familiar surroundings—you will feel as though you've lived another lifetime, and yet for your classmates it will have been several months like any others."

"Don't talk about going back!" Sophie said. "I've just tried to get Brooke to *stop* thinking about it!" Her voice had an edge of genuine pain. "Besides, we might not even *go* back."

"Ah"—Alex smiled—"there is an escape plan? New names, new passports? How very James Bond!"

Sophie smiled and shrugged.

"Oh!" I was startled by the appearance of a whole fish staring up at me from its platter that had materialized silently at my right elbow. We all laughed. Alex gave a nod of approval to the waiter, and in a snap it was returned to us perfectly filleted.

In those days I didn't eat fish, but I had resolved to pretend to love it either way. This proved to be unnecessary; the fish was unimaginably light and flaky and perfect. Alex was right. Each moment in this place I discovered a new part of myself, while the things I thought I knew dissolved effortlessly. It was both terrifying and liberating. And I was a person who liked fish now. Who knows what other mysteries might yet reveal themselves to me before I returned to the United States?

"Sea bass," Alex explained, just as the owner was approaching the table. "Guillaume swam out in the harbor and caught it with his bare hands when he saw us coming towards the restaurant."

The owner gave a hearty laugh and gripped Alex's shoulder.

"That's what he always used to tell me when I was a little boy. I believed him too!"

"But it's true, I will show you my wet swimming trunks!" Guillaume boomed, then turned to us. "How do you like the fish?" he asked in English that sounded as though it wasn't often used.

"It's wonderful!" I said in English.

"And you like it here, in Cap Ferrat?"

"It's the most beautiful place I've ever seen," Sophie said.

He beamed as though not only the delicious fish but Cap Ferrat itself were his doing.

"People are much more cheerful here than in the north," Sophie observed when Guillaume had left our table.

"Wouldn't you be with all of this surrounding you?" Alex asked. "Perhaps I will come here this summer, at least for July and August. I had forgotten how much I missed it."

"Let us know if you need company," Sophie said.

Alex looked thoughtful.

"I was kidding, Alex," she said quietly, perhaps embarrassed that she had seemed to be inviting herself. Even so, I knew she wasn't kidding. It was becoming evident that Sophie didn't intend to leave.

"I don't see why you shouldn't," Alex said. "Think of the time we would have! We could eat here every week and go swimming in the ocean. Brooke could write a novel. Sophie, you could paint all day in the attic studio. I will show it to you when we get home."

Sophie and I exchanged a look. Could he be serious? Could we delay the inevitable? *Too good to be true* would have been an understatement of massive proportions.

"Well," he said with a shrug, "think it over, *les filles.*"

And with that a new world opened before us, one that actually seemed to be within our grasp.

By the time we had finished lunch, the clouds were beginning to roll across the sky like slow-moving animals leisurely heading toward another pasture. A sunny afternoon was in our future.

We took our time wandering through the village, and with Alex a few steps ahead of us, Sophie dropped back, took my arm, and leaned her head on my shoulder for a moment. "I'm so glad we're here together," Sophie said, and I agreed. I knew somehow that I couldn't handle too much of Alex on my own just yet. I couldn't imagine the lather I would work myself into if I didn't have her here to create some kind of balance, to put me at ease.

Popping in and out of shops where all of the proprietors knew Alex, we picked up supplies for dinner at the house.

"We are going to have the only thing I know how to make for dinner," said Alex. *"Galettes! Au chèvre."*

We spent some more time on the beach that afternoon and were drunk with sun and good wine by the time we started dinner. We laughed and prodded each other with kitchen implements as we cooked, destroying a half dozen of the galettes before we got one right. I thought how much my mother hated wasted food. Then we sat down on the large stone patio and ate while the sun went down.

Alex began to tell us about the things we would do that summer, as if it had already been decided that we'd be joining him. It was as though he'd been listening in on our train conversation and was now joining the game of future tense that we had been playing. He told us about an older friend of his, Marie-Eléne, who had parties every other weekend on her yacht, and he told us about the people we would meet there. Artists, he said. People like us. Not like the people we'd met in Paris. As he talked, I remembered Sophie and me—how long ago it felt now—walking along the harbor in La Rochelle, telling each other about our boats. I snuck a look at Sophie and she smiled at me; she was thinking the same thing. And now here we were; she wasn't about to let it go.

Who knows how much wine we consumed; this house, like the one in Nantes, had an impressive cellar. After dinner, Alex ably built a fire in the elegant stone fire pit on the beach, and I noticed not for the first time that he seemed capable of drinking endless quantities of wine without much effect—unlike Sophie and me.

Though my own tolerance had been improved by my time with Véronique and Alex, by the time the fire was going and we were dancing around it and laughing like hyenas, my memories become a bit untrustworthy. Some flashes are clear as day, but between them there must be omissions. I don't remember, for instance, any discussion about going into the water; I only remember hanging back on the beach while Sophie and Alex ran toward the surf, tearing their clothes off as they went. I remember my initial reluctance, then the feeling of its disappearing as I pulled off my dress to their great delight, the rush of the elements hitting every inch of my skin: first the wind, then the waves. I remember the cold water hitting my ankles and rushing up my torso before I dove into a low wave. I remember the crazy, large moon and the way it highlighted the rippling water all around us.

I remember sneaking furtive glances at Alex. I remember admiring Sophie and for once not feeling so threatened and feeling instead that in this combination of moonlight and ocean, perhaps I was—at this moment—beautiful too.

Sophie stayed in the water when Alex and I returned to sit near the fire. We both watched her; she seemed lost in her own world. Her lower half was submerged and she was staring off toward the horizon; we could only see her back and a little of her face. I noticed that Alex was taking pictures, and without quite knowing why, I grabbed my small, disposable camera and began to quietly take a few of my own. I wanted to remember how his face looked when he was looking at her, when he was capturing her beauty as it slipped off into the night.

I don't remember how we managed going back up the path. I do remember dripping on the floor, and I remember Sophie and me clutching at each other, and I remember the three of us opening yet another bottle of wine after we'd dried off and curled up with Alex on the couch under a blanket—one of us on either side—and I remember almost crying from the feel of his bare skin on mine, wanting to dig in my nails just to get closer. I remember thinking that at any moment Sophie might slip away and leave me with my chance.

I also remember thinking it was the best night of my life. After that, nothing more.

I'M SURE that I didn't sleep well that night, but my mind was too drowned in wine to notice, and mercifully I was down for the count for at least a few consecutive hours. I woke to the sun shining so brightly in my eyes that it felt as if a klieg light were trained directly on my face. Not only were the blinds all pulled back, but one of the French doors to the balcony was flung wide-open as if someone had just come through moments before. Blinking, I reached for one of the silky couch pillows to put over my eyes. My head was spinning in a way that told me that the alcohol was not yet gone from my system and that the worst pain of the hangover was still to come.

It occurred to me that I'd been dreaming of water, and I knew that I'd be much better off if I could just rally myself to get some. These physical concerns distracted me momentarily from the questions that would assault me in merciless succession once my head had cleared enough to begin asking them.

Why was my hair damp?

Why was I sleeping on the couch and not in my room?

Where was Sophie?

Where was Alex?

Where were Sophie and Alex?

I pulled myself slowly upright and surveyed the clues left around me. There were two empty bottles of wine on the table and six glasses, three with tiny triangles of red in their bases. I was briefly amused by the fact that we had had enough presence of mind to switch out the glasses. There was a much-worked-over cheese plate and a gold box that had held chocolates. I made note of these details with the care of someone accessing a crime scene. I took in the three pairs of shoes that were together by the door, the towels hung carelessly on the balcony, the faint spots of damp on the back of the couch where our heads had been. I dissected every detail to protect myself from what was plainly obvious: the *two* of them were missing.

I pulled my knees to my chest in a reflexive attempt to comfort myself and quickly devised a scenario in which I was the first to fall asleep and I'd appeared so exhausted that no one had had the heart to disturb me. After all, a pillow was tucked under my head and a blanket was over my legs. Clearly, someone had attended to me. They had then gone up the stairs, laughing and stumbling a little along the way, and then when they'd reached the landing, that crucial territory between Alex's room and ours, they'd parted ways. For credibility's sake I granted them a drunken, meaningless kiss on the landing right before Sophie turned to go to our room. She would feel bad if she remembered it today, but then recall how much we'd had to drink and decide it wasn't even worth telling me about, that it had meant nothing, had barely happened.

Yes, I decided, my thoughts weaving through a minefield of their own making, that was all plausible. I listened closely for echoes of life in the large house. Nothing yet. I could imagine Sophie coming down at any moment and the two of us groaning and commiserating about our terrible hangovers. Her explaining to me that they couldn't move me an inch after I'd passed out on the couch and hoping that I hadn't felt abandoned.

I lay back down and several minutes passed, during which I envisioned going down to the beach, where we would let the alcohol sizzle out of us just in time to begin the whole process again. Perhaps there was somewhere close by where we could go for omelets.

Yet, with all these visions of the day to come—a day that had dawned brilliant and sunny without a hint of the clouds that had rolled in and out the day before—why this fear of approaching the stairs? This was the last moment that I wouldn't know one way or the other; I wouldn't be able to get that innocence back. But there was nothing to know, I reminded myself, and with that I pulled myself up a little too quickly, laughing out loud as I nearly lost my balance.

I made my way up the stairs and hesitated for the briefest moment when I came to the landing. Alex's door was the tiniest bit ajar. Nothing, I told myself. It meant nothing. If anything, a completely closed door would have been more forbidding. I walked slowly toward Sophie's and my room, pushing the door open quietly. My heart nearly burst when I saw Sophie, sleeping soundly. I admonished myself. How could I ever think she would sleep with Alex now that she knew about my feelings for him?

I could only see much later that her being there told me nothing about what had gone on the night before.

Tiptoeing over to the bed, I pulled back the covers. Sophie grunted a little in her sleep. I climbed in next to her.

"Sophie?" I whispered. "Are you awake?"

"Mmmmugggh."

She reached back and pulled my arm around her.

"Oh, God," she murmured, "I'm so hungover."

"Me too."

"I don't even know how I made it up to bed last night."

"I didn't. I slept on the couch."

For a few minutes we were quiet and I drifted back to sleep. A little while later, a knock came at the door. I looked up to see Alex standing there.

I shook myself awake and propped myself up to look at him. "Good morning," I whispered.

"My goodness, what have I missed here? This is so unfair that the two of you are together in this little bed and I am all alone in mine. Whatever have I done to deserve such treatment, *les filles*?"

Sophie looked over at him. "Whatever you did, you're forgiven. I can't remember anything that happened after skinny-dipping."

"Good thing you're both so young; at my age the hangovers last all day. Yours will be gone by lunchtime."

"You say that like you're so much older than us," I said, sitting up and reaching for Alex as though to pull myself up out of bed.

"But it is worse at my age, you'll see." He grabbed my hand with a smug smile. I pulled him down on top of us so that we were pig-piled on the bed, limbs sticking out in every direction. Sophie gave a loud groan and Alex and I laughed.

"See, this is how it should be," he said, "all in one bed *tous ensemble*!"

⁓☙

We showered and drank some French-press coffee that was strong enough to sufficiently revive us for the journey into town in search of breakfast. We ate at a restaurant that served café au lait in large bowls and *pain au chocolat* so light and heavenly that I could have eaten half a dozen. Soon my hangover was breaking away, releasing its hold. I was gripped with a sudden wave of love for Alex and Sophie and found myself wishing the others were not on their way to join us, that we could stay for a time just the three of us: a week, a month, until the end of the summer. At least the rest of this weekend, this bittersweet interlude. The energy had changed between the three of us and I wanted to savor this new thing that we now had: this feeling of having no limitations, of being naked together, which though we were now fully clothed seemed to remain present in some deeper way. I suddenly couldn't imagine ever needing anyone else besides these two people or anywhere else but this beautiful place.

As we let our breakfast settle, we smoked cigarettes—I had a full-blown habit at this point, as did Sophie—and Alex told us about the friends who would be joining us later. Henri and Isabelle were friends from Paris who lived in Saint-Tropez during the spring and summer. Isabelle was a dancer.

"Henri is a rich boy," Alex said with a barely disguised touch of disdain that made me wonder what exactly one called Alex if not that. "He is a classic dilettante. Every time I see him he has a new life ambition. He has been at different times a writer, painter, and photographer, so we will all have a lot in common."

I smiled. *Not like us* was the insinuation. Not devoted and passionate. Not the real thing.

"Who else?" Alex said, leaning forward and flicking a light dusting of cigarette ash into a delicate blown-glass ash-tray. "There's Sebastian, who works for his *papa* in wines, he is down from Bordeaux. Maybe with a woman. He is sweet, you will like him. I do not know who *ma chère cousine* is bringing with her. It's always possible she has fallen in love with someone new since I spoke to her two days ago. *Alors, on verra!*"

As we drove the sleek little car back along the narrow ocean road, I thought again how we were in a place where trouble couldn't touch us, and that the rest of my life, Nantes, my family, America, would simply wait patiently for me, to be dealt with later. I couldn't see all that was beginning.

When we got home, we went upstairs to the bedroom and changed into our bathing suits. I noticed Sophie pulling out one I'd never before seen.

"Ugh, I should have brought an extra, mine is still damp from last night," I said. "Is that one new?"

She nodded and smiled, stopping to admire the white bathing suit with its gold hardware. I had wanted to buy a new suit for this trip as well; mine was a little faded and not chic enough by half for the Riviera, but much as the desire was there, the money was not. Each time I looked at my bank balance I felt a little spasm of guilt, and an image of the many hours I'd spent behind the coffee bar floated through my mind. I felt a tiny flicker of jealousy and pushed it away. It wasn't material things that mattered at this moment in my life, not really. It didn't matter if Sophie looked more the part than I did.

Alex was waiting for us by the kitchen. I noticed that he was a little sunburned across his chest and biceps, and this got to me for some reason, this sign of humanity, of vulnerability. *"Sophie, quel joli maillot de bain!"* That he complimented her bathing suit shouldn't have mattered; he was the kind of man who noticed these things, who could get away with no-ticing these things. But I ached, and the nylon of my still-wet bathing suit suddenly even *felt* ugly. "You two go on ahead, I will be down a little later. I need to nap for a bit."

Sophie and I made our way down the path. I was happy to be alone with her for a moment. Despite my relief that I hadn't found her with Alex that morning, I had also not been with him myself. Out of nowhere I remembered the expres-sion on his face when he'd taken the picture of Sophie in the water, like a child who'd caught a beautiful insect by its wings. I wanted her here, of course. But did he understand that she was off-limits? Did she?

Alex came down an hour later, and one by one the guests arrived and joined us on the beach. Henri was pale and kept his face shaded under an expensive-looking fedora. He had a shy smile that made him seem vulnerable for a grown man, which surely anyone so wealthy and so lost must be. Everything about Isabelle, from her perfect dancer's legs to her pert little nose, gave you the impression that she had always been beau-tiful and mean and felt guilty about neither of these things. When we were introduced, she regarded me as though I were an exotic dish of food that someone was trying to convince her would not taste disgusting. She barely glanced at Sophie, an omission I could only take to mean she was threatened. Henri sat between Alex's and my beach towels and asked me polite questions about my time abroad in a slow, lilting French that denoted a certain ease with foreigners. Sophie lay on the other side of me either sleeping or doing a good impression of it.

At last Véronique arrived with someone she introduced as Grégoire, apparently the same Grégoire from her past, since Alex made an ostentatious show of being glad to see him again.

She kissed me on both cheeks and sat at the edge of my beach towel. Her shiny black hair whipped in the wind, glinting almost blue in the bright sun.

"Et bonjour, Sophie," she said, leaning over me to where Sophie lay with her hat pulled over her eyes. I smacked her in the leg when she didn't respond.

"What?" she said in English. *"Ah, bonjour, Véronique."* Sophie leaned over me to kiss her hello, smelling of salt water and sunscreen. Sophie, I was sure, was also wishing it were just the three of us here.

We discussed plans for the evening and Henri eagerly offered use of his boat, moored in the harbor at Cap Ferrat. When the sun began to go down, we headed back to the house to get ourselves ready for the night. Back in the room again I despaired over what to wear while Sophie showered. Pulling shorts and tank tops out of my bag, I held them aloft and examined them with caution as if they belonged to someone else, as though my suitcase had been switched with another on the train. Véronique, Isabelle, Sophie, even the boys, seemed so effortlessly lovely—where had they learned it? When I thought of my life in the future, I always envisioned a slightly thinner, more stylish person living it. Perhaps this was how I began to become that person. For now I just wanted to toss out everything I owned and start over. More than toss it out, I wanted to burn it, to leave no evidence.

There was a knock, and Véronique poked her head around the door. I put down the faded sundress I was holding.

"*Allô, chérie.* What are you doing in here? We were going to open a bottle of champagne on the terrace before we drive down to the marina."

I sighed and sat down next to my bag. "Trying to figure out something to wear tonight."

Véronique sat down on the bed.

She tilted her head, assessing me. "You can borrow something."

"Your clothes won't fit me," I said, smiling ruefully at her.

She made a face. "I have some things that are a bit bigger. Come, we will try them on." She bounced to her feet and grabbed my hand. I felt absurdly grateful to her.

Véronique was staying in one of the guest bedrooms down a long corridor. Though the *rez-de-chaussée* was dominated by large, open spaces, designed to accommodate the sunlight that flooded in from the windows, the top floor was surprisingly labyrinthine, with unassuming doors that opened onto grand bedrooms and hallways that could swallow you.

Véronique began to sift through what was hanging in her closet. "So, have you girls been having a nice time down here with my cousin?" She stopped to pull a hanger out, then seemingly decided against it.

"Wonderful. It's so incredible, this place. I've never been anywhere even half as beautiful."

"Really? *Oui, c'est vrai—Cap Ferrat est très beau.* But there are places in California that are very beautiful also."

"Not the part I'm from." I thought of the strip-club billboards that cluttered the freeway exits to Chino, the chain-link fences outside the houses with scruffy pit bulls pacing the dusty yards.

Véronique pulled from the closet whatever she had her hand on. She looked at me thoughtfully, coming to take a seat beside me on the bed. "But I think this is better in some ways. To not come from a place that has everything."

"If you say so."

She sighed a little. "It's not really that valuable, to be unimpressed with everything, to feel like nothing will ever be better than what you've already had. This is why I like being at the university in Nantes. If I had gone to the Sorbonne like all my friends, I never would have met anyone new. They're so small-minded and insular you wouldn't believe. Look at Isabelle, who is here now: an impossible bitch."

"She is awful, isn't she?" I had the traitorous feeling that we were also talking about Sophie.

"Terrible. *Chérie*, all I am saying is, don't be fooled. What you are is worth a thousand Isabelles. *En tout cas*, try this on." She handed me a dress.

I turned my back to her as I pulled my own top off and pulled the dress over my head. The cut was forgiving enough that it fit me perfectly, and the white looked lovely against my newly bronzed skin. I looked at myself in the mirror and had a pleasing sensation of being more myself than I had been a moment before. My cheeks were a bit pink from the sun, and my unwashed hair had a beachy fullness to it.

"*C'est parfait!*" Veronique said. "So what did you all get up to last night?"

"Oh, lots of wine. A swim in the ocean. Some more wine. Oh, and Alex made galettes."

She laughed. "*Mais bien sûr.* That is the only thing Alex knows how to make. Well, there will certainly be plenty more wine tonight. And with that moon that's rising, it should be very romantic."

"For you and Grégoire?"

"And anyone else who might be in the mood," she said, smiling over her shoulder as we walked out of the room.

~·~

We joined the others on the terrace to drink a glass of champagne before heading to the boat.

"*J'adore cette robe,*" Alex said when he saw me. He was sitting down with his elbows on his knees; he reached out and tugged gently at the hem.

"*Merci. Elle appartient à Véronique.*"

"And yet it seems made for you." He reached for my hand and pulled me onto his lap. I put my arm around his neck. How natural it felt. How right.

Sophie emerged a few moments later, looking gorgeous in an orange floral dress. Her eyes stopped on the two of us and she froze for a moment before she smiled and sat.

Henri handed me a glass of champagne with a cautious smile. "*Alors,* Brooke and Sophie, when do you return to the United States?"

"Four weeks," I said, frowning.

"*Arrête!*" Alex told him, circling his arm around my hips

as though trying to keep me from running away. As though I ever would. "We are not talking about that, it makes us sad."

Sophie opened her mouth as if to speak but then said nothing.

"Right," Henri said.

I noticed Alex mentioned nothing about us staying for the summer. I tried not to think of Chino and of the Starbucks. Alex began to stroke the outside of my thigh softly with his fingertips, and that brought me back into the moment, back into my skin with force.

Over the ocean the bright moon seemed many times its normal size.

Eventually we headed to the cars and I rode alone with Alex in the blue convertible after Véronique cajoled Sophie into riding with her and Grégoire. As we made our way along the winding road, Alex put his hand on my knee almost absentmindedly. I craved being the thing he could touch without asking permission. I uncrossed my legs. He ran his fingertips along the inside of my thigh, then let them rest at the top, maddeningly close. My breath was getting shallow and I stared fixedly at the empty road ahead. Henri and the others followed behind us, and to know they were there increased the thrill. We came around a curve in the road and the lights from the harbor became visible. Alex watched the road, smiling serenely. My skin was burning from his touch and blood rushed to my head, extinguishing rational thought. I felt as though I'd been shot up with some dizzying drug.

Just as we pulled around into the lot by the harbor, Alex's hand moved just far enough up my thigh that his little finger rested atop the fabric of my underwear. He stroked me gently before removing his hand to put the car in park.

My face was hot and I knew I must be blushing. I fumbled with the car door. I was certain that when the others saw me, they would somehow sense what I was feeling. I wasn't sure I could behave normally or form a coherent sentence.

Alex put his arm around me and chuckled a little as we walked toward the marina. Henri's "little boat" was in fact a fifty-foot yacht with a sullen-looking captain and two lovely female crew members, whom Isabelle seemed to take great pleasure in ordering around. The seven of us had a magnificent dinner on the stern of scallops and striped grouper as we sailed out toward Nice, the lights twinkling in the distance. Throughout dinner I noticed Henri sneaking looks at me. I felt as though he was studying me, waiting for me to do something. I had the now-familiar sensation that I was missing something.

When the dining table had been cleared, Henri appeared at my side.

"Brooke, you must come see the front of the ship. It's wonderful to look out and feel yourself moving along the water."

I nodded tentatively and followed him around the side of the boat. Alex and Véronique were cloistered together, laughing covertly about something, and Isabelle was talking to Grégoire with a look that said it was taking all of her energy not to yawn in his face. Sophie was by herself at the stern, staring fixedly into the wake from the boat. She seemed a little distant tonight, but I didn't have the energy or inclination to find out why just now.

Henri offered his arm to me in a gentlemanly fashion and I took it, glad to have something to steady myself on as we made our way down the narrow walkway. He asked me some more questions about Nantes, what my host family was like, what classes I was taking. His earnest sweetness made him seem almost childlike. Then he was quiet for a long time.

"I have known Alex for many years," he said, looking out into the dark water in front of us. "You should—"

"Henri!"

We both jumped at the sound of Alex's voice.

"What are you doing out here?" he asked, smiling and coming to stand between the two of us, leaning against the ship's railing.

"I wanted to show Brooke the ship."

Alex laughed. *"Ah, mais Brooke est très intelligente.* That sort of thing won't work on her, my friend."

Henri blushed and shrugged. For a moment my mind reeled, wondering what he'd been about to say, but once I was in proximity of Alex again, it barely mattered, and my mind was flooded with the memory of his hand between my legs. For the rest of our time on the water, Alex stayed close to my side. The latter half of Henri's sentence added to the cache of mysteries that I would obsess over in the years to come.

When we said our goodbyes to Henri and Isabelle at the docks, I again caught the melancholy look Henri was giving me. But maybe I was imagining it.

Back at the house, Véronique and Grégoire quickly disappeared, and then it was the three of us once again. Alex went back inside to get another bottle of wine and left Sophie and me alone for a moment on the terrace. I asked her if anything was wrong, trying to keep my voice even, to not show any of the irritation that I guiltily realized I felt. I loved Sophie but I wanted tonight for myself.

"I don't know." She stretched back on the chaise with her arms crossed above her head. "I wish it was still just the three of us. These other people being here, it's bursting my bubble."

I laughed. "Why is that?"

"I can tell they think we're silly, that they think they're his *real* friends. But if they'd known all the time we spent with him, with his grandmother . . ."

"Why does it even matter, Soph?" I asked gently.

She shrugged and turned to look up at the stars, her features etched sharply in profile in the moonlight.

Alex came back out and handed each of us a glass.

"Ah, bon," he said, "the three amigos alone at last."

For a moment we sat there silently while Alex poured our wine. As he filled my glass, I looked up at him, and for a blistering, electric moment we stared right at each other. He smiled and I felt it in my whole body.

"So quiet tonight, Ms. Sophie," Alex said at last, sitting down on the edge of my chaise. I let my shins relax against his back and looked out to where the calm ocean stirred, just beyond the treetops lit up by moonlight.

"Too much sun," she said dreamily. When she looked over at us, I thought I caught something pained in her eyes. Was this the real reason? Was she upset that I might be with Alex tonight? But she couldn't be, I thought defensively, I *told* her.

"In fact"—she pulled herself upright—"I think I may head up to bed. I'm exhausted." She leaned over to kiss Alex's cheeks.

"*Ah, non*, it's so early," he said, cupping his hand to her cheek. I wished that he wouldn't try to dissuade her from leaving; it stung a little.

"Yes, yes," she insisted, coming over to kiss me lightly on the lips.

"Are you sure?" I said, in my quiet way of asking for her blessing. She smiled and nodded, but there was something beneath it.

She disappeared into the house. I leaned forward and took a nervous sip of my wine, feeling the weight of Alex's body against my legs, the weight of being alone with him.

Alex leaned over his knees and stared thoughtfully into his glass of wine. The moment in the car seemed like long ago, and I wondered if that had indeed been meant as a promise, a preview of what was to come, or if it had been a complete whim, forgotten as quickly as it had happened. He put his glass down and turned around so that he was sitting cross-legged on the edge of the chaise facing me.

"*Et toi, chérie?*" he said, smiling, "you're not too exhausted, I hope?"

I shook my head.

He reached out for me and pulled me closer to him. "*Vas-y.*"

He put his lips to mine and pulled me up by my legs so that I was straddling him. Drawing me close to him with one hand around my back and the other in my hair, he took his lips away from mine, pulled my head to the side, and kissed my neck.

"Can I tell you a secret?" he whispered.

"Yes," I said, my voice slow and muddled as though I were underwater.

"Something I have noticed, a beautiful little coincidence of a woman's body," he whispered in my ear. "The underside of the lip here"—he bit my bottom lip softly—"is precisely the same color as the *mamelon*."

He pulled away from me and smiled. I blushed intensely.

"May I have a look?" He was already pulling one strap of my dress to the side. "Yes," he said, leaning down to my nipple as if to examine it, "the same exactly." He traced his tongue over my nipple and I gasped. I let my head fall back and felt as if all the breath escaped from my body in one sharp exhale. I was only vaguely aware that we were outside where we could be seen; it felt as if no one would have the audacity to intrude on this moment, that the universe wouldn't allow it.

"Ma belle Américaine." He kissed me again. *"Vas-y."*

He got up and offered me his hand. I returned the strap of my dress to its place and stumbled woozily to my feet, knocking over one of the glasses.

"Oh, no"—I looked down to where the wine was running out of the overturned and now-cracked wineglass—"I'm sorry."

Alex laughed and tugged on my hand. "Leave it."

I laughed too without knowing why and followed him into the house.

"Shhhhhhhhhh," he said as I followed him to the top of the landing, hesitating for a moment to glance briefly at the door to Sophie's and my room. It was closed, and for some reason I felt this as a reproach, though it couldn't be, could it?

In his room, Alex kissed me again and turned the lights down. He pulled my dress over my head, then laid me back on the bed. He hooked a finger around my underwear and tugged it gently down my legs. As my eyes adjusted to the dark, I could see every detail of the room and of him, so brilliant was the moonlight that shone in the window. He was still mostly dressed with the exception of his bare, brown chest, and it made me feel twice as naked to be beside him like this. I rolled onto my side to face him and covered myself with my forearms.

"*Non,*" Alex said quietly, softly taking both my wrists in his hands and gently drawing my arms down by my sides. "*S'il te plaît, chérie,* I want to see you."

It occurred to me that I had never before been naked like this with someone. Regan had only ever seemed halfway present when we were together, as though his guilt wouldn't let him fully absorb the situation. I had never been scrutinized like this; it was both terrifying and thrilling.

Alex ran a finger across my lips, down the middle of my torso, out onto the side of my hip.

"*C'est parfait.* All of it. Your body is so beautiful, *mon amour.*"

He lifted himself up over me and I closed my eyes for a moment, almost overwhelmed by his closeness.

"Open your eyes," Alex said quietly. "I want you to watch me."

I complied, and soon enough I was transfixed by him, forgetting to be nervous about my nakedness.

"People don't appreciate the body the way they should." He removed his pants and positioned himself between my legs. "Especially American men—with them it's all tits and ass. There are these little curves and swells, like your thighs here." He traced the insides of them. "When I felt that in the car, I knew how much I needed to see them, to get between them. I have been able to think of nothing else all night."

He maintained eye contact as he went down between my legs. I stifled a moan, burying my face in a nearby pillow.

When he came back up, I was nearly delirious.

"You taste sweet," he said, his lips close to my ear now, "like a good girl."

"Alex." My voice sounded weak and faraway. What did I want to say? I wanted confirmation that what we were about to do would change things between us for the better and not in some other, painful way. Should I tell him I loved him? Ask him if he loved me? I couldn't. What if he lied or realized I was in over my head and stopped? Which of these things would be worse? I didn't know.

"Yes, my darling?"

"Nothing. I'm just . . . very happy right now," I said awkwardly.

He laughed softly. "Good." He turned me on my side and pulled himself up behind me. "It's all I want. To make you happy." His fingers parted me and then I felt him inside me, deep on the first stroke. He grasped my hips from behind and bit the skin on the back of my neck lightly.

When it was over, he stayed inside me, his arms wrapped around me, until I fell asleep.

T HE SUN beamed through the uncovered window in the morning. I stirred and turned over. It took me a moment to remember where I was, and with whom. When my brain emerged from its half-asleep fog and I looked at Alex lying beside me, I felt a wave of bliss run through me, an almost nauseating thrill. I pulled myself close to his sleeping back. He didn't stir. I was happy to have these few moments of being alone but with him at the same time—to process what had happened, to have it all to myself. I let the memories of the night before come flooding in, let them radiate in the places where I felt small and pleasant pains from having had him inside me, from the effort of trying to bring our bodies together as close as we could.

I felt lighter than I had the day before, as though the effort of concealing my desire for Alex had been physically weighing me down and now I had been released from it. I felt cleansed, as if I'd been stripped of everything: defenses, armor, my souring memories of Regan. A new self had emerged in the night. Alex had broken down what was hard in me, my certainty that my inferior beginnings would forever separate me from the best of life, from people like him.

As my mind eased in and out of sleep, I felt him turning over. I moved my arm out of the way and he drew me back in so that my head was on his chest. And with that I was no longer alone in my new reality. I giddily realized that I'd missed him while he slept.

"*Bonjour,*" he said, his voice still raspy with sleep.

I looked up at him and smiled. He was propped up on his elbow now, squinting in the dazzling sunlight.

"*Merde*, that sun is so bright." He pulled himself out from under me to get out of the bed and go to the window. Normally, something about the sight of a naked man performing a manual task was a bit grotesque. But as Alex reached for the window shade, bending as he dragged it down almost to the floor, he remained beautiful, perfect from where I was watching, with a stripe of brown across his lower back where the edge of his swim trunks hid him.

"Much better," he said, looking back over at me with a grin. I was sitting upright with the sheet pulled up over my bare chest. I nodded. He rubbed his eyes in an appealingly childlike way and gazed down at me as if we had a secret, something that didn't need to be said aloud.

"*Comme j'ai faim!* You must be as well, *chérie*. Shall we go downstairs for some breakfast?"

I nodded again. What I wanted was for him to come back to bed. But his momentum told me that wasn't where he was headed. He was hungry, I assured myself, and that was fine. There was no rush now, we'd already crossed over and there was no need to cling to him. We had other moments ahead of us, infinite moments.

"*Bon,*" he said, and headed for the bathroom. He stopped as though he'd just remembered something and stooped down to kiss me, too briefly, on the lips. I smiled and let myself fall back onto the pillow that smelled of him, luxuriously breathing in his scent.

It was later than I'd thought, and by the time Alex and I came down to the kitchen—me following closely and only a little sheepishly at his heels—Sophie and Véronique were moving busily around the kitchen. Grégoire was nowhere to be seen. There was tension in the air that I couldn't quite pinpoint.

"What have we here?" Alex asked.

"Sophie is showing me how to make omelets!" Véronique said. Sophie smiled but didn't look up from her frying pan. I wanted to pull her away so that I could tell her everything, so that I could relive the night once again by recounting the details to my best friend. I had been too unsure about the first kiss, too embarrassed by the night in Paris, but now I had to tell her.

"Fais attention!" Alex came over and put his hands on Sophie's shoulders. "My cousin is very dangerous in the kitchen."

"Stop, you!" Véronique whacked Alex with a dry spatula.

I sat carefully on a stool, drinking coffee out of a wide-brimmed mug that Alex had poured for me. Véronique and Sophie conferred chummily over the frying pan; it was curious to catch the two of them like that. But the scene warmed my heart: Alex, *my* Alex, leaning against the counter sipping coffee and my dearest friends being friendly with each other at the stove, making breakfast for all of us as though we were a little family.

Alex ground some more coffee beans. Despite my best attempts not to, I found myself following him with my eyes.

He glanced over and flashed me a quick grin, which fired up the raw endings of my nerves and went straight to my heart.

"Brooke," Véronique said, "you will be our—*comment dit-on?*—guinea pig!"

Sophie brought the herb omelet over to me and set it down. "Good morning," she said quietly, smiling and looking me in the eye for the first time since we'd come down. I felt a little relieved.

"This omelet is great!" I said after a first, enthusiastic bite. "I didn't even know Sophie was such a good cook!"

"I helped," Véronique said, sticking out her bottom lip.

"Of course, both of you are amazing cooks. Alex doesn't know what he's talking about."

Alex laughed and leaned over to kiss me on the forehead. I blushed and caught Véronique smiling at us.

Once we'd finished our breakfast, Sophie, Véronique, and I took the rest of our coffee out onto the balcony. The soft breeze and the bright sun on the calm ocean seemed to slow time down nearly to a halt, but it was an illusion, as our departure time drew near.

"It's incredible," I said.

Sophie nodded but said nothing.

"I'll never forget this weekend," Véronique said, "first of many, I hope."

꿍

Sophie and I waited until the last possible moment before going upstairs to pack our things. I felt a heaviness in my limbs as I rolled my clothes and put them in my bag, as though my entire body were resisting the idea of leaving.

"I wish we didn't have to go so soon," I said to Sophie as I packed my bag sitting atop my conspicuously still-made bed.

She shot me an enigmatic smile. She'd been quiet all morning, since last night. I had barely been aware of it earlier in my blissed-out state, but now that I was alone in the room with her, it was almost palpable.

"But we'll be back," she said finally.

I nodded, trying to believe it was true. "Right. But for now I will miss it."

She nodded.

"Hey"—I stopped for a moment and stepped toward her—"is everything okay?"

"Of course." Her voice didn't quite convince me. "Just sad to leave, like you said."

⁓§⁓

Sophie insisted I ride in the front with Alex on the way back into Nice. Grégoire was with us as well, having been sent off to town to meet up with a friend who lived in the area. I wondered if he'd done something to offend the volatile Véronique and if he even knew what he'd done to warrant dismissal.

I tried not to stare at Alex as we drove, focusing instead on the scenery, which now felt familiar. He saw me looking over at him once and ever so briefly squeezed my knee.

We dropped Grégoire off first, then headed for the station. Alex parked the car and walked with us to the platform. We all stood still for a moment, bags over our shoulders, people flowing around us. Many unsaid things hung in the air, but I tried to reassure myself that there would be space and time to say them all if I could only be patient.

Alex spoke first. "*Alors*, thank you for coming along this weekend, *les filles*. It was marvelous."

He kissed Sophie first and then me. I waited for him to give me an extra acknowledgment, a quick kiss on the lips or even a meaningful look. But after a simple kiss on the cheek I was watching him walk away, bright and weightless in the early-afternoon sun.

Sophie and I took seats by the window. We sat silently as they called the final all-aboard and the train lurched into motion. As we pulled away from the idyllic town, I thought I could feel the ocean getting farther away and with it Alex, the space between us expanding every second. Sophie gazed out the window, her eyes forlorn. I asked her again if anything was the matter.

She shook her head. "People always think something's wrong with me whenever I'm not talking nonstop. But sometimes I'm just thinking, you know?"

"I know," I said a little defensively. I didn't like being grouped in with "people" as though I didn't really know her. "It just seems like something's on your mind, that's all."

Sophie looked down at her hands and let out a long sigh. "This is going to sound so petty." She was twisting her fingers around each other, interlacing them the way she did when she was anxious.

"Sophie." I put my hand on her knee. I was relieved that I wasn't imagining things or misunderstanding her after all. It was important for me to know that we were as in sync as I'd believed. "Just tell me. You can tell me anything."

She seemed to rally her courage. "I think it's great, you and Alex. It's just that everything's been so wonderful and now . . . I'm afraid it will be different with all of us." She glanced quickly up at me and then out the window. "I guess I just don't want things to change; I know it's selfish."

Did I question her reasoning then? I wouldn't have, because I thought I understood. She worried that Alex and I would retreat to a world of two with no room for her. It was the same thing I had feared.

"Ah." How good it felt to hear her acknowledge the existence of an Alex and me; it was proof that I hadn't imagined the whole thing. "It's not going to change anything, Sophie. I promise you."

"I'm sorry. Should I not have even said anything? Am I being silly?"

She spoke in such a childlike way, how could you suspect her?

"No, I want you to tell me when something is bothering you. But you don't need to worry. It isn't going to be like that, Soph. There will always be room for you."

"Okay." She looked at me now with a peaceful smile and took my hand. *"Je t'aime, chérie."*

"Et toi aussi." I closed my eyes, shielding them from the countryside racing my window.

B Y THE time we got back to Nantes it was dark, and Sophie and I shared a cab back to our home stays. The streets were so quiet that it felt almost as though we were sneaking back into town.

The next morning, I woke up stiff and parched from the long weekend of drinking too much and not sleeping enough. I readied myself for school with a feeling of dread. Now that I was back from Cap Ferrat, nothing stood between me and my impending final exams. My grades in France had been on the bad side of mediocre, and I was trying to convince myself that this didn't matter. I had no plans for graduate school, so what was the point of grinding for grades? But after a lifetime of feeling as if getting anything other than straight A's was a gamble with my future, the habit was difficult to break.

Maximilian was in the kitchen eating cereal when I came in to make myself some toast.

"Bonjour, Maxo." I ruffled his hair.

Nicole came around the corner, taking me a bit by surprise. She was never usually up this early. "Ah, Brooke, I am up way too early this morning for a school meeting. How was your weekend in Cap Ferrat?"

"Very nice, marvelous actually." I stopped for a moment, realizing that I had never used that word before getting to know Alex and Véronique.

"Is your boyfriend rich?" Maximilian asked.

Nicole gasped and swatted the back of his head lightly. "Maxo! That is not polite."

Max gave me a sheepish look.

I laughed. "He is very generous," I said simply, and leaned down to kiss Maximilian's cheek. *"Bonne journée, tout le monde."*

Outside, the weather was warm with just a little breeze. I found myself checking my phone again and again, waiting for something to appear. Alex had my number, and though he didn't normally send me messages or call, I was half expecting to hear from him despite having left only a day ago. Things were different now, weren't they? I resolved not to think about it, which only seemed to further my obsession.

It felt strange to come back to the institute after the weekend away, to return to the kitchen and make the Nescafé as usual. Which one was closer to my real life now? This slightly shabby place full of nondescript Americans, or Cap Ferrat and Alex? The answer, of course, was neither. My *real* life was far away and I would be thrown back into it soon enough. *Actual* reality loomed just on the other side of the dreaded exams, and going home after all this seemed too brutal to contemplate. Just as I was beginning to spiral into these untamed thoughts, I heard Sophie approach, chatting with Adam.

"I am *si jaloux* that you two spent the weekend in Cap Ferrat. I did exactly *nothing* glamorous over my long weekend. *Bonjour,*" he said to me, kissing my cheek. "All I did was study. I must admit I'm a little anxious about the exams."

Sophie and I groaned in unison. Of all the things we

talked about, studies and grades never entered into the conversation. It was as if school were a bit beneath us now. We
preferred to concern ourselves with higher planes of thought:
art and freedom of the spirit. And love. And our perfect,
shining futures.

"You two have been in some kind of alternate universe
with those fancy friends of yours," he said.

"But they're so wonderful," Sophie said. "You should
come out with us the next time we see them."

"Yes! Véronique loved you," I added.

Adam smiled and rolled his eyes. "Only because I told her
she's a good actress. But, okay, *les filles*, let me know."

"Oh, God," Sophie said after he'd walked out, "I really
don't want to think about the exams."

"You'll be fine," I said, believing it for her if not for myself.
Sophie didn't seem to need to study much back at home and
she was a natural with the language.

"No, I won't. I mean, my spoken French has gotten better
and I've been reading a lot. Olivier Cadiot, like Alex told us."

"He didn't tell me that," I said a little too quickly, a little
too sharply.

"Oh, well, anyway. It doesn't even matter probably, right?"
she added unconvincingly, sipping her Nescafé through
tightly pursed lips.

"Tell you what. I don't have any plans this afternoon—
let's go to the park and study for a little while after school.
It's so nice out."

"That's a great idea!" Sophie's eyes lit up. "We can get a
bottle of wine. It'll be like a picnic, a study picnic."

I laughed. "If you think it will help!"

❧

A closet near the back of the institute was full of odds and ends left behind by previous students. Sophie and I found a picnic blanket among the miscellany, then stopped at the Monoprix to pick up a bottle of wine and plastic cups.

"Won't you miss being able to get such good, cheap wine at the grocery store when we go home?" I said as we got in line to check out.

Sophie said nothing but smiled as though she had a secret.

"What?"

She shook her head. "Nothing."

All day since we'd made these plans, I'd felt a small but mounting sense of relief. I'd been worrying about the exams and now I was going to do something about it. I was going to put my head down and focus and it would all be okay. We spread out the blanket on a grassy knoll between two trees. I took a little bite of the Toblerone we'd bought and cracked my heavy textbook to the page I'd marked. Any feelings of calm quickly left me as soon as I began to review the materials and realized I had only a passing familiarity with the information. I looked up at Sophie, who had her books open but was focused on uncorking the wine. The bottle gave a satisfying little pop as the cork came out.

"Here you go." She handed me a plastic cup. She looked calmly back down at her open textbook and sipped her wine. A few more minutes went by.

"Sophie?"

"*Oui, chérie?*"

"I don't know . . . any of this."

She looked up at me, eyes wide, and whispered, "Me neither."

We both suddenly burst into nervous, near-hysterical laughter. We laughed and laughed for a few minutes before either of us could pull it together enough to speak.

"We did *go* to class, right?" she said. "I mean, I seem to remember it."

"Oh, God, Soph," I said, trying to compose myself, "what are we going to do?"

"Have another drink." Sophie held her glass aloft.

"I'm serious. I'm worried I'm going to fail these tests!" I said, a little relieved to admit it aloud.

Sophie swiped her hand in the air as though brushing away the possibility. "You won't *fail*. It's not like the point of being over here was to get perfect grades anyway. I mean, think about it," she said quietly and emphatically. "Who's had an experience like we've had here? It's worth more than grades, you know it is."

I tipped the rest of the wine in my cup down my throat and mulled that over.

"Brooke, what was the point of you coming here if you're going to keep looking at everything just as you did before you left?"

"What does that even mean? I'm just facing reality. You know we have to go back soon. What exactly is the alternative?" I was growing a little irritated now.

"To stay," she said evenly.

"For what, the summer?"

Sophie shrugged. And suddenly I knew that she didn't

mean the summer. I let out a sigh that sounded more exasperated than I meant it to.

"I don't even want to talk about it if you're going to get so angry with me," she said softly.

I sighed. "Sophie, I'm not angry with you. I'm just freaked out about the exams. And I don't think you're being practical. What about school? Volleyball team? Our parents? Any of this ringing a bell?"

"I don't care about any of that anymore. And I don't think you do either; you're just afraid. Why do you immediately assume that staying isn't even possible? Look how good our French is now! We could transfer to the University of Nantes! Or the Sorbonne!"

I looked down at my hands. It was too painful to imagine that staying in France was a real possibility, only to then lose it—which somehow I knew I would. She was right, I was afraid. I knew how easily I could give in to her, to all of it.

"Are you telling me you actually want to go back to California?" I noticed that she didn't refer to it as *home*. "That you want to leave France? Leave Alex?"

I shook my head. "I don't want to leave, no. But at some point we have to face facts. Where would we live, for one thing?"

"Alex would help us. He loves us. He would look out for us. His grandmother wouldn't even notice if we lived in that house! We're there all the time anyway."

I wanted all of this to be true. Looking at Sophie, at the fervor in her eyes, I could see she believed it was. I rubbed my eyes with my thumb and forefinger. The late-afternoon sun was still warm, and more than anything I had the urge to lie down on the picnic blanket and sleep.

"Let's just focus on the test for now, Sophie, can we please?"

"Fine. But I'm going to find a way for us to stay here."

"You do that." I smiled at her.

"I will," she said with a defiant smirk. "And you just need to keep an open mind."

As THE days passed, it began to feel less and less as if my night with Alex had ever happened. I called him late in the week, longing to hear his voice, but was met with his voice mail. I hung up without leaving a message, afraid the desperation would be plain in my voice, trying to comfort myself with the knowledge that he was never one to keep in touch in between the times we saw him. With Regan, I'd always known when I'd see him next, there was never the opportunity for these chasms to open between us. But Alex inhabited the moment he was in or else was just easily distracted. The thought of a vague *someone else* began to materialize in my mind. But it didn't matter. He and I were something, we had something. I knew it in my soul. I told myself the story of us again and again to soothe my troubled mind. I remembered, it seemed, every touch, every point of contact. But as I endlessly replayed these memories, they began to lose the visceral power they once had; they'd become emptier, more like memories of a dream.

I tried to focus on studying and enjoying the time I had left. With its lurching toward the end, each day felt monumental. I tried to memorize everything: the taste of the ham sandwiches, the smell of the aged wood in the house, the way the place Cigale bustled and came alive in the mornings. But Alex was never far from my mind, and I found that I was always either thinking of him or vigilantly trying not to. The elation of remembering his touch alternated with the desperation that I wouldn't see him again. It felt like the heat and chills of a fever.

By the time I did see him again, a week later, I was so consumed with yearning that I felt it bubbling beneath my skin, felt flammable with it.

Sophie told me that he was back in town and that we were meeting him at a bar we liked off the place du Commerce with low lighting and a small, cheap-looking dance floor. When I found out she'd been in touch with him before I had, I felt myself light up with jealousy. Then I reminded myself that while I had been trying to focus on studying for the exams, Sophie had been scheming to stay in France. So I assumed she had called Alex, maybe over and over, the way she did when I didn't answer her calls right away. I was a little mortified to think that she was asking him to help us, but I figured there was no stopping her. Truthfully, it gave me some pleasure to think of her embarrassing herself in front of Alex. She would have to snap out of it when the time came to go home. Yet I had to admit that a small part of me hoped she would come up with a plan so perfect that I would be compelled to relent and stay.

I called my mother after several weeks of delinquency and too-brief e-mails. I could hear the loneliness echoing in her voice, could hear the emptiness of the house around her. She was straining to sound chipper, to transmit only her happiness for me for the experience I was having. She wouldn't admit in a hundred years that she was anxious for me to come home, wouldn't impose that upon me. I could scarcely imagine telling her I was going to stay. But I would leave her someday soon either way, so perhaps it wasn't so much a matter of if as of when.

In the meantime, since returning from Cap Ferrat, I had made some progress with my studies. I had even spent a terrifying twenty minutes after class one day with Adam and our *traduction* professor. We asked Sophie to join us but she declined. In general, I had tried to avoid studying with her after our first less-than-productive session; in any case, she didn't seem very interested. I figured that she was a better student than I was in general and was perhaps expecting to have an easier time with the tests.

I spent a long time getting ready that Friday night. I tried on half my clothes, wishing I had the cash to pop down to the Galeries Lafayette for something new the way Sophie always seemed to be doing. I ended up with a black cotton dress that I'd worn dozens of times but, as far as I could remember, never with Alex. For at least half an hour, I fussed with my hair, without much success. I felt that the first moment he saw me tonight, after this time apart, would be crucial, and I wanted this vision of me to be an improvement on whatever impression he'd been left with. I had to move a step beyond the girl he hadn't thought to call since we'd slept together. I promised myself I wouldn't ask him why he hadn't called, wouldn't even acknowledge that I'd noticed. Let him think I had distractions, even other men.

As I'd planned, I arrived a little bit late, trying to cultivate a breeziness that I didn't actually feel. Véronique was habitually late, and I'd told Sophie I would meet her at the bar, so I headed upstairs and searched the empty couches. I heard Sophie's laugh, high and bright as it echoed through the space, then spotted Alex leaning forward on his knees, listening intently to Sophie chattering and twisting her long hair around her fingers as she sat angled toward him. She was wearing a frothy, embroidered white dress that nipped in at her narrow waist and splashed out over her tanned legs. As she leaned toward him, her breasts strained against the scooped neckline. I froze for a moment as I saw Alex reaching out to Sophie. He brushed something from her cheek, an eyelash maybe, and his fingers lingered there for an excruciatingly tender moment. What was I seeing?

They saw me just as I was approaching. Sophie shot out of her chair, startled, and put her arms around me as if she hadn't seen me in ages, though it'd only been several hours since we'd been at school together.

Alex stood and kissed my cheeks. I looked at him for a moment as we both stood there. He gave me a searching gaze, then sat down and promptly pulled me onto his lap. So it had been nothing. Or was this now a flurry of overcompensation?

"Sophie and I were just discussing how you plan to move here and be French forever," he said, sounding amused.

I blushed and held my hands up to indicate that I knew nothing about Sophie's scheme, then laughed and was embarrassed by how giddy I sounded. To feel the warmth of Alex's body next to mine brought the memory of being with him rushing back through my every nerve, obliterating every other thought. I let my fingers curl around his shoulder, and he looked up at me warmly. Maybe we could stay in France. I felt as if the blood were draining from my brain, heading elsewhere.

"Merde," Alex said, "this waitress is terrible! I am going to get us a bottle of wine and bring it over myself."

Reluctantly, I got up from his lap and moved to the seat next to Sophie.

"What have you been up to?" I asked, narrowing my eyes, meaning several different things at once.

She shrugged and smiled innocently. "I told you I would find us a way. Alex has been saying all along that we could stay with him in Cap Ferrat for the summer. I don't know why you refuse to take him seriously. You should just have some faith in people, Brooke, faith that things can all work out for the best."

"Easy for you to say." I stared fixedly at the rapidly filling bar.

"What's that supposed to mean?"

I was growing weary of her defensiveness. I knew that she had her own struggles, but I thought she was too smart to be so blissfully unaware that not everyone moved throughout the world with the same freedom that she did. Money was among the things that never seemed to concern her, and I wondered what that must be like. Her parents must have been keeping a steady cash flow going to her while she'd been here. She never seemed to want for it, insisting that we go out to eat and then blithely paying the whole bill, showing up with adorable new dresses all the time. Nor did she seem to have any concerns about being cut off.

"It isn't just the question of where we'd live or go to school. I have to work during the summers, Soph." It embarrassed me to have to point this out to her. I got the feeling that it some- how embarrassed her as well. She was quiet for a moment.

"I bet Alex could help find you a job. Maybe at that café where he knew the owner! Think of how much money you could make in tips from all those rich tourists," she said excitedly.

"Maybe," I said, a little touched by her enthusiasm. Maybe, maybe.

Alex returned looking exasperated. "The service is terrible at this place, *les filles*, I don't know why you come here. Let's get some dinner at La Cigale and then go back to the house."

Véronique met us at La Cigale. When she arrived, she looked rather relaxed for someone who was running so late.

"Where have you been, *ma chère cousine*?" Alex asked.

Véronique smiled and lightly flipped her hair over her shoulder. "I was seeing Jean-Marc and I forgot the time."

Jean-Marc, I thought, smiling at Véronique, who could even keep track?

The waiter came to the table and Alex ordered champagne.

"What's the occasion?" I asked.

"Why, don't you know, *chérie*?" he said. "It's a toast to you and Sophie, who are never leaving France."

Véronique looked intrigued. *"Ah, oui, c'est vrai?* When was this decided?"

The waiter arrived nearly instantaneously with the champagne. I was aware from his demeanor that he was familiar with the de Persauds.

"It was always decided," Alex said slyly, "only the girls have just realized that this is their fate. And you cannot fight fate, isn't that right, *chérie*?" He leaned over and squeezed my knee under the table. Smiling at him, I felt jumpy and short of breath at his nearness. After my first glass of champagne I felt sure he was right; it was fate and I should just let go. What was the worst that could happen? That I would lose a year in school? It could surely be made up. People did this. I didn't always have to be responsible. And with another summer, another year, what Alex and I had together could only grow stronger. We could finally spend some real time together without my departure looming.

"That's marvelous!" Véronique said.

"Véronique, you must come to Cap Ferrat too!" Sophie's voice was so buoyant it seemed to be coming from above our heads.

Véronique sipped her champagne with a little smile. "Well, yes, of course. *Merci bien*, Sophie, for the invitation."

After a tiny but certain pause, all four of us laughed, assuredly for four wholly different reasons. I suddenly worried a little for Sophie.

"I am so happy that we don't have to say goodbye to our American friends, Alex," Véronique said.

"Yes," Alex said, again looking at me across the table, *"on a de la chance."*

It was I who couldn't believe our luck.

We ate oysters and steak and went through the champagne and two more bottles of wine. Véronique regaled us with stories of her favorite pastimes on the Mediterranean: sailing and sunning and a nightclub in a cave that we simply had to visit. Suddenly, the exams and schoolwork that had so preoccupied me, along with my worries about my mother, had disappeared as though they'd never been. I was back under the spell without knowing it was a spell. It not only all seemed possible, but likely. Certain. Fated. All I needed, all I desired, was here with me at this table.

❧

Back at the house, Alex's mother was nowhere to be seen.

"Back to *la campagne*," Alex said when Sophie asked him where she'd gone.

We returned to the atrium and took off our shoes. The tile was still warmed from the late-spring sun that had beaten down on it all day. To be in this room again—this room designed to remind Virginie of her beloved Cap Ferrat house that she would likely never see again—made me slip one degree further away from the world I'd once thought myself so chained to. I allowed myself the fatal thought that only someone in such a malleable state could believe: maybe I did belong here after all.

Other people came, including Véronique's friend from all those months ago. How could I ever have thought she was a threat? She seemed like such a silly thing now.

"What ever happened with Grégoire in Cap Ferrat?" I asked Véronique when it seemed obvious that he wasn't going to show up.

Véronique huffed, "He doesn't understand me!"

"In what way?"

"People like him never understand anyone with artistic ambitions. He's too political. Fucking Marxist."

I nodded as if I knew the type, though I didn't. "Sorry about him. You should be with someone who gets you."

She looked at me. "You know something about that these days, do you?"

I blushed. "So you know?"

"Of course I know. *Chérie*, it's obvious." She smiled broadly. "Speak of the devil, where has he gone?"

I looked around, and as she said, Alex was nowhere in sight. Sophie was also missing. I felt a momentary lurch of panic but then reminded myself how unnecessarily worked up I'd gotten when I'd woken up on the couch in Cap Ferrat, how silly I'd felt when I'd found Sophie lying in her bed alone, innocent. And it was doubly unlikely—impossible even—now that Alex and I had actually slept together, now that we weren't merely theoretical.

I told Véronique I would be back and wandered into the corridor. Met with the silence of the hallway, I realized I didn't have much of a plan, and I'd had a lot of wine: a bad combination. Plus, I didn't know my way around the house as well as one would think for all the time I'd spent there. Despite its tidy appearance from the outside, it was vast and confusing inside, and my visits had mostly been confined to a few of the rooms in the house: the atrium, the dining room, and of course Alex's darkroom. I understood that there would always be parts of this house that I wasn't meant to see, wasn't meant to know, and it felt like a transgression to be outside the rooms where I knew I was welcome.

I heard a voice from a few feet away expressing alarm at the sight of me. I looked up to see Virginie standing two doors down, clinging to the doorframe and looking startled, frightened even. She was in a long nightgown that covered her frail arms down to her wrists, and her white hair was flowing loose around her shoulders. I had never seen her like this, for whenever she'd spent time with us, she'd always been made up and coiffed, her hair pulled back and pinned. I'd never realized it was so long.

"I'm so sorry, Madame de Persaud," I said, coming a little nearer, then stopping in my tracks when I saw that she was recoiling.

"Who are you?" she demanded.

"I'm Brooke," I said dumbly. Sometimes she had seemed to remember me, but perhaps she was only ever playing along, and she would naturally drop the pretense when caught alone in the night.

"What are you doing here? Why are you in my home?"

My heartbeat sped up as though I were actually an intruder and not an invited guest. "Alex," I stammered, "I'm a friend of Alex's."

She looked none too relieved. I hoped that I was not going to find myself in the awkward position of explaining who her grandson was.

"Then why aren't you with him, young lady? You shouldn't just go wandering around people's houses. You shouldn't be here."

"I'm very sorry," I said, backing away. "I was trying to find him and I got lost." I smiled at her weakly. *Bonne nuit, madame,*" I said as I walked away. She didn't go back into her room until I had left the corridor, and I could feel her eyes on me as I retreated.

I felt as if I might burst into tears. What a sad creature I was, drunk and wandering around a house where I didn't belong, looking forlornly for my disappeared Alex and my erstwhile best friend, startling old ladies in the middle of the night. I made my way downstairs to the empty kitchen to compose myself. All I could hear was an echo of the din from the atrium. Of all the things one could say about the rooms in this beautiful old house, they were far from soundproof. The door that led down to the wine cellar and Alex's darkroom was open, and when I crept toward it, I could hear muffled voices from below.

I tiptoed down the stairs. My heart sank as Sophie's sudden laughter rang through the passageway. Putting one foot in front of the other, I prepared myself for whatever might meet me at the bottom.

Their backs were to me and I was able to watch them for a moment before they were aware of my presence. They stood innocently side by side with no part of their bodies touching or intertwined as I'd envisioned. I was paranoid, I told myself, I was the bad friend for being so suspicious.

"Brooke!" Sophie said, turning around as though hearing the sound of my heavy thoughts out of the thin, stale air.

"I was showing Sophie some of the pictures from Cap Ferrat. Come and see." Alex held his hand out to me. I smiled and folded myself under the shelter of his arm. It was as though they'd told me to meet them here, so unsurprised were they to see me, as sure a sign of pure intentions as I could imagine.

I glanced down at the photo that Sophie was holding; she was looking into it searchingly as though trying to place the person in it.

"Let me see," I said gently. She handed it over. It was a picture of her, standing in the ocean with the water up to her waist. She was looking back over her shoulder, her face in profile, nearly obscured, her wet hair splayed over her bare shoulders. I vaguely recalled that Alex had had his camera with him that night, but then didn't he always? He was surreptitious; his gift required stealth and trust, a talent for both disarming and disrobing his subjects. Sophie looked, if possible, even more perfect in this picture than she did in real life. I glanced at her standing next to me, and she too appeared transfixed by this image of herself. And I knew, of all the things about Alex that made him desirable, the eyes through which he showed you yourself—a self perfected, a self that he made you certain you could be, perhaps even were already—was the most seductive.

"Beautiful," I said. We all stood there quietly for another moment.

"We should probably go back upstairs, *les filles*," Alex said, "before Véronique's friends start stealing the silverware."

Our footsteps echoed throughout the empty house. When we were back in the atrium and had refilled our wineglasses, Alex went over to comfort Véronique, as it seemed something in her night had gone wrong and she appeared on the verge of tears. I sat quietly with Sophie on the bench, waiting for her to say something, and at last she did.

"He's so incredible," she said dreamily, her eyes flashing quickly over to Alex and then down into her glass, "as a photographer, I mean." She looked over at me and smiled.

I smiled back cautiously. "Yes, he is. He has a gift."

"I've never really seen any of his photographs before tonight. I don't quite know how to describe it. It's as if it's more than an image, it's like he . . ."

"Really sees you."

"Yes! It's like you look at one of his pictures and you feel understood."

We were both quiet for a moment, considering this.

"I don't think I could ever do what he does," she said.

"What do you mean?"

"With my art. Make someone feel like that, like they're more understood. That's what good art does, doesn't it? I don't think my paintings have that, I think they're empty." Sophie looked desolate.

"I'm sure they're wonderful." I cringed at how false this sounded, despite my good intentions. "If you'd ever let me see them."

"Like you ever let me read your stories."

"Point taken. But you know we just have to keep working on it. Maybe Alex wasn't any good when he was our age either."

"I bet he was. I bet he was always good."

"Well, we'll have lots of time to learn from him." The wine had gone to my head and I'd decided we could stay.

Her face finally perked up. "Don't say we'll stay if you don't mean it, Brooke. I want to so much."

"I do mean it," I said quietly, feeling once the words were out that it must be true.

Sophie took my hand and squeezed it. "I just want us all to be together. I don't want it to end."

"Come on." I stood up and pulled her by the hand. "Let's see what's going on with Alex and Véronique."

"Brooke!" Véronique said as we approached.

"Yes, *chérie*?"

"Come outside with me. I need a cigarette and some air."

I smiled a little at the contradiction, then briefly locked eyes with Alex and felt something pop in the air between us.

I wanted so much to move the night forward to when I could climb in bed next to him, feel his skin on mine, but it seemed as if I'd been waiting forever, so what was another hour? I followed Véronique around the shrubbery to the almost-hidden door that led to a small balcony overlooking a side street.

She pulled her cigarette case from her pocket, drew two out with her delicate fingers, and handed me one.

"Is everything all right?" I asked finally when she had taken her first drag and had still said nothing.

She sighed. "I just had to get out of there for a little while. I was going crazy. You three left me alone with all of Alex's horrible friends."

"He said they were your friends."

She shook her head. "See, he probably doesn't even remember where he met them. He picks up strays everywhere he goes."

I blanched a little at this, but Véronique had introduced us to Alex, so she couldn't mean us.

"Anyway, I told him to make everyone leave. I thought if we came out here, no one could blame me. He always makes me look like the one who isn't any fun. I swear, sometimes I feel like I'm the older cousin."

"I could see that."

Véronique leaned in and nudged me. "I'm glad you're staying, I would really miss you."

"Me too."

"Alex would also."

I raised my eyebrows at her. "He is something, your cousin."

"Oh, yes, he means well. He just doesn't live on the same

planet as the rest of us most of the time. But some people are just that way, the rules do not apply."

I nodded.

"Your friend Sophie is growing on me," Véronique said after a pause. "I'll admit I thought she was a little silly when I first met the two of you. Head in the clouds, as they say, such a California girl. But she's smart, just not very serious. You and I are a little serious."

I laughed. I wanted Véronique to like Sophie, as I wanted Alex to like her. So long as each of them preferred me. "Sophie also doesn't always live on the same planet, but . . ."

"She means well?" Véronique said, stubbing her cigarette on the railing.

"*Exact*. So you want to tell me about this Jean-Marc?"

She smiled in the way one smiles when one absolutely cannot help oneself, with her whole face, her whole body. "He is a very wonderful man but there is the small issue of a wife."

"The issue being that he has one?" I said with a little chuckle.

"Perhaps. Though he says he's not happy with her. But I don't want him to leave her or he'd start acting like all of the rest of my boyfriends. Always around."

"Wouldn't want that. But I'm in no position to judge you. The heart wants what it wants, I guess."

"And wants nothing more than what it can't have," she said as I nodded. "Maybe when we're older, we'll understand how to have something and love it all at the same time. Really have something I mean, not just for a night or, in my case, an afternoon."

"Maybe. Maybe sooner than we think."

We lingered on the balcony a little longer. The street below us was empty and it suddenly felt late.

"What do you think?" I asked. "Safe to go back inside?"

Véronique nodded. "He'd better have gotten rid of them. If he's back in there chatting and drinking . . ."

We moved back through the foliage into the main room, ducking under palm leaves. The detritus of the party remained—the full ashtrays and empty wineglasses—but all of the guests had gone. Sophie and Alex were gone as well. I surveyed the room as though in the midst of a crime scene.

"Well, Alex did his job"—my voice was overly bright, a little shrill—"everyone is gone. I didn't think he'd send Sophie home as well, though."

I watched Véronique carefully for a reaction. She was hugging her arms to her chest as though cold. She didn't look me in the eye as she walked slowly to the table where her handbag was. "Poor Magdalena, look at this mess."

"Should we clean up a bit?"

"*Mais non.* Of course not. She hates me anyway."

I waited, rooted in the spot where I was standing, expecting Alex and Sophie to reemerge. They could be in the darkroom again, I thought, my mind pushing up against its own walls.

"Maybe they've gone downstairs to get something to eat," Véronique said softly.

We walked silently down the stairs into the dark kitchen, then stood there for a moment, their palpable absence surrounding us.

"Let's get a taxi," Véronique said finally.

I couldn't move. The image of him brushing her cheek caught in my mind, stubborn as a burr.

"They could be anywhere," Véronique said gently, "you know how Alex is, he might have suddenly decided that he needs to show Sophie what the power station looks like in the moonlight. He does these things, Brooke."

Nodding helplessly, I followed Véronique out the door and into the quiet night. We walked to the corner without speaking and hailed a cab. The buildings went by in a blur as we headed down familiar streets; my mind and body reeled from the wine, the adrenaline of my suspicions, my pent-up and unresolved desires.

When we pulled up outside my host family's house, Véronique finally spoke. "Don't worry." She leaned over to kiss my cheeks. "It will be fine."

I smiled weakly at her. As soon as I was alone in my room, I sent Sophie an SMS asking where she was. It was after two in the morning.

I opened my window to let the cool night breeze into my stuffy bedroom, then checked my phone once more. Nothing. My situation seemed unimaginable, so much so that I felt I couldn't really be in it, that if I went to sleep, I would wake to a different reality from the one I was now in.

I pulled back the covers and got in bed, repeating to myself again and again the futile phrase *It will be fine. It will be fine.*

I WOKE TO my alarm blaring in my ear after a brief and fitful sleep. I had forgotten to turn it off for the weekend. As my mind first surfaced from my dreams, I was blissfully untethered from reality. Then slowly the facts came back to me in all of their pernicious detail, ending with me in my bed alone and the whereabouts of Sophie and Alex unknown.

I rolled over, wanting to go back to sleep in hopes of waking to some different outcome, to something other than this terrible uncertainty. I looked at my phone, but there were no messages. It was too early to get out of bed on a Saturday, but I didn't feel as if I could fall back asleep. The house was oddly quiet, and then I remembered that Pierre was away on business and Nicole had taken the children to see their grandmother in La Baule for the weekend. It was a small mercy to have the house to myself. I lay there for perhaps another hour on the drowsy threshold of sleep but unable to give myself over to it. Best to get up, I decided, drink some coffee, and figure out what to do. My legs and arms felt leaden, as though they had registered and physically manifested my despair.

The morning was warm but cloudy and the air heavy with humidity. It was going to rain at some point today. You could feel the moisture gathering. I ground some coffee and put it in the press, staring out the window as the teakettle heated up. Suddenly, I heard my phone ding.

Sophie had sent me an SMS. My hands shook as I opened it.

Hi! Just saw your message. What are you doing? Come meet us for breakfast!

The teakettle screamed and it startled me so much that I dropped my phone. I bent down to the linoleum to pick it up: there was a tiny dent but it was otherwise unharmed. I put it carefully on the small kitchen table and went to pour the boiling water into the press.

Us.

Surely Sophie wouldn't be inviting me to come and join her and Alex for a postcoital breakfast? It was beyond the realm of reason. You do not betray someone and then cavalierly invite them to breakfast. So she must be at home; she must have gone home after all.

I sat down and sent Sophie an SMS: *Where are you????*

I repeated my text, my heart now pounding: *Where are you?*

The de Persauds.

Putting my phone down, I steadied myself with one hand on the table; her words had a dizzying effect. My phone beeped again after a few seconds. I stared at it for a moment before reaching out to pick it up and read her message.

Come over! I'm making breakfast!

I walked to the counter on shaky legs. I pressed my coffee down, watched the liquid go jet-black, then sat at the table and stared at my phone. *Maybe,* I thought, and stopped. What could I even tell myself now?

Suddenly my phone rang. The noise filled the room, the

whole house. It was Sophie calling, and when I didn't answer, she called again.

Why aren't you answering?? What's wrong??

An odd and sudden calm came over me; the thing I had feared all this time had finally happened. Had the fear been worse or the thing itself? It would certainly be the latter, but just then I felt only numb. Dazed, I looked down at my phone, which was ringing again, then leaned forward and turned it off. I refilled my coffee cup and went out into the backyard, wearing only my sweatpants and a thin T-shirt. I sat on the back step and pulled my knees in close to my chest.

I felt a deep unease, as though I were still in the stages of uncertainty, as though I still suffered only from the fear that this thing had happened instead of the knowing it had. And as I sat there, I could feel my future slipping away, the summer in Cap Ferrat, Alex, Sophie. And so another fear was confirmed, that none of it had ever been quite real, that none of it was really mine to have or lose. I saw what would happen now: I would call my mother later that day, burst into tears, and tell her it was just homesickness. I would take my exams. I would get on my flight in two weeks and go home, as it had always been my destiny to do.

Some tiny, desperate part of me wanted to believe there was an alternative to all of this, an alternative in which Sophie had a reasonable explanation, but I knew in my heart the truth, the terrible, inevitable reality. His fingers on her cheek. Sophie's odd behavior that morning in Cap Ferrat.

Sometime later there was a knock on the door. At first I ignored it, thinking whoever was knocking was looking for the family, and I didn't feel like explaining that they were gone. It was convenient, this city house with no car in the driveway to betray your presence. But the knocking persisted, became more urgent. And, of course, it wasn't for the family.

She was standing there with an anxious smile when I opened the door. The sight of her made me queasy with the dueling instincts of wanting to shut the door and wanting to tear her to pieces.

"Brooke! I was about to send out the gendarmes! Why aren't you answering your phone?" Her eyes looked frantic. Though I felt actual, visceral pain at the sight of her, the street was no place for this discussion.

"Come in." I closed the door behind her, staring all the while at the floor, unable to look her in the face. I walked silently around her—studiously avoiding any contact—through the kitchen and back out onto the porch. I returned to where I'd been sitting and stared up into the branches of the trees. How could I look at her? She wasn't the Sophie I'd known, not the Sophie in my head and in my heart. Not my Sophie who loved me and whom I loved. Had she ever been?

"Brooke, what's wrong? What's happened? Did you get bad news?" Sophie sat beside me and put a hand on my knee. I froze and briefly stared at the audacious hand before shrugging it off and turning to face her. There was, I saw, no other way to have this conversation than in plain, frank language.

"Sophie," I said, bravely now, looking her in the eyes— those eyes I thought I'd known—"did you or did you not stay at Alex's last night?"

Her surprise appeared genuine. "That's why you're upset?" She blinked at me.

"Just answer the question." I looked away from her, unable to sustain eye contact.

"Well, yeah, I did but . . ."

"And you slept with him?" The words burned my tongue.

She paused for a moment, and from the corner of my eye I could see her whole body go rigid. "Brooke . . ."

I got up from my seat and walked down onto the lawn, unable to stand being so close to her. I raked my fingers through my hair. My hands needed to be occupied, to be restrained from what they might otherwise do.

"Brooke, I don't understand why you're so upset. It isn't like that. You know I would never do anything to hurt you!"

She was standing now too, a few paces from me in the yard as though we were preparing for a duel. Who was this girl? She looked so much like my friend. She looked so much like someone I trusted.

"That doesn't even make sense, Sophie! Those phrases together don't make any sense! How did you think it wouldn't hurt me?" I was aware that the neighbors could hear us and I didn't care.

"Because I just thought we were beyond this. We're not like everyone else, Brooke! Don't you know that? Don't you see that? I wanted to be free like you are, like Alex is. I thought it was something we could share, all of us. You said there would always be room for me." She was gesturing wildly and her eyes were lit up like a zealot's.

I felt a series of tiny implosions in my mind and heart, a swift collapsing. Her face was earnest, a mask of innocence.

She believed what she was saying, but how? Had Sophie made her world so small that only we three were in it now? That the distinction of who was a friend and who was a lover no longer even mattered? Had she just decided to rewrite all of the rules and expected me to follow along? Impossible. Yet the tiniest part of me saw a glimmer of reason in it all. Didn't I want both of them too?

"You thought we could share Alex? You cannot be serious." My voice was quiet with rage. What I really meant was *How could you make me compete with you?* Because that was the truly cruel part of what she'd done.

She looked down at her hands, fingers twisting around each other.

"He said it would be all right. I was worried, but he said it would be all right." She spoke directly to the ground, suddenly childlike.

Only now did it occur to me that Sophie wasn't the only one who'd betrayed me, but Alex as well. My anger doubled accordingly. Did he not think he owed me anything? Not even the decency not to sleep with my best friend?

"Oh, he said that, did he? I *wonder* what his motivation could have been. I refuse to believe that you're this naive, Sophie. And after all your talk about how sex should be special."

"It was special," she said, landing the blow.

I took a few steps away from her, back toward the house. "I really didn't need to hear that," I called over my shoulder. I had to get away from her just then.

"It was special because of our time all together, because of the three of us."

"Stop, Sophie. Just stop." My tears came suddenly, the anesthesia of the shock wearing off at last. I choked them back and turned toward her. "We are not some bohemian artists, Sophie, this is not a ménage à trois. We are Americans and you've slept with the man your best friend is in love with. Stop trying to make this something else. You know what I think? That you just have to have *everything*. It's not enough that you're beautiful and rich. You couldn't stand to just let me have this one thing! This *one thing*."

She looked at me as if I'd slapped her. "You never said you were in love with Alex," she said quietly, carefully.

"I did, Sophie. On the train to Cap Ferrat. Is that really your excuse?" My voice was shrill and I was nearly screaming.

"No! It's just that it didn't get through to me. I'm so sorry, Brooke, you have to believe me that I wouldn't have done it if I'd known. I only thought . . ."

I said nothing, just shook my head. I wished so much that I weren't crying.

We stood for another couple of minutes without saying anything.

"You should go," I finally told her.

"I can't leave it like this, Brooke." She came over to me and reached out to touch my shoulder. "Please say you can forgive me." She had begun to cry as well. "You're my best friend in the world. I won't even so much as talk to Alex ever again if you don't want me to. I won't look at him!"

"I don't see what good that would do," I said, shrugging her off.

"Then tell me what I can do, tell me anything. You're the one I care about, the one I love." Her voice rose in octaves of increasing desperation, her fingers clawed at the fabric of my T-shirt.

I shook my head again and walked back into the house. She followed me through the corridor to the front door.

I drew close to the doorframe to let her pass, and when she was safely outside, I looked at her again.

"Brooke . . ."

"Sophie, I just need you to go right now. I need some time."

She gazed at me plaintively.

"I'll speak to you Monday," I said, my voice a little softer now.

Sophie relented and took a couple of slow steps toward the street. "I'm so sorry, Brooke. So very sorry."

I nodded once, looking down at the pavement, and said nothing. Then I closed the door.

I DIDN'T EMERGE from the house for the rest of the weekend. Normally I was careful about how much of the family's food I ate, but unable to face the prospect of going to the store, I took liberties. I gave myself over completely to my anxiety about our upcoming final exams—this being far preferable to whatever else I'd be feeling if I let myself—and buried myself in studying, taking breaks only to eat and watch a couple of badly dubbed American movies that the family had on DVD.

I heard nothing from Alex but had an SMS from Véronique on Saturday asking if I was okay. I stared at the message for a long time, wondering how on earth to answer that question. I wondered whether to tell Véronique the whole story but decided I couldn't face it. It would somehow be that much more true if someone else knew. I lied and said I was fine but busy studying: a half-truth. Somehow I knew that I wasn't going to see Alex again, that he would remove himself from the picture, leaving Sophie and me to deal with the wreckage. I had the miserable realization that Sophie and I were probably just two of many. I thought obsessively about Alex's and my night together, but now with the melancholy realization that it had always been doomed, that there wouldn't be another one like it.

At night I couldn't keep imagined scenes of Sophie and

Alex together out of my head. Along with these troubled fantasies came an insidious sense that it was somehow partially my fault, that I had let this happen. How many times had I almost told Sophie my feelings for Alex? And why didn't I? In plain English, not as a part of some fantasy future that we were spinning, not in a theoretical, faraway time, but now, in this instant. How hard would it have been, really?

That didn't mean she wasn't at fault for sleeping with him—there was no way to play the facts to leave her without culpability—but what if it all could have been prevented by my having had the courage to say the words? I wanted not to forgive Sophie for what she'd done but instead for it never to have happened. I wanted to have never seen her weakness, to have never known that she was capable of this. I wanted to not have to think of him comparing the two of us: the shapes of us, the sounds we made, our scents. I could have told her on the train to Cap Ferrat, going or coming, and we wouldn't be in this mess. Maybe we'd be spending the summer there as we'd planned.

It wasn't that Alex had broken us up but that we were all intertwined. He was between us, and I between them, and Sophie between him and me. It was all just impossible.

I had tidied the house and positioned myself in front of my desk when Nicole and the kids came home from La Baule. I heard the happy noises of their return, the house coming alive with its inhabitants, and I felt a wave of wanting to be home. For the first time since I'd arrived in France, I thought longingly of California. I yearned suddenly for the quiet evenings when my mother and I would sit on the porch with our tea, making believe that we were somewhere other than a dried-out street in Chino; even the thought of that sorry cul-de-sac was comforting. My former life had been remote and unappealing, but now I saw that I was only ever on sabbatical; my future was entirely nebulous.

◦§◦

I skipped the train that Monday morning and walked the long way to the institute. The morning was bright and warm with no clouds in the sky. The schoolchildren in their uniforms walking in lines were louder and more squirrelly than usual. It's the sunshine, I thought, smiling for the first time in days, they know the jig is just about up. I found myself full of nervous energy, knowing that I had to see Sophie.

I wanted to be able to coolly look at the facts, to say that all that mattered was that she'd slept with Alex. But part of me knew that it wasn't quite so simple, that in the context of the past few months it could never be so black-and-white. There was a world that only she and I now lived in—a world that we shared with neither Véronique and Alex nor the other Americans. We had been making up the rules as we went, but she had pushed it too far, and her vision of what we could be to each other had become too elastic. She'd gone somewhere I couldn't follow. And now, most painfully, I knew I'd never be like her.

What I feared most was her pleading. I loved her and she'd hurt me. To beg for my forgiveness seemed to be requesting a shortcut. What had happened couldn't be undone or minimized, I wouldn't allow it. Yet we would always be bound together in this hellish threesome. I could never be alone with Alex again as I could never be alone with her again. The other would always be present.

When I arrived at the school, I went into the kitchen. To my relief Adam was there, and to my greater relief he was filling a French press with hot water. I felt myself dragging with exhaustion, the stress having burned through all of my energy reserves.

"Bonjour, belle fille!" he said. I went to him and kissed his cheek. It filled me with a strange regret to see him. I suddenly wished I'd spent more time with him, wished I hadn't depended so much on my friendship with Sophie. Then maybe I wouldn't feel so alone right now.

"What have we here?" I asked, leaning my head up against his shoulder for a soothing moment.

"Can you believe? I found this in the closet of lost things. I cleaned it up and *voilà*! Too bad I didn't find it earlier." He looked down at me then and perhaps noticed my dark circles. "I thought maybe we could all do with some real coffee today."

He pulled two mugs out of the cabinet for us. "So, I heard a rumor that you're staying the summer with your beau."

Though it hurt to hear Adam call him that, I figured it would have been worse to hear Alex's name. I looked at the ground and shuffled my feet a little. "No, no, we got a little carried away after a few too many glasses of *vin rouge* is all and began planning our lives as expats. But it's the real world for me, I'm afraid I'll have to go back to my summer job after all."

He shrugged. "*C'est la vie.* Maybe you can come back and visit someday when—" He stopped abruptly. "Good morning, dear," he said over my shoulder. I turned around to see Sophie lingering in the doorway. "Would you like some coffee? I made some good stuff, not that *dégoûtant* Nescafé."

Sophie nodded and walked cautiously over to where we were standing. Her eyes flickered back and forth from the coffee to me as though gauging whether I was going to allow her to come any closer.

"Good morning," I said coolly.

"Good morning."

We caught eyes for a brief moment; hers were puffy underneath her makeup, her lashes spiking out from raw-looking lids. I looked away.

"Well, I'm going to get some time in the *salle d'ordinateurs* before it fills up." Adam blew us a kiss over his shoulder. "See you later, *les filles.*"

We stood there silently as Sophie poured herself some coffee. From the corner of my eye, I could see her hand—or was it her whole body?—shaking.

"It's almost time for class," I said, glancing up at the clock. Mostly I just didn't want to be in this small space alone with her; it felt suffocating.

"Brooke"—she lightly touched my arm as I went to leave, her voice raspy—"can I please talk to you?"

"Later," I said as gently as I could, "we can talk after class, okay?"

"I have class at the university this morning. Should I just come back here after that?" Her voice wavered as though she feared I'd change my mind.

"If you want." I shrugged. "Or we can talk later."

"No, I'll meet you," she said quickly.

∽∾

We met at our favorite sandwich shop to pick up lunch. The bread was warm and slathered with butter as always, the woman smiled imperceptibly when she thought you weren't looking as always, but it all suddenly felt alien and it made me indescribably sad. We ate the sandwiches walking through the park, and for a while we said nothing.

"I don't want to just keep saying I'm sorry," Sophie said, "because I know it probably sounds empty. That you don't believe me."

I sighed and kicked at a small stone. "It's not that I don't believe you're sorry . . . I know you are. But, no, you don't need to keep saying it."

We took slow, quiet steps and I bit into my sandwich. We'd been in this park a hundred times. Everything was the same and yet everything *felt* different. It was as though I'd discovered that I was on a film set after having believed all this time that it was real.

"I just feel like I've ruined everything." Her voice caught. "Part of me wishes you would just scream at me and call me a whore or something."

I laughed a little ruefully. "I'm not going to do that." I understood what she meant. I was angry, yes, but it waxed and waned, and in between I slipped into something that felt far worse. There had been a seismic shift between Sophie and me, and fury seemed preferable to the bleak new reality: that our friendship might be beyond repair.

"I know," she said, "because you're a good friend and you're too nice to say something like that."

I bristled at the words *too nice*; it didn't seem to me to be complimentary, it implied that I was someone who could be taken advantage of. She couldn't really think it was so simple, could she?

"I just—" She stopped, choked by tears. "I don't know what to do to make it right. You know I'd do *anything*. Whatever you ask, name it! I don't care about anything else, only you."

Her eyes were wide and her fingers curled around her uneaten sandwich, as though she were trying to strangle it to death. She raked her free hand through her hair. I leaned subtly away from her; she seemed to be almost vibrating, to be giving off heat. I couldn't bear to look at her.

Take me back, I thought, take us both back to the train, let us start this over again. Let me never have to think of his hands on you, of him admiring your naked body, of what he might have said to you, of its all having been so close together: me and him, you and him. Let me never have to relive that night when I knew you'd gone off with him. Let me never have to know what that feels like.

"There's nothing you can do, Sophie," I said finally. Perversely I felt a fleeting desire to comfort her, and this in turn made me angry. I have cried too, I wanted to tell her, but not to you, not anymore. This would likely have hurt her most of all. We stood there for a moment, conscious perhaps that we'd reached the middle of the park and that we had to come to some sort of resolution before we reached the other end.

"I need you to understand the way I saw it." Her voice shook. "I thought that we would share him like we've shared everything, that we would laugh about it and it would be just one more part of this whole experience. After you slept with him, I just thought it would be okay. I see now how stupid that was. I know I don't have any right to ask you for anything, but do you think you can ever forgive me?" Turning away, she stared at the ground. "I need you to forgive me."

She clutched at my hand so suddenly that it caught me off guard. Almost on impulse, I squeezed her hand and then quickly dropped it.

"It's not that I can't forgive you," I said softly, although as the words left my mouth I wasn't so certain, "but it doesn't make it all go away."

She looked up and gave me a small nod, trying to compose herself. I could hear her ragged breath, she seemed to be trying to slow it down without much success. Her hands clenched and unclenched into fists by her sides.

We began to walk again.

"Can we ever . . . " she started to say, then exhaled as though gathering her nerve. "Do you think we can ever be friends again? Like we were, I mean."

I was silent. The answer was something I didn't want to acknowledge any more than she did. What's done is done. What's marked can never be unmarked. All you can hope is for the mark to fade, but it can never be pure again. I would never again have a friendship like that to lose.

"I guess time will tell, Sophie," I said finally. I couldn't imagine feeling anything other than what I felt at that moment, but I wanted to think that this anger and this sadness had an end somewhere down the line.

My answer must have wounded her because she said nothing else until we reached the edge of the park. I had a sudden and overwhelming need to be away from her, away from her palpable regret and sadness, her beauty none diminished by the tears, her naive desperation. She repelled me.

"Promise me that you'll still consider staying," she said.

"Sophie." I shook my head. *This again?*

She put her hands out as though to stop me in my tracks. "No." She shook her head. I had a wild and fleeting desire to shove her away, to push her down. "Don't answer right now. Don't say no just like that. Just tell me you'll think about it?"

I sighed and nodded. Not because I really would consider staying, but because I knew it was the fastest way to remove myself from the situation. She had become, within days, someone I didn't feel the need to be honest with. I reminded myself that I owed her exactly nothing. Perhaps I was too soft even for hearing her out.

I took the long way home. I felt deeply sad and, strangely, a little closer to being free.

AFTER THAT, Sophie and I fell into a holding pattern that nearly resembled normalcy, or so it would have seemed to an outside observer. It was too much effort to try to keep her at bay. But we were like a cake missing several key ingredients: fine to look at but all wrong to taste. I focused on studying, and Sophie mostly went out to our bar in the evenings. She wanted me to go with her as was our habit, but I begged off. God knows what she got up to in that place on her own; since our fight she'd developed a wide-eyed look that made me nervous. Or perhaps she'd had it for a while and I'd only now noticed. One time I let her talk me into joining her for drinks, a day when I'd spent so many hours studying I feared my brain might emulsify. It felt tense to be alone with her; we got drunk and reminisced about our trip as though it were already a long-past fond memory. We carefully avoided any mention of Alex.

At the end of our penultimate week we took our final exams. They were long, arduous, and occasionally terrifying, but to my relief it wasn't a repeat of the entrance exams. I was resigned to my academic fate and only hoped for a passing grade. As I kept telling myself, I had another year of university ahead of me.

"How did it go?" I asked Sophie as we were leaving an exam.

"Fine. Okay." Her eyes were glazed over, perhaps the result of filling in so many of those bubbles in a row.

 ❧

After the exams the faculty threw us a party at the institute. Véronique and some of the other students who had attended the conversation club also came. I happily availed myself of the array of sweets and mediocre wine; once my appetite had returned after finding out about Sophie and Alex, I could hardly keep myself away from sugar, let alone wine.

I was relieved to see Véronique. I knew I wouldn't go into what had happened. Even though Véronique probably had an idea, it just didn't feel right to talk about it, and I felt vaguely embarrassed about the whole thing.

"Alex said to say hello," she told me when we'd stepped aside to pour ourselves a glass of wine. "He had to go back to Paris for work."

"Ah." I felt my heart constrict a little even though I had already resigned myself to not seeing him again, or at least so I'd told myself. "Well, you must tell him goodbye for me then."

"Goodbye?" Véronique asked with what seemed to me feigned surprise. "But I thought that you were staying, at least for the summer?"

I shook my head and drank my wine. Sophie was in the corner paying an unusual amount of attention to one of the white-hat-wearing frat boys, perhaps avoiding Véronique, perhaps even avoiding me. Sophie had said a quick hello to Véronique earlier but then meandered off to talk to some other Americans. The guy looked stunned by her flirtations, and the sight of the two of them made me queasy.

"I would love to, but it's just not the most realistic of plans. I have to work during the summer." It felt pleasantly shocking to mention to Véronique the necessity of something like a summer job.

She gave a gratifyingly reverent little nod. "Well, you must come back and visit us."

"Definitely, and you must come see me in California sometime." All this time I'd been making plans that would never happen, why stop now?

"Of course." She smiled quickly. She gazed into the plastic glass that held her wine, cupping it in her palm and twisting it with her fingers. Then she stared at Sophie for too long a moment to be meaningless. "So, work, that's the reason you're leaving?" She moved her glance back to me with eyebrows raised.

"Yes," I said with a rueful smile, "that's the reason."

I said my goodbyes to Véronique that night. With her exams also now finished, she was headed off to Mykonos with some friends. I kissed her cheeks and made my way into the night. Despite all of our promises to keep in touch, I knew it was the last I'd see of her. It will be easier, I told myself, if you just recognize this. Let it all be what it really is.

Sophie left with the frat boy before the party ended, perhaps trying to prove that Alex really hadn't meant anything to her.

❧

The night before I was due to leave, Sophie wanted to go out, but I told her I had to pack. She offered to come over and help, to bring a bottle of wine.

"So where did you run off to last night?" I asked.

She sat at my desk, working on removing the wine cork. She gave me a sheepish smile.

"I thought so." I laughed. *Slut,* my mind silently formed the word. "And?"

She shrugged. "Not terrible." Neither of us wanted to be having this conversation and yet we both wanted to pretend that we could still speak freely with each other. It felt strange to have her in my bedroom. I'd agreed to see her because, somehow, even after what she'd done, I was caught between my terror of losing her completely and my overwhelming desire to put thousands of miles between us. I couldn't be in the room with her without feeling waves of anger lashing up from the pit of my stomach, small torrents of revulsion when I thought of the two of them. Intertwined. Naked. Without me. I had seen too much of Sophie's body not to be able to picture it perfectly.

She poured me a glass of wine and I sat down on the bed next to my overflowing suitcase. I looked over Sophie's shoulder, out my open window. Was it really the last time I'd see the view from here? The last night I would spend in this room? In France? It felt surreal that all this would so soon become my past.

"Look," Sophie finally began, her voice uneven, betraying the effort it took to say whatever she had to say, "I know things haven't been the same between us."

"Sophie," I said, cutting her off but trying to keep the edge out of my voice. I wanted something, but I didn't think a fight was it. "We really don't need to do this."

"Just listen, please?"

I nodded. I rolled my last few items of clothing tightly and pressed them into the corner of my suitcase.

"I know things haven't been quite the same between us," she said again as though starting a well-rehearsed speech, "after what happened. And I know you said you need time, and I respect that, I do. But I really think that your deciding to go home because of this is something that you'll regret." She paused as though gathering her strength. "I think you should call and change your ticket. I think you should stay."

She reached for her phone and held it out to me, her hand shaking slightly, as though she meant for me to agree and call right then with no further discussion. I felt a sudden and almost overwhelming exhaustion. I wanted to laugh in her face, or scream at her, or bury my head in her lap and cry for hours.

"It's not just about that, not just about you. I couldn't even afford the change fee on the ticket, let alone spending a summer in France. I couldn't stay even if I wanted to."

"Well, do you *want* to stay?"

Did I even know the answer to this question? *Did* I want to stay even after everything that had happened?

"Part of me does. But it doesn't matter," I said finally.

"It does matter!" She got up from her seat and came to kneel by the bed, taking my hand in hers, her skin hot and fevered. "I can cover you. My parents sent me some money for the summer. I told them I was joining an arts program. It would get us through until we find jobs in Cap Ferrat."

"Sophie, stop." I pulled my hands away. "Just stop." She got to her feet and sat back in her chair, looking despondent. Couldn't she see she was humiliating both of us? "It's just not going to happen. This is not a fairy tale, we are not like Alex and Véronique, we don't live in their world. Or at least I don't. . . ." I sighed.

Sophie's eyes brimmed with tears. "I knew I'd ruined everything," she said under her breath.

"Sophie, not everything is about you." A little wave of surprise passed over her face. "We have to go back to the real world eventually. At some point you have to be practical. I wanted to believe it was all possible too, but it isn't. It's not the right thing. And maybe you shouldn't be staying either." I wondered how well her parents knew her, how much they had any idea what sort of life we'd been living over here.

"I can't go back," she said—she had a hell-bent look in her eyes, daring me, or anyone, to challenge her.

"Why not?"

"I just can't. I want you to stay with me, but even if you get on that plane tomorrow, I'm staying here."

Sophie turned and stared out the window. In profile I could see a tear rolling down her cheek, leaving a blackened trail of mascara.

I shrugged, though she wasn't looking at me. "Oh, well," I said quietly, "none of my business." I closed the suitcase with a violent *zip* and stood up. I crossed my arms over my chest.

She turned back to look at me, her eyes huge and hollow. "Don't say that, please don't say that. I want to be your business."

I wanted to hug her. I wanted to tear her to pieces.

"Come on," I said softly, "help me check the rest of the room to make sure I didn't leave anything behind. I'm always doing that."

Then it was time for her to leave. I walked her down to the street, her feet falling unsteadily on the stairs.

We put our arms around each other. It was the first time since the incident that I had really touched her, and it was almost more than I could handle. She shook a little in my embrace and I thought I might faint.

"I wish you'd stay," she whispered into my ear. "I'll miss you so much."

"I know."

"I'm going to write you. You don't have to write back immediately, just read my e-mails, and then when you're ready, you can write back, okay?"

The bargain had a girlish desperation to it. I wanted to say something to soothe the moment, but there was nothing for it. No more playing pretend, I thought. I managed a little nod as my eyes found a spot beyond her shoulder on the street. I couldn't bear the weight of her gaze anymore.

"Oh!" Her eyes lit up. She rummaged in her gray bag and pulled out a tiny red box. "For you."

I smiled nervously and for a moment was still.

"Take it."

Inside the box was a delicate gold chain bracelet with interlocking circles. "Sophie, I can't . . ."

"It's just a little friendship bracelet," she said with a wave of her hand.

"Sophie, it's from *Cartier*." I whispered the name with reverence.

"I know, I know. But it's not the expensive one or anything. Look, I got one for myself too!" She pulled the sleeve of her cardigan up to display it. "So we match."

"This is too much." I shook my head. I imagined how horrified my mother would be if she saw it; she'd probably call Sophie's parents about it.

"It's nothing." She moved away from where I was standing trying weakly to hand her back the box. "I insist you keep it." She stepped away but her eyes stayed on me until the very last second.

"*À bientôt, chérie,*" she said as she walked away. See you soon.

I watched her go. Even then it seemed I felt the need to memorize the image of her hair swinging back and forth. Part of me was waiting for her to look back over her shoulder, to smile or to say something, but she didn't. Somewhere in my heart I feel that if she'd turned around, things could have gone differently, that knowing I was standing in the doorway watching her would have been enough to make her realize I still loved her, even after everything.

But I didn't want her to know it then. At that moment I was ashamed that I still cared about her at all. I wanted to be finished with her. I couldn't let her believe that what she'd done could be fixed. She needed to know that we weren't kids anymore, we had to face the fact that our actions could change the course of everything, that they had terrifying power. Like so many things that had happened that year, Sophie and I learned this lesson together, learned the bottomless pain of asking ourselves what might otherwise have been. When I think of her now, when I see her in my dreams, her swishing hair and her lovely long legs bare in the moonlight, I know I am still waiting for her to turn around. Those are the dreams that haunt me the most.

I FLEW HOME early on Saturday morning. My mother met me at the airport and I cried when I saw her; whether out of relief or out of guilt that I would've left her if things had gone differently, I wasn't sure. I had a week to rest, recuperate, and get over my jet lag before beginning work at Starbucks.

With frightening speed, my time in France felt far away and remote. Some days I had to remind myself that I had been there at all. The events of the months since I'd been standing at the drive-through last summer seemed so extraordinary that they were like a hallucination, a fever dream. Yet, as Alex had said, I felt different being back in my own life: it felt more like playing a role than actually living. I knew what to do and when to do it. I knew how to put one foot in front of the other and get from morning to night, but it didn't seem authentic; it felt as if I were trying to convince an audience that I was this person. I reminded myself that I had responsibilities and that school was an opportunity that shouldn't be wasted. I tried to look to the future. I put the Cartier Love bracelet in the bottom of my jewelry box. Part of me hated the thing. I felt like wearing it would only call attention to the rest of my very non-Cartier life. And yet. It was a symbol that I was loved. I imagined my customers at Starbucks catching sight of it as I handed them their lattes, wondering about what kind of life I must lead to have been given it. As with everything else, I was stuck in the middle.

I suppose I'd expected to feel that way that summer. What I didn't know was that my sense of not being in quite the right life would never completely go away, that I would always feel as if I were waiting for something to come along and return to me all that I felt my life might have been when I was in France.

I thought Sophie was deluded for staying in France, but then again, we were never playing with the same rulebook; some days I felt smug about being more sensible. Other days I just felt jealous. I understood why she'd stayed; it was hard to shake the feeling that by putting us on a collision course with Véronique and Alex, fate had given us an opportunity, had opened a door. Sophie was there pursuing it, and part of me resented her for her courage, perhaps even more than I resented her for everything else. Some days I was angry at her, and other days I longed for her. Whenever I received one of her frequent e-mails, I felt both converge with a force that made my stomach flip. One day I got a postcard, a black-and-white vintage photo of the newsstands along the Seine.

Dear Brooke,

I've found a charming little apartment in the 18th arrondissement. I wish we had spent more time in Paris. To think it was here all that time and we only came once! I'm not far from Montmartre, and there are lots of ex-pats but not many other Americans. It's really so French you couldn't believe. I do my shopping with a wicker basket and drink wine with lunch and the couple

who live next door are always either fighting or having
sex, and let me assure you they make plenty of noise
doing both. Loving Paris, the only thing missing is you!

Love,
S

⁓

In the beginning of the summer, her e-mails were cheerful.
She told me in great detail about her neighborhood and what
she spent her days doing: painting mostly and reading a lot.
She was thinking of making good on her fib to her parents by
actually joining an arts program. She had met some colorful-
sounding friends in her neighborhood, a young French guy
who worked at a bar near her apartment—whom she seemed
likely to be sleeping with—and a couple of rowdy German girls
who were living one floor above her. She'd even run into one
of the old guys from Alex's party, she told me. He'd remembered her, naturally, and had insisted on taking her to a fancy
dinner—one of the best she'd ever eaten. She said frequently
that she had room in her little bed for me if I wanted to come
spend the rest of the summer there. I didn't ever consider it,
but nor did I want to tell her no, to tell her to stop writing.

⁓

About a month after I returned home I received my exam
scores. I saw the official-looking envelope with its clear address window and felt myself overtaken with panic. I took it
with me to the kitchen and opened it slowly. What would I
even do if I'd failed?

I'd passed. Barely.

Relief washed over me. So at least the consequences of my trip wouldn't last into the following year.

At first, being back home, being out of France, separated from my best friend and from the only other two people I'd spent any time thinking about during the past year, was like an open wound I tended to daily. I still thought about Alex constantly. I would stand behind the drive-through, watching customers approach and leave, or behind the register making change for the long morning lines that snaked from the counter to the coffee bar and observe the people with a mild disgust at their sheer ordinariness. They had never bothered me like this before, but I was spooked at the idea that here, among them, was where I belonged. I couldn't even imagine Alex in the same room with these people; it seemed as if it would violate a law of the universe.

Some days I was certain that getting on that plane was the right thing to do; other days I felt regret twisting in the pit of my stomach. Maybe I had overreacted to Alex and Sophie's sleeping together; maybe I could have made it work to stay at least for the summer. I fantasized that I could even have ended up with Alex. Maybe. Visions of what I might be doing if I'd stayed sometimes kept me awake long into the night. I saw myself on the beach with Sophie, picking my way among the cobblestones with Véronique, wrapped in Alex's arms watching the sun come up over the ocean through the giant windows of the master bedroom in Cap Ferrat. I would wake from the turbulent nights during which I had these visions feeling hungover and beat-up. June and July crept past, dragging me along.

Dear Brooke,

I wish you'd write. I know I said you didn't have to but I wish you would. To be honest, I've been lonely since you left. I've found people to spend time with, but it's not the same. There's no one who really understands me here. The Germans are sweet but they're silly, the kinds of girls who'd end up as dental hygienists if they were Americans. I don't know what girls like that do in Germany. Probably get married, chiefly. It's so hard for me to make myself understood. Everyone just sees "pretty rich American," although I think people here think all Americans are rich. I guess it's like you said, reality will always catch up to you.

Love you and miss you,
Sophie

I nearly responded. But as I tossed around the words I might say to her, I couldn't bring myself to write them. So things were falling apart? Okay. So what? I was working at a Starbucks in Chino for the summer—was I supposed to feel sorry for her? So her money and beauty followed her everywhere. *Poor thing.* In my heart I was stranded between wanting to go back and feeling as if her own vanity was the only reason Sophie wanted me there. Had I only ever been reflecting her light?

It wasn't supposed to be like this. We should have had each other there to process everything that had happened, to go into our senior year as best friends, to have our time in France be a precious thing between us, to be full of inside jokes, and to annoy everyone else by making asides to each other in French. She carried on thinking I'd left her, but in reality she had left me.

My mother occasionally expressed worry at how morose I seemed, but she gave me space and was judicious with her questions. I suppose she knew I'd tell her the details when I was ready.

By August, the initial omnipresent ache had begun to fade a bit, but I wasn't much happier. If anything, I missed being in the throes of all of that early pain and longing—it had at least still connected me to those experiences. Now, as I looked over the course catalog for school and started researching internships for the following year, I just felt that something huge and essential was missing.

To pass the time, I started sleeping with Peter, my Starbucks manager, a surly but reasonably attractive college dropout. I nearly laughed in his face when he told me—clearly worried that I would get attached—that he didn't have room in his life for a "serious girlfriend." I promised myself daily that I would leave town as soon as I could, that I would not spend even one day working there after graduation. I received a few more e-mails from Sophie that were back in her upbeat tone, and then another telling me how lonely she was. Exasperated by this, I finally wrote her back.

Sophie,

Have you ever been to Chino in the summer? Probably not, so I'll tell you what it's like. It's hot and dry and it smells. The smog out here gets so bad you can feel it in

your lungs, and when there were forest fires in the valley
two weeks ago, the Santa Anas blew so much smoke in
that the sky was black and the sun turned red. We couldn't
go outside for two days, it was like the apocalypse. Most
days I get up at 4:00 in the morning to open the Starbucks
in time for the morning rush. I also never don't smell like
overroasted coffee beans.

I'm sorry to hear that your summer in Paris is not all that
you imagined. I guess you've got to know when to quit.

Brooke

She responded quickly, but it was as though she hadn't
actually read my e-mail. Now she was right back to sounding
cheerful.

More and more, her letters seemed strangely frozen in
time, as though they were letters from the past that I had
unearthed rather than active accounts of her current life. She
simply felt so remote now, like someone who didn't quite
exist any longer. Until one day I received the e-mail I realized
I'd been dreading.

Dear Brooke,

You will never guess who I ran into in Paris? Okay, that's
a lie, you've probably guessed already. Alex! I ran into him
in the train station when he was coming back from Cap
Ferrat for the weekend. We had a long dinner and all we
could talk about was YOU, my love. I didn't tell him we'd

had a fight. I didn't want to embarrass you, let him think
we'd been fighting over him. It is pretty silly when you
think about it.

Ma cherie, you must come back to France. I'll buy your
ticket. No excuses! You must send us your travel dates tout
de suite!

All my love and kisses,
Sophie

I was stunned by her e-mail. The tone as though nothing
had ever happened. I began e-mails to her over and over. *Of
course* I couldn't come to Paris, and what was she thinking
telling me all of this? Of all the spoiled, stupid, harebrained
ideas about how to get me back . . . But I sent none of them.
To think of the two of them, *in Paris*, without me twisted
the knife. Surely they had slept together. Everything I started
to write felt pathetic, made me feel petty and beneath them.

A week later I received yet another e-mail.

Dear Brooke,

I think we're at a point where I need to be frank. Because
I've tried being loving and conciliatory and it seems to
have no effect on you. I see your side of things, I really do.
I know you were hurt when you found out about Alex and
me, but I think you're being childish drawing things out
like this. And honestly, I think I'm being really generous
offering to pay for your ticket out here, and it's pretty rude

to just not answer my e-mail at all. I know you're upset but you're letting your pride get in the way and it's ruining everything.

Love,
Sophie

Somehow the accusatory tone of her e-mail made me panic momentarily. I hadn't realized how secure I'd felt, having the moral high ground. I felt a flash of feverish contrition and began typing an apologetic reply. But a moment later, I was banging the backspace button on my keyboard. What was I doing? She couldn't just *demand* that I come to her in France. This whole thing was absurd.

Two days later, I got home from my evening shift and grabbed some leftover potato salad from the fridge. I collapsed into a kitchen chair, exhausted from being on my feet all day. I started idly pawing through a stack of mail and discovered a thick envelope with numerous stamps addressed to me. It was from Paris.

I pulled out an Air France ticket: LAX to Charles de Gaulle, leaving Tuesday afternoon and landing midday Wednesday in Paris. My jaw dropped. Was this real? The ticket must have cost thousands of dollars. There was a note inside.

Dear Brooke,
Still waiting to hear from you. But I realized the other day that I've been letting you labor under a false belief all of this time and that it's fueling your

stubbornness. Namely, I've let you think that Alex was yours first. I've let you go on thinking that because I figured it would hurt you even more to know the truth. But now I see it's the other way around, you think I stole him from you but I didn't! The night you know about wasn't the first time. So there it is. We were sharing him all along and we could have gone on doing so if you hadn't been so small-minded about it. We're supposed to be more than this to each other. My love, your jealousy is unbecoming. You should really let it go. Not a good look.

I'm heading out to Cap Ferrat this weekend. Alex wanted me to come before but I felt bad about going because of you.

Just get on the plane on Tuesday and we'll figure things out when you get here.

Love,
Sophie

I had the queer feeling of realizing something I had always known. Not suspected: known. Alex had never been mine. Behind my back, she'd always had him. And now she was going to reclaim her prize. Memories rapidly unspooled in my mind: the drunken night in Cap Ferrat when I'd fallen asleep on the sofa—had they then? What about in Paris? What about every time I wasn't with one of them? I saw their bodies coming together over and over, their luminous, mirrored smiles facing each other, breaking into laughter between kisses.

"Mom?" I hollered.

"Yes, dear? Must you scream?"

She had already been heading into the kitchen and was right behind me.

"Sorry," I said. "Do we have mailing stuff?"

"Hmm." She pulled open a drawer. "I only have one stamp left, I need to get some more. What do you need it for?"

"Never mind, I'll go to Kinko's." I shoved the ticket in my purse. I walked by my mom and back to my bedroom. I grabbed the Love bracelet from the bottom of my jewelry box and dropped it into my purse.

"Honey, what is that? Are you okay?" my mom asked from my doorway.

"Yeah," I said bitterly.

"Are you sure?" My mom gently grabbed my elbow as I tried to brush by her. I stopped for a moment, tempted to fling myself into her arms and tell her the whole story. Yet I knew that she couldn't understand.

"I am, Mom." I forced a smile. "I promise. I just have to run an errand."

⁓

I sat down at the Kinko's console to type out a letter to go in with the package. Some new fury boiled up inside me and my fingers felt hot on the keyboard as I typed.

Sophie,

I suppose I should have known. Maybe I did know and I just didn't want to believe it. No wonder you don't want to come back home; if this is how you treat your friends, you've probably got none left here. I know you want so desperately to believe that you are more than a pretty rich girl, and yet you use your looks and your money as weapons every chance you get. I suspect you know you'd be nothing without them, that they're the only reasons people tolerate you to begin with. This whole thing isn't half as daring and original as you think it is. After all, you're not the first dumb American to confuse being a free spirit with being a slut. You always said you thought I could see the real you, and I guess I finally do. And I suspect that Alex does too.

Brooke

The words came from somewhere inside me that I'd never seen. I'd never called someone a slut before. It seemed like an outlandish word to call another woman. On some level I knew I didn't want to say these things to Sophie, didn't want to hurt her even if she'd hurt me. But I was propelled by something deeper now. The plane tickets had caused something to come loose in me. It felt as though she were taunting me: *Look how I have everything you want, look how easy it would be for me to give it to you. Look how generous I am.* I shredded the plane ticket into many pieces and deposited them in the envelope with the letter. I dropped the bracelet in and sealed the envelope closed, placing it in the outgoing mailbox before I could give it another thought.

I went home in a blur of tears. That night I raided my mother's prescription sleeping pills and went to bed.

I had an e-mail from her on Monday.

Dear Brooke,

Are you happy? I went to Cap Ferrat and they sent
me away. Alex was there with another woman and he
pretended to barely know me, acted like he'd never invited
me. But YOU heard him, he said anytime. ANYTIME. And
Véronique was there, she threatened to call the police if
I didn't leave. Some guy who was with them drove me to
the youth hostel in Cap d'Ail and they took me in after he
bribed them. I spent the night on a cot.

What else? I failed my tests and my parents are insisting I
come home. I can't go back. I can't.

I know you didn't mean to ruin everything. Write me back.
Come to France. I need you.

S

I was confused until I realized that she couldn't have received my package yet. She didn't know. I shook as I read her
e-mail. I closed my computer and went to work.

Several days later our phone rang in the middle of the
night. I was awakened from a deep sleep, and as I stumbled
for the phone, I realized: Sophie had gotten her mail.

"Who's calling?" my mom asked blearily from her bedroom.

"No one, Mom." I took the phone carefully from its cradle

and swiftly hung it up. I unplugged it. Sophie tried several more times over the next few days and I managed to intercept nearly every call, screening the calls and deleting the messages as soon as I heard her plaintive voice on our ancient answering machine.

Then one day she called while I was at work and spoke to my mother.

"Brooke, honey." My mom was sitting at the kitchen table when I came in from work. I'd only worked an afternoon shift and the sun was still high and blazing.

"Hi, Mom." I came over and deposited a kiss on her cheek.

"Sophie called for you," she said, her voice serious.

I froze for a moment before shrugging and turning my attention to searching through the pantry for a snack. "What did she say?"

"That she's coming home in a few days. Not much else, but she sounded very upset. She wasn't making a lot of sense."

I felt a tiny wave of gratitude that Sophie had chosen not to emote all over my mother and tell her the whole sordid story. I wanted to protect my mother from it, I wanted her to believe that my experience in France had been only good.

"Brookie"—I turned and faced my mom, stopped short by the seldom-used nickname—"I know you two had a falling-out of some kind. I gathered. You don't need to tell me all of the gory details, but I think you should reach out to her. Whatever it is, I'm sure it can be sorted out. I wish I'd treasured my girlfriends when I was your age. It's important." She shook her head.

"Okay, Mom." I put my arms around her. "I'll call her next week when she's home."

The guilt from my letter was starting to eat at me, my mom's directive notwithstanding. The letter had felt right—even righteous—in the moment. But I'd never before said such cruel words to anyone, and now, knowing she'd read them made me feel nauseated.

❧

On the day I had decided I would call Sophie, I woke with lifted spirits, with new hope that somehow things could work out. Maybe it was easier for me to imagine accepting her back into my life knowing she was humbled by having failed her exams and by having been tossed aside by our friends. I was still angry, still hurt and humiliated, yes, but now she was too. Could we find our way back to each other now?

After working the morning shift that day, I was home by early afternoon. I'd ignored Peter's suggestive glances and declined his invitation to go out that night. "I can't," I'd told him, "a friend of mine just got back to town and I'm seeing her." I hadn't told him about Sophie or much of anything about France. We didn't do much talking.

When I got home from work, my mom was in the other room ironing clothes. "Hi, sweetheart," she called down the hallway.

"Hi, Mom!" She put her iron down and came to join me in the kitchen, where I was making a sandwich for myself. "You want one?" I asked, smiling.

"No thanks, I had some of the lasagna from last night."

She then said cautiously, "You seem cheerful today," as though afraid I might suddenly decide I wasn't.

I shrugged and grinned at her. I put my sandwich on a plate and sat down at the table across from her.

"Just looking forward to school?"

"I guess. Better than the five a.m. shift at Starbucks."

She looked at me expectantly.

"I'm about to call Sophie," I said quietly, relenting.

My mom's face lit up and she came over to kiss me on the forehead. "Good, I'm proud of you, sweetie. You never really lose by forgiving someone. All my love to Sophie, then. I'm going to finish up my laundry and leave you here to negotiate the Treaty of Versailles."

I rolled my eyes at her playfully.

⁓

The phone rang several times on the other end before an unfamiliar male voice finally answered. For a moment, I wondered if I had dialed the wrong number.

"Is Sophie there?" I asked tentatively.

There was a strange and pregnant pause. "Who's calling?"

"Brooke Thompson."

"Are you a friend of Sophie's?"

"Yes. Sorry, who am I speaking with?"

"This is her uncle Bernard. . . . This isn't really a good time."

"Oh," I said, confused. "So, um, should I call back later? Do you know if she'll be around?"

He made a small, pained sound, then was silent.

"Is something wrong?" I asked after a moment, my voice

echoing in my ears, small and plaintive. I was suddenly finding it harder to breathe, as though the air in the room were thinning.

"Hold on a moment." I could hear him putting his hand over the receiver and speaking to someone in the room. "Okay, Rebecca, okay," he said, his voice sounding far away. Rebecca was Sophie's mom. "Are you there?" he said to me.

"Yes."

"So, look, I really hate to be the one to tell you all of this, but Rebecca and Frank really aren't in shape to talk to anyone right now."

What he said after that is blurred in my memory as though I'd suddenly half lost consciousness when he said the words. And such strange words: *Sophie has passed away.* It sounded peaceful when he put it that way, as though she had slipped away in her sleep like some octogenarian who had come serenely and half willingly to her end. I realized once he'd said it that I'd known from the moment he'd answered the phone; that I could hear it even in the voice of a stranger.

Sophie had not been on the flight from Paris. Her parents had tried to reach her but could not. They got ahold of the landlord—which made sense, as I assumed they'd been paying her rent. He'd opened her apartment and discovered all of Sophie's belongings, her passport and phone, and a note for her parents. The police told them a tourist couple had reported that they'd seen a girl who matched Sophie's description throw herself from the bridge in the Parc des Buttes-Chaumont the day before. Her uncle didn't go into much detail about the note except to say that she had apologized but not explained why. I had many more questions but he had no answers.

The next thing I remember was hanging up and slumping to the floor, where my mother found me screaming.

❧

For the first semester of my senior year, it was all anyone could talk about. There was a vigil and a memorial, and for a time I seemed to warrant a strange, morbid celebrity. Girls from the volleyball team whom I didn't even remember ever having met before wanted to discuss Sophie for hours on end. She's still the most interesting thing about me as far as this school is concerned, I thought, and then felt guilty for letting it bother me.

For my part, I didn't want to speak to anyone about her. Rather, the only person I wanted to talk to about her was a world away and I had no way of contacting him. I purposely hadn't even kept his number, either out of spite or to keep myself from calling him in a weak moment, I wasn't sure which.

I saw a grief counselor, with whom I shared a great deal about my feelings and virtually nothing at all about the actual circumstances or my guilt. I knew she'd only tell me it was misplaced, and I wasn't interested in having it alleviated. It was keeping me company. It turned out no one had talked much to Sophie while she was in France. So it seemed that she and I shared many secrets, and I hoarded them all—despite the prodding from her friends, who wanted to know what could have made her do it. What I kept private felt sacred, and that was what *I* needed; that was all I had left.

Much harder to face were Sophie's parents, whom I drove up to see about a week after I got the news. They had me over for a strained and painful dinner at which her mother repeatedly burst into tears and I awkwardly tried to comfort her. When she wasn't sobbing, I had the uncomfortable feeling that she was searching for something, in my eyes, in my words, some clue or perhaps just some hint of her daughter. And every once in a while I would say something or do something that she would tell me reminded her of Sophie—unsurprising, I supposed, since we'd spent so much time together—and this would appear to both light her up and break her all at once. I got out of there as quickly as I could.

I went through the next year on autopilot. I kept my head down and studied hard and was relieved when graduation finally came. After college I spent a summer with my mom—though not at Starbucks. Instead, I got a job copyediting the Web text for Chino's local paper. In the fall I moved to New York and have been here ever since.

For years I dreamed of Sophie at least once every couple of nights. To this day I still do—though somewhat less often as other things have come along to crowd my brain. My dreams of her always seem to be brief, and in them she is always happy. Mostly we're just sitting somewhere together or walking along in our park; sometimes we're on a pier watching the boats. There is always the sensation that she can't stay long, that she's going to have to leave soon. Sometimes I already know she's gone and I tell her I miss her; she smiles and says she knows just before disappearing. But every so often I dream she's not yet gone, that there is still a chance to change things, and I am back on the doorstep watching her walk away, just waiting and waiting for her to turn around.

I AGREE TO see Alex the Thursday night following the party. We meet at a little café south of Union Square, convenient both to his hotel and to the train back to Grand Central. The place has a bit of a faux-French vibe to it, and the irony of this isn't lost on me. If I'm honest with myself, it's a relief to get out of my new house for a few hours—with all its shiny, unused appliances and unpacked boxes. It seems as if it will take a lifetime to settle in; this alone could make me never want to move again.

As I walk down from Union Square to the café, I try to answer the question I've been asking myself ever since I made this dubious appointment: What do I really want from Alex? To have him say, I remember you. I knew you when you were young and hungry for a life you would never have. I see that you are grown and not that girl any longer, but I remember her. I am your link to her, the only one now that the other is gone. I wouldn't, *couldn't* forget you if I tried. I know what happened and it wasn't your fault.

I consciously try not to primp for him. I tell myself that this is not in any way a date but simply something I have to do. I can't explain my reasons for needing to see him. It's only coincidence that we ran into each other, and I'm long past the point in my life where I try to impose meaning where there isn't any. But I am looking for something from him, and what that is, I'll only know when I see it.

I've been thinking about Sophie and about my younger self almost constantly since I ran into Alex. These two girls seem frozen together forever in time—the memory of Sophie and the piece of me that would always be there with her. What would she think of me now? I gave up writing shortly after school, and without much of a fight I settled into the kind of job that my twenty-year-old self never wanted. Even worse, I ended up being pretty happy with it.

Though rationally I know that Sophie is gone and has been gone for a long time, because she was so far away when she died, some part of me can't be reasoned with, thinks she might still be in Paris waiting for me to join her. Perhaps this is why people want to see a body at funerals, so that their heart can catch up to what their brain knows to be true.

What would Sophie have become if she'd lived? I wonder if someone like her was ever meant to be forty, to age, to find coarse, gray hairs stubbornly going in the opposite direction of the rest the way I do now. I can't imagine she'd have settled for anything less than everything she'd wanted. I fear she might have been disappointed by me, that I'd become so boring. I couldn't shake the brutal suspicion that she'd have left me behind one way or another, and maybe this hurts more than anything else. We're not supposed to be selfish about other people's deaths but we are. We're left behind, after all, it's the dead who couldn't care less.

Is it more painful for me to think that Alex doesn't remember me or that he doesn't remember *us*? I don't know. Perhaps I just need to know that I'm not in love with him anymore.

Young loves just get into your bloodstream that way, their image looming so large in your memory that no real person who comes after ever compares. The other night had felt like a hallucination, so much so that I remain unconvinced that he will actually be there when I walk in the door to Café Deville. It's not only Alex that threatens to pull me under now but the whole of the path not taken that he evokes. What if seeing him tonight breaks my heart all over again?

I'm a few minutes late but I try not to rush. At least he'll hopefully already be here. There's something appealing about the idea of making him wait for me after all of these years.

I push the door of the café open and it's warm inside. I unwind the heavy scarf I'm wearing, peel off my winter coat, and hang it over my elbow. Scanning the near-empty bar, I see Alex sitting at one of the small bar tables on the other side. He's seen me already and is watching me remove my outer layers. He smiles and raises his hand.

I walk over to him. "Sorry I'm a little late."

He takes my folded coat from me and puts it on the seat beside him. "It's okay. I'm happy to see you. I was worried that you might not come," he says, though his face tells me he was not actually worried at all.

My stomach is churning and I realize—a little horrifyingly—that I have no idea how to begin a conversation like this; the waiter comes over and gives me a temporary reprieve by asking me for my drink order. I stick with my usual and order red wine.

"So, have you been enjoying your time in New York?" I ask. It's not helping my cause that all I want to do is stare at him outright, to catalog the tiny changes that I can only now see, up close, in the geography of his handsome face. He has aged beautifully; the tiny lines only make his expressions more dramatic, more intense.

"I have. I always love to come to New York. I lived here for a time."

"I looked at some of your work online after I saw you the other night," I say as evenly as possible. "You're very talented."

"Do you think so?" He shrugs and looks out into the middle distance for a moment. "To tell you the truth, it feels like it's been many years since I've connected with my work in any real way. I still take many pictures, of course, and I am grateful that people are still interested, but I'm not sure why they are. It makes me immediately suspicious of people who say they are fans."

"Including me?" I smile, conscious that I am flirting, conscious of how easy it feels to do so.

"Not you. I can sense that you have taste. And I am certain that you prefer my old work to my new work. True?"

I laugh and nod. "I hope you don't mind me saying it."

He smiles. "Well, it must make you nostalgic, no?"

Only now do I notice that his eyes have darkened, and it makes me inexplicably nervous. I wanted to be holding all the cards, and until this moment I thought I had been.

"You could say that," I finally reply when the pause becomes unbearable.

"But then, it can be distressing when an image from our past comes upon us unexpectedly."

He gives me a sly smile that feels like a challenge. He softly rattles the ice in his glass.

I release a breath I feel I've been holding for years. "I thought you didn't recognize me the other night."

"I didn't, not at first. But when you said you were leaving, I saw you again, staring at that picture. It was the oldest one they chose. At first I thought you just had good taste, but then I realized."

"But you came over to talk to me before that." I feel as if I've been caught in a lie. I want to run.

"I was intrigued. You looked so out of place."

I'm mortified by this. Had I thought he'd just found me irresistible? I look down at the table, my cheeks burning.

"It's not a criticism, just an observation." Without warning he reaches over the table and takes my hand. "Would you really want to blend in with those people?"

Contemptuous of the beautiful people as ever, I think, no matter how much he belongs to them. But, no, I realize, no. I have stopped wanting to be anyone other than myself. Progress of a kind.

Alex is still holding on to my hand.

"I still have that photo," I say quietly, "the one you took of me in the garden." Not only do I still have it, I know its precise location: in a small box of important miscellany that includes my passport and my grandmother's wedding ring. It wouldn't appear to anyone else like a memento of another man, though that's precisely what it is.

"Ah, yes," he says in a way that tells me that he hasn't any idea what photo I mean. "My work used to mean so much more to me." He takes a sip of his whiskey and looks thoughtfully into his glass for a moment. "Perhaps I will get through this phase. I know I'm ridiculous to complain. It just used to seem so different. I keep waiting for the feeling I had when I was young to return. But then perhaps no one would even notice."

"I bet that isn't true. I bet you have more fans who are real believers than you think you do."

"I don't remember you being such an optimist. But then, I suppose people change."

"It's easy to be optimistic about other people's lives." This is mostly true. In recent years I've felt a cautious optimism about my own life, adding up its parts—good job, fiancé who loves me, Mom still healthy—and deciding I was pretty lucky.

"And you, Brooke, whatever came of your painting?" He leans forward across the table.

I wince. "That was my friend." I'm unable to say her name. "I wanted to be a writer back then."

"Ah, that's right. Forgive me, it was such a long time ago."

Yet that photograph of Sophie still hangs at his parties, one of his best. And I still have the photograph he took of me, secreted away after all this time.

"So? Your writing, how is it going?"

I shrug. Suddenly I can't admit that I've walked away from it entirely. "You know how it is," I say vaguely. "I work away at it when I can."

Mercifully the answer seems to satisfy him.

The conversation carries on in a decidedly neutral direction. He talks to me about his book tour and asks me thoughtful questions about what I'm reading and what I like to do in the city. He was plenty polished when he was twenty-five, but the years have only made him smoother around the edges, so refined that his words seem to slip through the air and surround you on all sides. It can't be like this, I think, I didn't come all this way to chitchat.

"Do you live in the neighborhood?" Alex asks, hailing the waiter for another drink.

I shake my head. "I just moved upstate. Not too far, it's practically like staying in the city with the train being as fast as it is."

"I had not taken you for a suburban girl."

I shrug and smile, tempted to add that I hadn't either.

"So it must be the fiancé, in that case."

I blush. He has noticed the ring. Then does he wonder what I'm doing with him if I'm engaged? No, I think, he probably doesn't wonder that. I'm sure I am not the first girl with an occupied ring finger to have sat across from him, falling for all of it. And yet, I remind myself, I have another purpose for all of this, which is why I didn't remove the ring. I am not here to seduce or be seduced.

"He's starting to think about children," I say.

"How lovely. Probably enough about him now, no?"

A pang of guilt surges through me as I nod. "Is the whiskey helping you stay warm?" I say rather helplessly as the waiter brings him another. I am dancing around the point, unable to find a way in.

"Oh, yes, you should try some, although red wine can do the trick nicely as well. Honestly, I don't mind the winters here. It's the summers I can't stand. I always used to leave for those."

"Where do you go for the summer?" I refuse to use the word as a verb as people on this coast are so fond of doing.

317

"I suspect you can guess, my dear."

I smile broadly. He remembers. "Cap Ferrat. How wonderful. The most beautiful place I'd ever seen."

"Yes, *Mamie* left me the house," he says impishly, "so I feel quite compelled to spend every summer there."

Ah, Sophie was right, then. He got the house and, I suspect, quite a lot of the money, and so he was able to pursue his dreams. I'm lost for a moment, the visceral memory of him returning full force as he sits across from me, my mind traveling back through the years. I've never been back to France after what happened there. I find myself overwhelmed.

"And your friend, what was her name?"

"Sophie." My voice comes out in a squeak.

"That's right, my girl in the ocean."

"Excuse me for a moment." I get up shakily from my chair. My legs feel weak and wobbly as I make my way to the ladies' room.

I sit for a moment in one of the stalls. What am I doing here? What did I ever hope to gain from this?

I start to cry, and once I begin, it takes over my body and I'm suddenly heaving sobs. I've thought about Sophie plenty in the past ten years, but it's been a long time since I've cried for her. Alex looks so much the same as he did the last time I saw him that it fools my mind into thinking we're back in France, and if we're back there, then there's still a chance I could do something differently. I could have stayed. I could have helped her. I didn't have to make her feel so guilty about what she'd done, about being with him. The letter I sent. The torn-up plane ticket. The bracelet. I hear her desperate voice on the answering machine.

Looking in the rearview of all these years, the pain I felt over Alex seems so faded as to have never existed. Because it is nothing compared to the pain that came after. I should have known that she was fragile, that her regret could destroy her.

So what *did* I want from Alex? To acknowledge that we'd mattered to him? That we'd had some impact? That we'd at least been memorable to the person who'd been everything? But we were just two girls he'd slept with a decade ago. Undoubtedly two out of many. And it wasn't his fault. I'd always known he meant more to me, more to us, than we'd meant to him. That was never really the question. But Sophie had been so separated from everyone she knew at the end that if he didn't remember her, it was as though that version of her was never known by anyone but me. And I couldn't bear the weight on my own. I needed him to know and be sorry that she was gone. To shoulder the burden just a little, to spend at least one night as I had spent so many nights, wondering if he could have done something to help her. Part of me wanted to know if he had seen her after I left, if her stories had been true. But despite what he might tell me, the end would always be the same. She would still be gone.

But it isn't just about Sophie. I can't pretend that I am selfless, that her death is the only reason for my regret. The last time I saw Alex was the last time a certain kind of life, and a certain version of myself, had felt possible. Enough years had gone to temper all of my expectations. It's just what happens when we grow up.

Even Alex was disillusioned. He too seemed fonder of his younger self.

Then a truly dangerous thought takes hold. What if we could bring each other back? What if we were each the key for the other?

But then I think of James, how real he is. How he's sweet with my mother and sends me text messages from work in the middle of the afternoon when one of his coworkers does something funny. How he can make me laugh until I have tears in my eyes. How he always makes me dance with him at parties and how I always love it. How he still looks at me with gratitude and wonder when I undress before him.

A girl knocks on the stall door. "Hey, are you okay?" She sounds drunk, wasted, and embarrassingly this makes me laugh out loud, that she is trying to save the day.

"Yes." I pat delicately under my eyes with a few sheets of toilet paper. "I'm okay. Thank you."

"Okay," she slurs, then stage-whispers, "he's not worth it, honey."

Taking a few deep breaths, I emerge from the stall. I have a particular talent for bouncing back quickly from a sobfest. I clean up the residue from my eye makeup and my face appears as though nothing has ever happened. I look at my watch. I can make it back to Grand Central in time for the nine o'clock train if I leave soon. I resolve to go upstairs, pay my portion of the bill, and say good-night to Alex. Let him think I'm a soon-to-be-married woman who's had a change of heart just in time.

⤙⤚

I approach the table to reach for my purse, but I can tell by his expression that Alex has been waiting to ask me something.

"It's all coming back to me," he says, smiling, "you and Sophie. The two beautiful American girls. What fun we had that weekend!"

A weekend, that's what he remembers. Yet my entire year, and some years since, had been consumed by him.

"So did you keep in touch? You were such good friends then." His voice is nostalgic.

"No . . . I . . . No, we didn't."

"She stayed on in France for a time, didn't she?"

I nod and feel ill. This is it, I realize, I have to tell him.

"Véronique saw her out and about once in a while that summer. And then she came out one weekend to Cap Ferrat." His smile seems too perfectly French.

I nod. I realize now that I've only ever had Sophie's version of anything that went on with her and Alex, that there might be another side to all of it.

"And then, actually, I saw her several years ago in Paris. I don't know if she was visiting or living there, though she was looking very French." He paused to take a sip of his drink.

I feel the blood draining from my face. "You . . . saw her?"

"Yes, she came lurking around one of my shows, just like you! It was one of those parties where everyone was grabbing me by the arm and pulling me into conversations as I tried to make my way across the room. I missed talking to many people that night, but I was especially sorry to have missed her. We caught eyes at one point and she gave me a little wave, but, alas, she didn't wait around for me."

"But—" I begin quietly, only to be interrupted by the waiter.

"Miss, would you like another glass of wine?"

I should say no, just the check. I will spend a few more

minutes here waiting for the bill, and then I will go back into the cold night, back to the subway, back to the train, back to my house where my whole life is waiting for me.

Yet, much as I try to tell myself that he didn't see Sophie—because, good Lord, how many lovely, lithe blondes are running around Paris?—that he *couldn't* have seen her, an alternate reality plays out in my head. Sophie no longer Sophie but some Parisian version she'd chosen instead. *Could* she be alive? My insides suddenly feel as though they're coming apart, my head is clouded and dizzy. I've made my peace with her death, and I can't just resurrect her because Alex saw a blond girl. But . . .

"I should . . ."

The reluctance in my voice gives me away and Alex grabs my wrist lightly, shaking his head. "No, you can't leave. Not when we've only now found each other at last. Please stay."

Please stay. If he'd only said those words to me ten years ago, would I ever have left France? He does not release my wrist, but begins to stroke the inside of it with his thumb. I feel it, what I'd had then, all that slipped through my fingers. All those years ago, he and Sophie had made me believe that I could be more, that anything I wanted was possible. Maybe it still was. If Sophie could come back from the dead, why couldn't I?

The waiter looks down at me, his eyes both expectant and bored.

"Okay," I say. "One more drink."

Grand Central is nearly empty by the time I catch my train later that night. Once I'm seated, I open my book out of habit, but I can't focus on the words. There's no space in my head to absorb them.

Alex is exactly the same; other than the gray at his temples, it's as though not a day has passed. In the moment, the sameness of him seemed to compress the years, to take me right back in time, the nostalgia dizzying. But now I realize I'm also a bit disappointed. I realize that it's actually a bit *pathetic* that Alex is the same as he was when he was twenty-five: charming and bright, yes, but also arrogant and shallow. Unwilling to go deeper than the superficial glamour that surrounds him, and unwilling to separate himself from it.

I am relieved to be going back to my warm house and my steadfast fiancé. I am relieved that I am relieved.

I stare absentmindedly into the blackness of the window of the train, the ghost of my own reflection looking back at me. A thousand questions run through my mind about Sophie. First of all, what did I really know about her death? Sophie hadn't been on the plane from Paris. All of her things were left behind. A police report was filed that a couple had seen a girl of Sophie's description jumping off the bridge. And they'd found the body in the lake below. Hadn't they? Was this simply a detail my mind had filled in? As I thought about it, I realized I was relatively hazy on the details. Her parents hadn't shared the forensics with me, but then why would they have? There'd been no doubts at the time that she was dead. Had there? If there had been any mystery, any scandal, word would have made it around the tight-knit alumni community of our little school like lightning; her death was a legend there.

I suddenly feel nauseated and bend over and put my head between my knees.

"Are you all right, miss?" a man in a sharply tailored business suit asks me, a middle-aged finance guy on his way back home after working long hours.

"Yes, yes, thank you." I smile weakly at him.

I think of Sophie, Sophie at thirty, Sophie alive but perhaps no longer named Sophie. Sophie speaking perfect French and wearing perfect French clothes and shopping at the market and smoking cigarettes, every trace of the California girl erased. How would she have pulled it off? She always seemed to have more money than she even knew what to do with. But her parents weren't *that* wealthy. For me back then, there was only rich and not rich, no gradations, but now I understood that they were unlikely to have had the kind of money Sophie acted like she had. Wasn't there a grandmother, though? Someone who'd left her something? I suddenly remember the magazine mogul she'd met at the party, the one who'd shown up in Paris and insisted on taking her to dinner. I imagine her: *Save me from going back to my dreadful American life! Help me disappear, I need you!*

I should be furious, I realize, at the very idea that this might all have been a charade, that Sophie has let me feel guilty for all these years. But I'm not, I can't be. Because the idea of it, of her living in some parallel, self-designed universe, sets us both free.

The train speeds me toward my comfortable home, toward James, and the life I was meant for. And I am smiling to myself with tears running down my cheeks, imagining that perhaps Sophie is sleeping somewhere on the other side of the Atlantic, keeping company with my long-lost dreams.

Epilogue

COME ON!" Sophie said to me. "I'm glad we get some beach time before everyone gets here. We don't have to share."

It was our second day in Cap Ferrat. Alex was napping up at the house and no one else had yet arrived. Sophie and I were too keyed up to rest, despite the day's relentless heat. I laughed and followed her. The sun was blazing above us as we made our way down through the scratchy brush that lined the trail.

"I always thought I'd want to live in Paris, but maybe I choose Cap Ferrat instead," Sophie said after we'd arrived breathless on the beach and plopped down in the sand.

"Nice to have the choice."

"I think our choices are whatever we decide they are."

"Yeah"—I looked out at the pure azure of the ocean—"maybe."

"We're young and beautiful!" Sophie shook my shoulder as though to snap me out of something. "*Anything* is possible."

I laughed. I wanted to believe her.

"I feel like I'm another version of myself here," she said, "like I'm living a whole other life and nothing back in California matters."

"Me too. I miss my mom, though. If it wasn't for her, I probably wouldn't want to go back at all."

"You're lucky."

"I'm lucky?"

"Your mom, she's amazing. I wish my mom was like her."

It had never occurred to me that Sophie would have envied me for anything. It had never occurred to me that my roots might have been deeper than hers. "I wonder if our moms knew what their lives would be when they were our age."

"I'm sure they didn't," Sophie said sadly, "or they probably would have done something differently. At least my mom."

"Mine too, I think." I'd never wondered much about it, whether she had regrets. It wasn't that my mother seemed particularly unhappy, but it also didn't seem like the kind of life anyone would deliberately choose.

"But"—Sophie bit the edge of her lip as if she could hardly contain her smile—"it's going to be different for us. We're going to *choose.* We'll make our own destiny." She dug her hands into the sand beneath us as though trying to hold on to it, to keep it from slipping away. She leaned her head on my shoulder. "After all, I'm nothing if not resourceful."

Acknowledgments

Much love and gratitude to my parents, who always treated my writing aspirations seriously and endured many years of my writerly angst. I won the parent lottery and I love you guys to pieces.

To my fantastic agent, Carly Watters, who helped make this book what it is and has been an invaluable support to me throughout the process. To my darling editor, Sarah Cantin, thank you for believing in this book and for your keen editorial eye and your unfaltering positivity. A big thanks also to Haley Weaver, Steve Boldt, and all the rest of the folks at Atria for their goodwill and hard work.

Many, many book friends have helped me along in my journey. To Lucy Silag: your belief in this book has made an enormous difference, thank you for all that you've done. To Meg Thompson, Susan Chi, and Colleen Lawrie: thank you for being such good friends, helpful readers, and shoulders to cry on over the years.

To all of my wonderful work family at Girl Friday Productions, especially editor extraordinaire Amara Holestein for all of her help with the original manuscript. Much love to Leslie Miller, Ingrid Emerick, Jenna Free, Christina Henry, and Kristin Mehus-Roe. I'm so lucky to have you as friends and colleagues.

Big thanks and all my love to Derek Vetter, who is always on my side.

Losing the Light
ANDREA DUNLOP
A Readers Club Guide

Questions and Topics for Discussion

1. "I'm more than willing to take an anthropological stance on the beautiful people." (Pg. 3-4) Early in the novel, Brooke positions herself as an "anthropologist" among attractive people—a neutral observer. Do you agree with Brooke's self-description? Why or why not?

2. One of the major themes throughout *Losing the Light* is the notion of belonging. What does it mean to belong? Using examples from the novel, discuss whether it seems like people naturally "belong" (in a certain crowd, country, lifestyle, etc.) or whether belonging is a matter of confidence or is somehow otherwise fostered. What are some moments in the book when Brooke feels she does or doesn't belong?

3. Alex has a critical impression of the wealthy, glamorous people who surround him, and yet Brooke notes both in France and in New York that he is, in essence, one of them. Why do you think he regards his peers this way? In what ways do his views parallel or differ from Brooke's opinions of rich, fashionable people?

4. As the novel goes on, Brooke becomes more aware of the socio-economic difference between herself and Sophie. How are class differences depicted in *Losing the Light*? What is their significance?

5. What role does Brooke's relationship with her mother play in the novel? How does this relationship influence Brooke, and what lessons does she learn (or fail to learn) from her mom?

6. Sophie responds defensively when Brooke suggests that her life is ideal or close to it. Do you think this tension between how Brooke views Sophie's life in comparison to her own—and Sophie's sub-

sequent objections—reveals a lack of understanding on Brooke's side, or Sophie's? Do things come more easily to Sophie?

7. How do Brooke, Sophie, and Alex use lies and secrets to cultivate the image they want to project? Consider how Brooke's affair with her professor is discussed, Sophie's "disclosure" that she is a virgin, Alex's latest photography project, or any other withheld or manipulated facts. When and why do these characters choose to reveal their secrets?

8. The trip to France in some ways marks the beginning of adulthood for Brooke and Sophie, giving them the opportunity to live away from their parents and invent themselves as the people they'd like to be. In what ways do we see them mature or develop over the course of the book? In what respects do they remain on the edge of adulthood?

9. Monsieur Boulu, the professor of translation, asserts that everything, even onomatopoeia, is understood through the specificity of languages—that language is "not just a way of speaking but a whole way of communicating with the world." Do you see this idea elsewhere in the novel? If you speak a foreign language, can you think of any examples of how differences in language can change how you understand something?

10. The conclusion of *Losing the Light* leaves Sophie's fate ambiguous. Discuss what you think happened to Sophie at the end of the novel. Do different possible endings change how you interpret Brooke, Sophie, or their relationship? If so, how?

11. What do you think would have happened if Brooke had taken the flight to France that Sophie sent her a ticket for? Would they have been able to mend their friendship? Would Sophie have continued lying to Brooke about aspects of her life? How might Brooke's life down the line be different?

Enhance Your Book Club

1. *Losing the Light* is told from the perspective of Brooke, and there is often a sense (especially after Sophie's emailed confession) that there is perhaps a very different story simultaneously taking place from Sophie's perspective. As a group, choose a scene with Brooke and Sophie, and rewrite it through Sophie's eyes. Share and discuss how you think the situation took place from Sophie's point of view.

2. Imagine you are planning a study abroad trip. Where would you want to travel to, and why? If you have previously lived abroad, would you want to return to the same place, or somewhere new? What would you want to get out of living in a foreign country?

3. Add some extra flavor to your discussion of *Losing the Light* by bringing some French wines and perhaps some French cheese and macaroons to share with the group. To complete the evening, put on some Edith Piaf songs to play in the background.

4. The characters in this book have the kinds of intense relationships that come with being young. Did you ever have a friendship like Brooke and Sophie have? The kind that burns bright and flames out? Or a crush like the one Brooke has on Alex that consumes her thoughts? What memories did the book bring up for you?